Where The Heart Leads

THE McPHEE CLAN
Book 8

Jillian Hart

ISBN: 1507756674
ISBN-13: 978-1507756676

CHAPTER ONE

Bluebell, Montana Territory, Spring 1877

"Have you told Aumaleigh?" Verbena asked the minute their aunt left the room.

"Told Aumaleigh what?" Magnolia hefted her end of the curtain rod as she balanced precariously on a chair.

"About Gabriel coming to my wedding." Rose went up on tiptoe, feeling the chair beneath her toes wobble unsteadily. They should have waited until Oscar came with the ladder, but she didn't want him climbing with his leg still healing. "Honestly, I haven't known how to tell her."

"I'll do it." Daisy shook out the freshly made curtains. Ruffles fluttered as she worked them onto the curtain rod. "I'll just pull her aside and tell her."

"As gently as possible." Iris fussed with a set of newly hung curtains, trying to get them to gather just right. "Maybe I should be the one."

"Are you saying I can't be gentle?" Daisy's mouth twitched in the corners.

"I'm saying I could be gentler." Iris teased. She smiled so easily these days now that she wore the sheriff's engagement ring. He'd surprised her with it a few days after his proposal.

"Maybe we should all tell Aumaleigh," Rose suggested, setting the curtain rod into its wooden bracket.

"Tell me what?" Their aunt's voice echoed across the charming parlor of her new two-story log house. She arched a slender eyebrow. "What is with you girls! You've all gone pale. What is going on?"

"Nothing." Rose eased down from the chair. She really didn't want to upset her dear aunt, not today, her moving in day. "Don't worry about it."

"Yes, no worrying, that's right." Magnolia leaped down from the chair. "We need to be talking about exciting things. Like where to put the sofa. Look, there's Oscar with a wagonload right now."

"Aumaleigh." Daisy accidentally dropped the curtain rod and stooped to pick it up. "Where do you want the furniture? This is such a spacious room, you could do so much with it."

They didn't give her much time to answer. Not at all. Iris rushed in with an opinion. "I'd want to look out these windows at this view."

She seemed eager to direct the conversation away from whatever the five of them had been talking about.

Those girls. Aumaleigh shook her head. They were up to something, and you never knew what. "Fine, I won't ask what you're keeping from me, but I have a long memory. I won't forget. I will get it out of you eventually."

"Why are you looking at me?" Magnolia asked innocently.

"Because you're the weakest link in the chain." Verbena finished dusting the window sill. "Our aunt knows you're the one who will buckle under pressure."

"I'd like to deny it, but I can't. It's true." Magnolia shrugged. "How do the curtains look? Are they straight? Oh, Oscar and Beckett are carrying something heavy. Open the door, Iris!"

"You're closer to the door, Magnolia."

"Yes, but I'm fixing the curtains. Are you sure you measured right, Rose?"

"Me? Maybe it's you that did the measuring."

Life was never dull when they were around. Aumaleigh laughed, shaking her head at her nieces. "I'll get the door. Goodness, Beckett. You men are doing too much. That must be heavy."

"Not for us." Her capable ranch foreman lumbered through the door, hauling her heavy carved oak headboard. "Where do you want this?"

"Upstairs, first door on your right."

"Your wish is my command." Beckett winked as he headed toward Daisy instead of the staircase. The two took a moment, leaning toward each other. Their voices dipped low, keeping their words just between the two of them.

Oh, it was good to see them so happy. Aumaleigh turned her attention to the other man hauling her furniture around. She held open the door for him and breathed in the fresh spring air. "Oscar, you are doing too much."

"My leg's better, Ma'am. I'm fine." Polite as always, Oscar Holloway crossed the threshold, balancing the bed rails and slats on his shoulder. "Whew, this is sure a nice place. Bet it'll feel like home in no time."

"It already does." She shared a smile with the young man and closed the door.

As he ambled away, she realized she was proud of how her nieces had hired him on to help both at home and in the bakery. Nor had she regretted for a moment asking Oscar to move into the ranch's bunkhouse. He insisted on doing work around the ranch to earn his room and board.

When his leg was fully healed, she was going to miss him. He was a logger in the forests up north. Surely he would be returning to that well-paying work.

"Verbena, guess what I see." Magnolia waggled her brows as she adjusted her chair in front of the last curtain-less window. "Your handsome husband is here."

"Already?" Verbena glanced at the little mantel clock ticking away above the fireplace. "Well, I guess the afternoon is nearly gone. Aumaleigh, I'm sorry I didn't help more."

"What are you talking about? You've been wonderful." She wrapped an arm around her youngest niece, so full of happiness for her that she could burst. Verbena was still battling morning sickness, but in the afternoons she had a rosy glow. "You need to head home and take it easy. I won't let you do too much. You have your growing baby to think about."

"I know." Verbena beamed with joy. Her hand landed on her still flat stomach. "But it's hard to leave. We're having such fun."

"Here, put on your coat." Taking charge, Aumaleigh grabbed the garment from the hook by the door and helped her niece into it. "You need a nap."

"A nap would be good. I get so tired these days." Verbena hid a yawn behind her hand.

Zane opened the door, an impressive, brawny man who looked tough enough to bend steel with his bare hands. But when he gazed at his beloved wife, he went soft inside. You could just see it. His Verbena meant everything to him.

"Looks like you're settling in." Zane slipped an arm around his pregnant wife. "Are you sure I can't help out around here?"

"No, we have it under control," she assured him. "Keeping track of the five McPhee sisters is a full time job. I don't want to add any husbands to the task."

"Understood. I just wanted to offer one more time." Zane tipped his hat, glancing around the room in a brief farewell before leading his wife away.

"They are so sweet together," Magnolia said, spying on them through the window.

"Yes, he's as tough as nails," Iris agreed, "but achingly tender with our Verbena."

"Well, he better be," Daisy went to the window to spy on the couple too. "Or he'll answer to me."

"To the five of us," Rose agreed.

Aumaleigh couldn't help stealing a peek out the window. Call her nosy. Verbena and Zane stood by their wagon, kissing. How sweet.

"They make me miss my Tyler. It's all that kissing. I wish he was here," Magnolia sighed from atop the chair. "Rose, is the curtain rod in the bracket on your side?"

"Yes. But yours isn't. Will you stop watching the kissing?"

"I can't. That's my favorite kind of kissing. True love kissing."

Aumaleigh opened the front door, sure her nieces could handle finish hanging the curtains. Their cheerful banter followed her onto the porch and into the fading sunshine. Clouds were moving it, swift and sure. She loved spring. The air was still a little crisp because of the snow on the nearby peaks. She savored the moment, this moving-in day. The start of her new life.

The rattling of another wagon caught her attention. There, passing Verbena and Zane's departing vehicle was a supply wagon heading her way. Funny, she didn't remember ordering anything from town.

"Hey, Aumaleigh!" Adam waved, drawing his draft horses to a

stop in the road. "Looks like it's moving day. How are you liking your house?"

"I love it. I need to have you, Annie and Bea over to supper sometime soon."

"We would love that." Adam, her nephew by marriage, touched the brim of his Stetson. "How about sometime after Rose's wedding? It's coming up fast."

"It is." Aumaleigh wrapped her arms around her waist, shivering a bit in the house's shadow. "Where are you headed with that delivery?"

"The place just up the road. Your new neighbor. He got into town this morning and ordered a wagon full of furniture from over in Deer Springs. Nice stuff, too." Adam slapped the reins, sending his horses forward. "I've got a second load to deliver for him after I get this one unpacked."

"It's good for your business."

"That it is. See you, Aumaleigh." His wagon rattled and rolled away, following the rutted road and rounding the corner.

Cottonwoods rustled their green leaves, keeping her company as she stared down the empty road. Interesting about her neighbor. According to the latest rumors, he was some well-to-do gentleman from Ohio.

Ohio. She winced. Did it have to be Ohio? She didn't like to think about the years she'd lived in the southern part of that state. Well, that was water under the bridge. She shrugged, meaning to turn around when another wagon loaded down with furniture and men rolled in her direction.

"Got your deliveries," Burton called out from the front seat. He was the number one wrangler at the Rocking M ranch, which she owned and loved.

"We couldn't stop ourselves," Kellan explained, hopping from the wagon seat the instant the horses stopped. "You can't keep us cowboys from lending a hand. You're good to us, Aumaleigh."

"You're the best cowboys around." She went out to meet them.

"We can't deny it." Kellan joined the other cowboys climbing out of the wagon box. Shep, John, Pax and Tiernan all got busy opening the tailgate and uncovering the new furniture.

Gratitude filled her right up. It was hard to believe she was standing in her own front yard, on the land she'd bought in the shadow of her adorable new home. She was surrounded by loved ones and friends, starting a new chapter in her life.

"What are you doing outside?" Kellan hauled the end of an overstuffed chair from the wagon bed. "You aren't thinking of trying to help move any of this stuff, are you?"

"What if I am?"

"Then I'm going to chase you back into that house, young lady." Burton hopped to the ground, his eyes flashing with humor. "I'm not going to take any guff about this."

"Really? I'm the boss around here. You do what I say."

"You're not the boss of everything." Kellan winked on his way by, hefting the heavy chair as if it was as light as could be. "I mean it, Aumaleigh, back in the house."

"Yeah, let us do this for you." Burton tossed a rolled up area rug over his shoulder. "If you don't, we might hogtie you and do it anyway."

"Yeah, we're cowboys on a mission," Shep added, carting a crate toward the door. "You know us."

"We don't stop until our job is done, come heck or high water." Tiernan grabbed another crate and followed the other cowboys in.

"C'mon, Aumaleigh." Pax wrapped his arms around the matching, overstuffed ottoman. "You need to tell those knuckleheads where to put everything. You can't leave them to their own devices."

"You're wise, Pax." A gust of wind blew over her, and she shivered. The sun was edging downward toward the craggy peaks of the Rockies. The afternoon was nearing an end. "I'm coming, and don't worry, I won't touch a thing."

"Okay, but I'm trusting you. The boys will never let me live it down if you start carrying this heavy stuff." Pax clomped up the stairs and crossed the porch. The girls inside called out to him, and he answered, stepping into the house.

She didn't know what made her stay in the cool air alone in the yard. Maybe it was simply nice to catch a breath of fresh air, or to stop moving after a day of constant demands. Moving day was fun, but it was also a lot of work. Or maybe it just gave her a warm-in-the-heart feeling watching her nieces through the lamp-lit window talking and laughing and fussing over the last curtain.

They were so amusing, the five of them. Iris, the oldest, shook her head, apparently deciding the curtain ties were all wrong. Her strawberry

JILLIAN HART | 9

blond hair, sweet oval face and gentle beauty made her stunning as she nudged fun-loving Magnolia out of the way to retie the sash.

Magnolia pushed a lock of gold hair out of her eyes and slipped an arm around Rose. The two sisters leaned into each other as sensible Daisy moved in to apparently give her opinion on the best way to tie back a curtain.

Adorable. Her heart filled up with love. The rattle of an approaching vehicle echoed through the yard. Probably Adam on his return trip from delivering the furniture. But it wasn't his big draft horses that rounded the corner.

She didn't recognize the matched, jet-black team as they moved through the shadows of the cottonwoods. With their finely carved faces and heads held high, they moved like poetry down the country road. The instant they pranced into the light, the sun glossed their coats and they shone with rare beauty.

She breathed out a sigh of admiration, even as her chest constricted. There was something that troubled her, that reached in and grabbed deep.

The driver in the buckboard remained in the shadows—nothing but a vague impression—and yet she couldn't fight the feeling that she knew him. How strange was that?

Then her breath caught, because the buckboard and driver emerged into the sunlight.

She blinked, sure it was a hallucination. But no, she wasn't that lucky. There he was, there, real flesh and blood and not make believe, tipping his wide-brimmed hat to her.

Gabriel. Gabriel Daniels. Her knees buckled and she grabbed the side of the cowboys' wagon for support. Maybe if she was lucky, her old flame would keep going, just drive on by and leave her be. *What was Gabriel doing here in Bluebell?*

And worse, why was he pulling his horses to a stop?

"'Afternoon." The familiar notes of his voice washed over her, stirring up dreams best left buried. "How are you, Aumaleigh?"

"F-fine." Which was a complete and total lie, a fabrication she would cling to with her last breath. The sun slipped behind a cloud. It felt like the whole world went to shadows. "How are you?"

"Passable." His gray gaze met hers without a wince of guilt. "You must be as happy as I am about tomorrow's wedding."

"Overjoyed." Of course. He must be in town for the wedding. She rolled her eyes. "My lovely niece didn't mention you would be attending."

"It was the least I could do, since I was invited." He sat there with his wide shoulders and mature handsomeness and just the right amount of amazing.

It was infuriating! The very least he could do was to stay away. He'd smashed her young heart to smithereens, which obviously was a fact he'd conveniently forgotten over the decades. She squinted at him. "What are you doing?"

"Getting out of my buckboard so I can lend a hand. You appear to be moving in."

"I don't want your help." There, she'd said it. Perhaps she sounded rude, but she didn't care. Seeing him, talking to him—it hurt. "Get in your buckboard and head back the way you came. You took a wrong turn at the fork in the road. Josslyn's place is to the left."

"Is that right?" Ignoring her orders, he ambled over in his self-assured way, more handsome than a man in middle age had the right to be. He brushed by her, and his nearness rippled through her like rings in a pond, radiating straight to her soul.

There was a time when he'd been her other half. Her perfect match. The man she would have given her life for.

Now she really wanted him gone. "Same old Gabriel Daniels. Nothing has changed in all these years."

"I'm still stubborn as a mule." He grabbed a drop-leaf table from one of the wagons. "Nice place you've got here."

"Don't even try to compliment me. I don't want your help, Gabriel. I don't need it." She grabbed the leg of the table to keep him from lifting it off the wagon bed. "This isn't the way I want things between us, but you won't stop."

"Aumaleigh." His voice dipped low, warm when it should have been cold. "I'm just trying to be friendly."

"I can't be friendly." She nearly choked on the words. "I don't think I can even try."

"You'll have to, for the kids' sake. Seth and Rose come first. We're here for them."

"Yes, that's true. I suppose a temporary truce is in order."

"I didn't know we were at war." He released his hold on the table.

Some measure of tenderness settled in his chest. It had been buried there all this time. "Don't make us enemies, Aumaleigh."

"I'm not the one who did that." Time had changed her, carving lines into her heart-shaped face. Those lines added character to her, like sunlight on a rose. She hiked up her chin. "Let's just agree to keep to opposite sides of the church, and we'll be fine."

"Is that what you want?"

"Yes." Sorrow darkened her bluebonnet-blue eyes.

The sight of her sorrow still got to him. It cut like a knife. He had to look away. He had to clear his throat. "All right. If that's what you want."

"The past is behind us." She sounded as if she was trying to convince herself of that. "Let's keep it there."

"Okay." Hard to argue with that, not without showing his hand. He could bluff with the best of them, so he backed away from the wagon as if he wasn't disappointed, as if his heart wasn't bruised. "As you wish. I'll leave you alone."

"Thank you." She wrapped her arms around herself, and something about her stance told him she wasn't as tough as she pretended to be.

That's how it always had been between them. He'd been able to see into her, to know her heart. What would she think if she knew why he'd sold his ranch and uprooted his life?

Maybe she'd laugh at him.

Or she'd think he needed to be locked up.

Either way, he didn't want to find out. A man had his pride, so he tipped his hat to her. "Have a good evening, Aumaleigh."

"You too, Gabriel." Lamplight from the parlor windows glowed over her, as soft as a touch. The gentle light added luster to her molasses-dark hair and polished her alabaster complexion.

She was beautiful. Time had not robbed her of it. Decades could not diminish it. Somehow she looked lovelier than ever. It didn't seem fair that she could still affect him like this, even after she'd decimated his heart.

The best thing to do was to walk away. Her dislike of him blew cold like the wind. He climbed back into his buckboard. Leaving was the only thing he could do.

He gathered the reins and gave them a snap. The horses responded, leaping into a fast walk. The rigging jingled, the wheels rattled and rain began to fall, but he knew without turning around she was watching him go.

He'd come a long way and given up a lot. But at least he knew where he stood.

And what he was up against.

CHAPTER TWO

"Was that Seth's uncle?" Iris poked her head out of the open door. Her periwinkle blue eyes pinched with concern. "It was, wasn't it? We waited too long to tell you."

"You knew?" Aumaleigh rocked back in her heels. Her gaze zipped back to the road where Gabriel had disappeared. A strange sense of disappointment battered her. "I would have appreciated a warning."

"I know. It wasn't fair for you to suddenly be confronted with him, and face-to-face." Iris breezed down the steps, oblivious to the rain. Behind her, a string of cowboys trailed out the door, talking to themselves, making a beeline for the closest wagon.

Over the scuffling sounds of them moving her furniture, Iris came over and took Aumaleigh's hand.

"Oh, you're so cold." Caring crinkles dug into Iris's forehead. "Come on, let me get you some tea and talk you into forgiving us."

"Forgive you? No need for that. I already know why you didn't tell me." She patted Iris's hand and they made their way toward the house together. "What were you going to say? And when? There would never be a good time to talk about Gabriel. He's here, he's coming to the wedding. It's great he's here for Seth."

"Okay, that's great. Personally, when my ex-fiancée came to town, all the old hurt rushed back." Iris stepped to the side as a pair of cowboys hauled a dining room table up the steps and into the house. "I felt like I'd been run over by a delivery wagon. A really heavily-loaded and speeding one."

"I was hit by that wagon too, but fortunately the shock wasn't lasting. I'm tough. I'm over it." A smile tugged at the corners of her mouth. "What about you? Are you and Milo talking about a wedding date yet?"

"Shh, I'm not supposed to say anything. Not until Rose and Seth are married. *Then* we'll announce it."

"Oh, so there is a date." Aumaleigh followed her niece up the porch steps.

"Say anything to my nosy sisters in there and I will deny everything." Iris waggled her brows as she crossed the threshold and cast a scolding look at the rest of the McPhees. "Aren't you done with those curtains yet?"

"We were, but I'm still fussing." Daisy gave one of the panels a final tug. The curtains framed the view of rain, vibrant green hillside and the misted glory of the nearby mountains. "There. Now they're perfect."

Boots scuffled in the door. Burton cleared his throat behind her. "Where do you want this, Aumaleigh?"

"Let's see. The sofa should go here." She gestured toward the middle of the room. Great. She intended to let the task of arranging furniture distract her from her feelings.

Gabriel was not worth her time. She shouldn't waste another thought on him. He'd been the one to leave her standing in the night, waiting in the meadow near the road for him. She'd stayed there until the morning star rose. She'd headed home with tears on her face and grief in her soul.

There had never been a word, a note or an attempt at an explanation. He'd simply stayed away, making his feelings clear. He hadn't wanted her.

Decades had passed, but it surprised her how much it still hurt. That was proof of how deeply she'd loved him once.

Not anymore.

"Aumaleigh?" Daisy's gentle voice broke into her thoughts. "I hate to say it, but school will be out soon."

"Definitely go pick up your sweet Hailie." Aumaleigh gently squeezed her niece's hand. "Thank you for helping out today."

"Where else would I be?" Daisy brushed a kiss to Aumaleigh's cheek. "You send word if you need anything. Maybe you should come over for supper. I don't see how you'll get everything unpacked in time to try and cook."

Aumaleigh opened her mouth to thank her, but Rose cut in.

"Too late. We've already got her, Daisy." Rose said, wrapping an arm around Aumaleigh's shoulders. "Unless you, Beckett and Hailie want to come over to have supper with us? It's going to be fun. Gemma and Elise are coming. I think Penelope is going to try and make it."

"I promised Hailie chicken and dumplings tonight." Daisy shrugged apologetically and slipped on her coat. "Where did my husband go?"

"You mean that handsome guy over there?" Magnolia gestured in the direction of the dining room as she fussed an end table into place.

"Yes. My Beckett." Daisy filled with light as she gazed upon her husband, radiant with a quiet but deep joy. "I need to say goodbye to him. Excuse me."

It was hard not to sigh as Daisy slipped away, crossing the room. That's how sweet they were, newly wed and so in love with one another. It heartened her to see. Some loves you just knew would stand the test of time.

"Aumaleigh, where do you want this?" Rose held up a precisely folded patchwork quilt.

"Oh! It's gorgeous." Iris breezed over, her coat in hand, to take a look. "Aumaleigh, did you make this?"

"Y-yes." The word caught in her throat.

"It's amazing." Rose traced her fingertip over the pink calico ring of the double wedding ring pattern. "Pink and blue."

"Oh, some of the squares are embroidered." Magnolia tilted her head, unfolding more of the quilt. *"Love is patient, love is kind."*

"We loved with a love that was more than love," Rose read.

"My bounty is as boundless as the sea, my love as deep; the more I give to thee, the more I have, for both are infinite." Iris brushed her fingers against the quote embroidered in gold thread. "Aumaleigh, you made this for your wedding bed."

"I did." She cleared her throat, trying to keep the hurt buried. "It was a long time ago. Maybe one of you girls would like it? Rose? Iris? Magnolia?"

"No." Rose shook her head.

"Not a chance," Iris seconded.

"Not me." Magnolia looked stubborn. "This is such beautiful

workmanship. It's a work of art."

"And a work of your heart," Iris said gently, taking the quilt from Magnolia and folding it with care. "Don't worry. We understand. At the wedding, we are going to make sure your contact with him is non-existent."

"That's right," Rose chimed in. "I am assigning Iris to be your lookout."

"My lookout?" Aumaleigh gave a soft laugh. Leave it to the girls to dream up something like that. "I don't need a guard, not from Gabriel. I'm perfectly capable of handling this on my own."

"No one said you weren't." Daisy breezed by, on her way to the door. "Don't forget I'm lookout number two!"

She slipped outside before Aumaleigh could argue, so she glanced at the remaining girls. "I don't need two lookouts. I don't need one. Iris, I want your word."

Instead of promising, Iris set the quilt on the sofa. "I need to go. I have to be right there when school lets out, or who knows what trouble Sadie and Sally will get into."

"Go get your girls." Aumaleigh loved the joy and love that transformed Iris as she waved and hurried away. Love was the only thing that mattered. Gabriel had turned his back on her—he hadn't wanted that with her.

She put away her sorrow with the quilt, folding it away inside the storage bench. Out of sight, out of mind. But deep within her was still that young girl so full of hope and belief in her wonderful Gabriel.

Well, she was no longer that young girl. Her life was full. She was mature and sensible enough to handle seeing her old flame for a day or two. He'd be leaving soon enough and she'd never need to think of him again.

"The wagons are empty. We've got everything moved in." Burton shook off the raindrops from his hat and glanced around. "Hey, it already feels like a home."

"It does," she agreed. A fire crackled in the river-stone hearth. Lit lamps cast a cheerful, cozy glow. Magnolia and Rose laughed together, trying to unroll an area rug and dropping it.

Aumaleigh treasured the moment, savoring the feeling of being happy. Truly happy.

This new chapter in her life was going to be the best yet. She just had a feeling.

* * *

"Pa, are you all right?" His daughter, Leigh, turned from the sink in the kitchen. "You seem upset."

"No, just got a lot on my mind." That was no lie, but it wasn't entirely the truth either. Gabriel propped one shoulder against the archway, studying his daughter with her bouncing dark brown curls and smudges of dust on her pretty pink dress. A father's love filled him up, pushing out the disappointment that had been troubling him. "Don't tell me you've got all those dishes washed."

"I'm speedy. No grass grows under my feet." She swiped her dishtowel down the handle of a fry pan. "I'm all set to fix supper here. We won't have to have another meal out."

"Your aunt Josslyn will be disappointed."

"She can come here!" Leigh brightened, hanging the dishtowel to dry next to the stove. "What a brilliant idea. I should have thought of it earlier. We can invite Seth over and make it a celebration. After all, it's his last night as a bachelor."

"Something tells me he probably already has plans."

"Oh, too bad. I should have thought of it earlier. I just didn't know we could get everything delivered so fast." Leigh threw open the pantry door and started pulling out ingredients. "We'll have our own little celebration anyway. This is our first night in the new house. I still don't know why you want to live so far away from me."

"I know, it's a dumb decision of mine." Grinning, he pushed off the wall and ambled into the kitchen. "Is the tea water hot?"

"Yes. I was just waiting for you to come in to steep your tea. Honestly, I miss Eleanor. You need to hire a maid, Pa. I won't go home until I know someone is taking good care of you."

"I can take care of myself."

"Foolish men. They always think that, but it's never true. Admit it, Pa. You men need us."

"I'll always need you, Princess." It was hard to believe his little girl was all grown up. It felt like yesterday when she was just a little thing, toddling around the parlor, tiny and precious, the owner of his entire heart. "You can always change your mind and stay here with me."

"What about my fiancé? No, my life is back home. You'll just have to find a way to survive without me." She winked, smiling airily.

"Yes," he agreed dryly. "Don't know how I'll manage."

He saw the shadow at the window in the back door and whipped it open before she could knock. His sister looked up at him with surprise and delight.

"Gabriel. I can't believe you, moving here." Josslyn pushed past him, her red hair wet from the rain. She shook off her coat and sidled in at the stove. "Hi, Leigh, my love. Why did you let your father do this? He never should have bought this place."

"I tried to stop him, but did he listen to me? No." Leigh set down the tea kettle to embrace her aunt. "You know Pa. Mules look weak-willed by comparison. Let me pour you some tea."

"Isn't that tea for me?" Gabe spoke up, giving a soft bark of laughter when both his sister and daughter gave him a look. He held up his hands. "Fine, fine. You two have tea. I'll go out and put up your horse, Josslyn."

"Good, because I left him for you." His sister winked, smiling her thanks before accepting a cup of tea—the one Leigh had brewed for him.

He grabbed his coat off the hook. "A man deserves better treatment."

"Some men, maybe." Josslyn took a sip of tea. Leigh nodded at him in agreement.

"I know when I'm outnumbered." He donned his Stetson and closed the door behind him. The ring of female laughter was muffled, but he liked the sound.

Rain pounded down to bounce off the brim of his hat and ping in the mud puddles. He took Josslyn's gelding by the reins and led the animal to the barn. The wind blew them in. He liked nothing better than a spring storm. They were quick, electrifying and they turned the whole world a little greener.

The team he'd bought from his nephew, Seth, looked over their stall gates, watching him with curious, bright eyes. Probably hoping for grain. Maybe he would spoil them with a treat. Buy their good regard. At the start of any relationship, it always worked out best for a man if he came bearing gifts.

Which brought his mind back around to Aumaleigh. He shook his head, gave the horses a little grain and started rubbing down Joss's gelding. He hadn't been able to get the woman out of his head since he'd seen her back in December—and earlier today.

She was still grace and loveliness. More than two decades hadn't diminished her beauty one bit.

But it had diminished his bitterness.

He traded the towel for the curry comb, patiently grooming the gelding. The sounds of the storm echoed in the mostly empty barn. If he were honest, the reason his bitterness was fading was because he'd learned that she was a spinster. She'd never married. She had no children of her own.

All the dreams he'd had for her as his wife—her happiness, a baby in her arms, the joy of watching their children grow up, sweet days filled with love.

That had never happened for her.

Hadn't that been the reason he'd stayed away? So that she could have those things with the right man, a moneyed man, one that her family was sure could provide a luxurious life for her?

Sorrow gripped him. He'd been wrong. He'd done the wrong thing, made the wrong decision, and they'd both paid for it. That dream of love and a happy life together never happened.

His throat felt tight as he untied Joss's gelding and led him to a stall next to Barney. The black gelding gave the newcomer a sniff, as if to decide if he was friend of foe. With a nicker, he conveyed his opinion to his brother who gave a whinny of welcome.

Thunder crashed overhead, rattling the barn. Rain turned to hail, drumming on the roof. Since he had a little time yet before supper, Gabriel climbed the wooden ladder into the loft. The last dregs of daylight edged between the boards, guiding him toward the loft door. He unlatched one side and pulled open the door, leaning his shoulder against it as the countryside stretched out below him.

Wow. Ohio wasn't anything like this. The mountains, close enough to touch, were shrouded in thick, black cotton clouds. Lightning undulating across the sky, grazing the underbellies of the clouds. Thunder cannoned, echoing across the fertile mountain valley. Sheets of hail turned the lush green meadows and foothills white. He breathed in the fresh, charged air and let the chilly wind blast his face.

And that's when he noticed small flickers of light through the dancing boughs of the cottonwoods. There, across the rise and fall of the land, was a two-story log house. Lamplight shone like gold in the many windows, one of which framed Aumaleigh to perfection.

He was too far away to see more than the blue of her dress and the fall of her molasses hair. An impression, really, of the woman he'd once loved with every piece of his soul. She moved away and the lamplight went out, but the past had a hold of him. Memories reared up, vivid and so sweet they hurt.

The boom of thunder chased them across the field. Her laughter filled his ears, sweet and melodic, the most beautiful sound.

They weren't going to make it to the shelter of the buckboard before the rain hit. Lightning blinded him, but he took her hand, so small and delicate against his big, rough one. The tenderness in his heart doubled from just touching her.

This second date of theirs was not going to plan, not at all, but it didn't seem to matter to her. She tilted her head to look up at him while they ran, and the heart and life shining in her bluebonnet-blue eyes stymied him. Just made him melt.

He had nothing but tenderness for her, tenderness that was so, so sweet.

"Oh no!" Her hand slipped from his, trying to catch a pretty pink bonnet that was spiraling up with the wind. "My hat!"

"Wait, I'll get it." He bolted after it, cursed under his breath when the wind snatched it away at the last second and dashed it to the ground. Sully snatched it up, clutching it between his big horsy teeth. "Hey! What do you think you're doing?"

The gelding merely arched his neck, proud of himself.

"That's no way to treat a lady." Gabe made a grab for the hat. "Especially in the rain."

Sully lifted his head high, keeping the hat out of reach. His brown eyes sparkled with mischief.

"It's too late now." Aumaleigh held up her hands in a helpless gesture. The skies opened up and rain hit the ground like bullets, drenching them both to the skin in seconds. As if they hadn't been wet enough.

So much for a romantic second date.

"I knew I shouldn't have worn the pink bonnet." Aumaleigh sailed up to him, lovelier somehow with the rain in her hair. "You did warn me."

"I tried to." He rescued the dainty bonnet from Sully's teeth. "Bad horse. I'll beat you later."

"Yeah, right." Aumaleigh came in close to him, her slender fingers curling around the hat brim. The way her lips hitched in the corners made a man wonder what they would feel like pressed against his. Her chin went up. "Clearly your horses are terribly abused."

"I try."

And then they were laughing and the entire world disappeared—the rain, the wind, the thunder—all of it. There was only the wild beat of his heart slamming against his chest and the quiet hope soft in her eyes.

Oh, he wanted to be that hope for her. To give her every last one of her dreams.

He leaned in without thinking, following the whispers of his heart. Her eyes widened with realization as he moved in but she didn't move away. Then their mouths were touching, his lips caressing hers in the gentlest of kisses.

Did she feel the reverence he felt for her? The adoration? He sure hoped so.

And then he felt her lips relax against his, softening in acquiescence, and he took her in his arms, kissing her without ever wanting to stop. Her hands lighted on his shoulders, such a sweet touch—

"Gabe?" Josslyn poked her head up into the loft, shattering his thoughts. She climbed up and headed his way. "Leigh almost has supper ready. That's one stubborn girl you've got there. She refused to let me help. Just shoved me right out of the kitchen."

"Yes. I think she may have gotten her stubbornness from our side of the family, especially from you."

"I do have a gift." Joss shook her head, her gaze darting out into the storm. "Interesting. You have a perfect view of Aumaleigh's house."

"I'm watching the storm." It was easier to admit that than the truth. It had been hard seeing how much Aumaleigh disliked him. It had been clear and stark in her eyes.

Which was a problem. Because the love he'd had for her had never completely died.

CHAPTER THREE

Aumaleigh held up her wine goblet in the McPhee Mansion's stately dining room and smiled at all the lovely faces surrounding her at the supper table. They had grown to be quite a crowd. "To Seth and Rose. May you two have a life of dreams."

"And infinite happiness." Iris raised her wine glass.

"Happily-ever-after," Daisy added, lifting her glass.

"A storybook life," Magnolia chimed in, giving her wine a sip.

"And a fairy tale love." Verbena lifted her wine goblet full of milk to finish the toast. "Welcome to the family, Seth."

As "welcomes" rang out and wine glasses clanked, Aumaleigh noticed that Daisy took only a small celebratory sip of her wine before setting it down. Her plate was largely untouched, and she looked unusually pale. Was the girl just tired? Or perhaps it was something more?

Aumaleigh remembered when Laura, the girls' mother, was pregnant with Daisy, she'd had evening instead of morning sickness.

"I'm going to bring out dessert." Iris rose and began taking the plates from the little girls seated beside her. "Sally and Sadie. Do you want chocolate cake?"

"Yes!" Sally answered. "And Mitsy too!"

"And Bitsy too!" Hailie gave a sweet, little girl smile and leaned against her stepmother, Daisy.

"I know that baby dragons like chocolate cake." Aumaleigh stood and began gathering plates too. "But do they like chocolate frosting too?"

"Yes!" the little girls chorused.

"Especially with the frosting flowers," Sally added, crooking one eyebrow hopefully.

"You're in luck." Iris brushed a kiss on the top of the girl's head as she moved past. "We made all kinds of frosting flowers."

"Oh goody! Mitsy is delighted!"

While the men at the table talked horses and ranch business, and the girls hopped up to run around the dining room with their imaginary dragons (guarded over by Sheriff Sadie), Aumaleigh headed into the kitchen. Her footsteps felt light and her heart full as she set the plates on the counter. She loved seeing how joyful her nieces were these days. "Rose, are you ready for tomorrow?"

"Yes, but I'm nervous. Verbena and Daisy, were you nervous too?" Rose lifted the cake cover to reveal a chocolate marvel of frosting and colorful rose frosting flowers.

"Was I!" Daisy grabbed a pile of dessert plates from the cupboard. "But it was a happy-nervous."

"Excited-nervous." Verbena counted out dessert forks from the drawer.

The clink of plates, the rattle of silverware and the melody of conversation grabbed Aumaleigh, bringing up a memory she'd thought long forgotten. Images flashed through her mind, carrying her back in time to when she was young.

"Aumaleigh, are you going to see Gabe again?" Josslyn whispered as she swished over in her ruffled apron, carrying a pie fresh from the oven.

The apple and cinnamon scent filled Mother's kitchen, and her stomach rumbled.

"He asked me out again for Sunday." She stopped slicing onions and blinked. Her eyes were burning. Whew, those onions were strong. "I can't believe it. He's taken me out twice and he hasn't changed his mind about me. Yet."

"Why would he?" Josslyn set the pie on the cooling rack and backtracked to the oven where more were waiting. "You're gorgeous. You're adorable. You're fun—"

"Now you're just making things up." Aumaleigh's cheeks heated. Honestly, she was terribly uncomfortable with praise. Compliments always made her feel unworthy because she knew they weren't true. "I don't know why he's still interested. There could be something really wrong with him. Do mental afflictions run in your family?"

"Funny, but no." Josslyn added another pie to the rack. "Gabe is as solid and

as sensible as a man gets."

"Hmm. If a mental disorder doesn't explain it, then I'm doomed."

"Why do you say that?"

"Because one day Gabe will take a good look at me and think, what am I doing with her?" She set down her knife. Her eyes were stinging so bad from the onion fumes, she had to wipe the tears on her sleeve. "I was actually hoping the mental thing would work in my favor."

"Don't even try and fool me. Gabriel is lucky to have you and he knows it." Josslyn shut the oven door and stopped talking the instant Cook looked across the large kitchen in their direction.

"What are you two doing?" The short, rotund woman scowled at them with her rat-like eyes. "If I catch you one more time, I'll tell Maureen and you both will pay dearly. No more talking. That's the rule."

"Yes, Ma'am." Josslyn needed the job and nodded contritely. Only Aumaleigh recognized the proud jut of her jaw. In her head, Josslyn must have plenty of sass she'd like to give to Cook.

Footsteps rounded the corner, pounding into the room with military precision. Aumaleigh's spine went straight, she took one final sniff and grabbed her knife.

But not quick enough.

"Aumaleigh!" Her mother, Maureen McPhee, charged into the kitchen, her mouth pressed into a tight line. "Don't even try and deny it. I heard what Cook said."

Aumaleigh's face turned hot. "I'm sorry, Mother. I'm not behind on my work."

"That's not the point." Maureen stormed to a stop at the work table, staring down her nose at the half diced onion. "You need to concentrate. How many times must I tell you? Work is the only thing you're good for, and you've got to get better at it. What will happen to you when I die?"

"Oh, Mother, please don't talk about dying." Her chest tightened. She didn't want to think of her mother gone. "Please go sit back down. I'll make you a cup of tea."

"With those onion-y fingers? I think not." Maureen glanced around, as if pleased to notice all the kitchen workers in the big farm kitchen had ceased their work and turned to watch another installment of the McPhee family drama. "The problem with you is that you never think, Aumaleigh. You're never considerate. Here I am, just trying to help you with your future. Do you think any man is going to want a girl like you?"

Yes. The treacherous word caught on her tongue. Her heart ached, thinking of Gabriel. Her mother must never know, so she bowed her head, feeling everyone's eyes on her. "No."

"That's right. A man wants a lovely and refined wife, not a mess of a girl like you. Look at those onions. You call that finely diced? Cook, make sure Aumaleigh stays through her supper, practicing until she can chop an onion correctly."

Aumaleigh's hand shook as she gripped the knife, angry words filling her head. Her vision blurred as she sliced the onion, listening to Maureen's heels tapping a cheerful rhythm on her way from the room.

"You've got to stand up for yourself, Aumaleigh." Josslyn whispered after everyone had turned back to their work. "You can't let your parents control your life."

"—isn't that right, Aumaleigh?" Rose's voice broke into her thoughts, stealing her away from the memory and that miserable time in her young life. She blinked, realizing all five of her nieces were staring at her as if waiting for an answer.

"I, uh—" She had no clue what to say. "Sorry, my mind drifted."

"That's the way it looked," Magnolia reassured her, holding a plate as Rose set a slice of chocolate cake on it. "You had to be a thousand miles away."

"And a few decades." Aumaleigh felt foolish. The past was gone. Why was she letting it grab hold of her again? Her regrets were over and done with. "What's the question?"

"It's me." Dottie lifted her shoulders in a self-conscious shrug. "Do you want me to leave in the morning so you all can get ready? I don't want to be in the way, and I'm not part of the family. You probably just want to be alone, and I completely understand."

The dear girl twirled a lock of dark hair around her finger, looking painfully nervous.

"No way are you walking anywhere. Or riding, for that matter." Aumaleigh lifted the tea kettle from the stove and poured steaming water into the teapot Iris had prepared. "I'm sure the girls will agree with me."

"Oh, we do." Rose spoke up, shaking the cake cutter for emphasis and a blob of frosting fell off.

Magnolia scooped it off the edge of the plate with her finger and popped it into her mouth, thinking no one was looking.

"You'll help me get the girls ready," Aumaleigh decided. "Come to think of it, you probably haven't had time to get a nice dress for the wedding. You only just moved in and started managing the bakery."

"I was going to wear what I already have. Ma always said it's good enough for me." Dottie shrugged self-consciously.

Aumaleigh winced. She had way too much experience with critical mothers. "Let's see. You're about the same height as Rose. After we're done demolishing the cake, let's go through her closet. I bet we can find a dress to fit you."

"Oh, no! That wouldn't be right." Dottie blushed bright red. "I'm fine, really I am. I couldn't wear someone else's dress. What if I spilled something on it? I might ruin it. I can be very clumsy."

"I have that green dress that would look perfect with Dottie's coloring." Rose cut a final piece of cake and slipped it onto a dessert plate for Dottie. "It's decided. Dottie, you have to wear it. I'm the bride and you can't disappoint me. It's a territorial law, I'm sure of it. You have to do what I say."

"Not to mention that we're your employers," Iris pointed out, handing Dottie a fork. "Let us do this for you. You have to get ready with us."

"And I'll do your hair," Verbena volunteered.

"Wait! Our shoes are about the same size," Magnolia hopped over to Dottie to compare feet. "I have some cute shoes that would look great with that green dress."

"Poor Dottie," Daisy sympathized. "She's going to be McPhee'd whether she likes it or not."

"Maybe she'll learn to love being one of us." Aumaleigh watched with fondness as the girls led the way out of the kitchen, carrying plates of cake for everyone. She snatched up the teapot, hanging back.

The memories in this house didn't seem to bother her anymore. The years she'd spent here taking care of her mother seemed distant. Guilt had kept her here, but love had too. She had to be honest about that.

However you looked at it, love wasn't easy. Families were complicated. Life wasn't fairytale perfect. Not even close.

But life could surprise you.

Aumaleigh whirled around, remembering to grab the honey jar. Laughter and conversation rang in the other room, echoing around her on the walls of the kitchen. Smiling, she listened to the sounds of the little girls running and playing, their shoes knelling merrily on the hardwood floor. The men's deep conversation paused while the women handed out cake, only to resume again once they had forks in hand. The women talked of dresses and how Dottie should wear her hair tomorrow.

The back door opened and Oscar slipped in with an armload of wood.

"Don't tell them I'm here," he whispered. "Just wanting to get everything ready for Rose's big day tomorrow."

"Thanks, Oscar." She nodded in agreement and in gratitude before slipping into the dining room.

This was the happiest she'd ever been. She savored every moment. With teapot in hand, she refilled cups, stopped to pet imaginary Mitsy and finally sat down with her nieces and Dottie. What an exciting evening, and tomorrow was Rose's wedding day.

* * *

Dawn peeked between the part in the curtains, stirring Rose McPhee from sleep. Her eyes popped open and she sat straight up in bed. Today she was going to become Mrs. Seth Daniels! Joy shivered through her as she tossed off her covers and leaped out of bed.

Okay, truth be told, she was shivering because it was cold too. She grabbed her warmest slippers and her quilted house coat and tossed open her door. Was that bacon frying? Following her nose, she headed down the hallway.

"Good morning!" Iris glanced up from the stove. "You're up early. Here I was hoping to get everything made before you woke up. You're the bride. You deserve breakfast in bed."

"You're going to be the next bride after me." Rose spotted the coffee pot and grabbed a clean cup. "Have you and Milo set a date yet?"

"Oh no, I'm not saying a word. You can't drag it out of me."

"Not even if I get some wild horses?"

"Go ahead and try. Nothing is going to get me to talk, not until after you and Seth are married."

"Well, that's in six hours." Rose glanced at the clock ticking away. "As soon as Seth kisses me, then I want to know. I'm the bride. You have to do what I say."

"You can pull that on Dottie, but it won't work on me." With a wink, Iris forked the bacon strips out of the pan. "How about at the reception? After the meal."

"That's a long time to wait." Rose poured a cup of coffee and returned the pot to the trivet. "Give me a hint right now?"

"You're as bad as Magnolia." Iris nodded toward the back door. "I think someone wants to see you."

"Seth!" Rose set down her cup and waltzed across the kitchen.

The sight of him fresh-shaven and tousle-haired set her heart to fluttering. The new light of dawn haloed him, making this feel like a dream as she went up on tiptoe for a kiss.

"You're not supposed to see me." She leaned back in his arms, grinning from ear to ear. "It's bad luck."

"Not for us, it isn't." He pulled something out of his coat pocket. The gold chain caught the morning's light, glinting like a promise of their happiness to come. "You need something new according to my ma."

"Yes, always listen to your mother, especially when it concerns presents for me." Rose took the chain. When their fingers met, it was as if their souls touched, leaving no doubt. This was true love.

* * *

Ashes banked? Yes. Aumaleigh poked her head into her new kitchen, surveying the half-unpacked room. *Lamps out? Yes. Back door locked? Yes.*

Satisfied, she grabbed her reticule, glanced in the newly hung oval mirror and frowned at her reflection. Gabriel was going to see her today, and she didn't feel ready for it. There just wasn't any way to stop it.

Oh, the girls might try, but she wasn't going to fool herself. Avoiding Gabriel was a waste of energy. Instead she was going to fortify herself, so that he would never guess how deeply he unsettled her.

Determined, she opened the door. A man was tethering her mare to the rail. She skidded to a stop.

"G-Gabriel?" His name seemed to stick in her throat.

"Sorry, I didn't mean for you to catch me here. I get the feeling you'd be fine with not seeing me again." His smoky baritone rumbled over her, friendly with a hint of something deeper, something she couldn't put her finger on.

Was it apologetic, perhaps? Well, he should be.

"I promised Seth that I would look after you this morning, get your mare hitched up since you had so much to do helping the girls."

JILLIAN HART | 29

Gabriel's maturity only made him all the more attractive. "I had planned to be gone before you came out of your house, but your horse had her own ideas."

"Yes, Buttons has always been a good judge of character. Doesn't she like you?"

"Apparently not." The docile old mare pulled back her lips, displaying her large and menacing horsy teeth.

"Good, Buttons." Aumaleigh swept down the stairs to praise her dear mare. "Well, your obligations as the groom's best man are done. It's been nice seeing you, Gabriel, but I'm in a hurry."

"Of course." He tipped his black Stetson in a gentlemanly fashion. The familiar movement stirred up a memory.

Seeing him in the moment, standing there in the morning sunshine and seeing him also in the past at the same time. The girl she'd once been, remembered.

But the woman she was now—the one who'd had her heart broken by him—wanted to give him a big push. Maybe he would fall backwards in the mud, new suit and all. Then she would drive off as if he'd never mattered to her one bit.

Okay, perhaps she had more built up animosity than she'd realized.

"I'll let you be on your way." He went to his black gelding standing patiently in the yard. "Isn't it funny? Who would have thought that after all these years we'd be neighbors?"

She blinked. Neighbors? What did that mean?

"You know the ranch next door?" Gabriel mounted up, a natural in the saddle. Back straight, wide shoulders squared, at ease as he gestured across the field to where the peak of a weathered red barn could be seen above the trees. "I bought it."

"Wh-what?" She crinkled up her forehead in thought, trying to marshal all her cognitive abilities, but her brain refused to function. "No, that's not right—I mean, Tyler would have told me. You're only visiting—"

"No, afraid not. I'm here to stay." Gabriel wheeled his horse down the driveway, riding into the east, into the sun, leaving her staring after him like a fool.

He was her neighbor? He was going to live in the same town? She would have to pass him on the road, see him in town, maybe shopping at the mercantile.

No, I can't do it. I just can't. Panic wrapped around her, making her stomach ache. She blinked into the sun, looking after him but he was gone, lost in the bright golden rays. She wanted to reach out, drag him back and demand why he was doing this.

But she knew. It was because of Josslyn. Gabe and Joss had repaired the rift in their relationship. It wasn't as if she could fault Josslyn for that, but Joss was her best friend. She could have given a warning, even mentioned it casually. *Say, you know the man who refused to marry you when you asked him to? The one who wasn't man enough to say no to your face? Well, he's moving to town. Just wanted you to know.*

Aumaleigh shook her head. Come to think of it, no wonder Josslyn hadn't said anything. There was no good way to bring that up either. None at all.

Well, it is what it is. She climbed into her buggy, set her bag on the floor and gathered the reins. As she steered Buttons down the road, her anger began to grow. Why had Gabriel come here after all this time? Did he *have* to move next door, of all the places in the world?

She was in a good mood to turn her buggy around, drive up to his house, bang on the door and give him a piece of her mind. He'd been the one who wanted to leave her behind back then. Why was he hanging around now?

She ground her teeth together. There ought to be a law. Former fiancés needed to keep their distance. He'd wanted another life, and he'd gotten it. Why did she have to be reminded of the mistakes she'd made?

Because that's what this was going to do to her. Every time she ran into him, spotted him down the street or across a store, she was going to be reminded of the biggest failure of her life.

If only she could borrow Magnolia's snake stick and chase him out of town with it. That would show him. The image of her chasing Gabriel down the road made her laugh out loud.

"Losing your mind?" a friendly voice called out. "Laughing for no reason is one of the first signs."

"Oh, I have a good reason," Aumaleigh assured Sheriff Milo Gray who'd pulled his paint gelding onto the side of the road, giving her plenty of room to pass.

That's when she noticed she was exactly in the middle of the road. She'd been too angry to see anything, much less a lawman coming her way.

"I'm guessing our new town resident is to blame." He seemed understanding, which was a good trait in a sheriff and in her future nephew-in-law. "I've heard all about it from Iris. Don't you worry, we're on your side."

Heard all about it? Did that mean everybody knew? And had thoroughly discussed it, all the while leaving her in the dark? Ooh, now she was mad again.

The subject of Gabriel Daniels sure struck a nerve. Best to take a deep breath, get rid of this anger and go back to her normal, non-angry way of handling things. "What are you doing out and about today? Shouldn't you be getting ready for the wedding? You're supposed to be Iris's date."

"True, I can't deny that, but I've decided to work today." The amiable smile died on his handsome, chiseled face. He was pure lawman, forged steel and integrity. "I've got all my deputies on duty today. We're going to make sure this town stays safe from our neighborhood vandals."

"That glint in your eye tells me you have a good idea who it is."

"I'm pleading the fifth on that. Have a good time at the wedding and save a piece of cake for me."

"I'll try, but maybe you should swing by the reception just in case."

"I'll keep that in mind." With a chin jut of farewell, Milo rode off, a man sure of his purpose.

Aumaleigh urged her mare a few more feet to park in front of the bakery. She'd slip inside and grab the wedding cake, boxed and ready for the reception. She didn't notice a man ease around the corner of the building and into the shadows.

Determined not to fall victim to any more bouts of anger at Gabriel, she hummed to herself while she left Buttons at the hitching post and let herself into the bakery.

CHAPTER FOUR

Junior Klemp had a bad feeling. He clutched the crock that once had held a very tasty stew the oldest McPhee sister had given him. It was a humiliation that she'd mistaken him for a homeless, vagabond sort and given him bread too, but her kindness stuck with him. There had been more times than he could count that he'd gone hungry in his life.

He set the crock and left it on the back door step. There. His obligation was over and done with. He'd never told his brother, Giddy, where the food had come from. Giddy didn't care about things like that.

But Junior's stomach had been twisted up in a terrible knot ever since. All because of his nerves. He was afraid Giddy was going to ask him to do something against Miss Iris. His brother was a mean one. Too much like Pa could get, when he was crossed.

Yep, it was a dilemma. Junior blew out a troubled sigh as he watched the sheriff from a distance. The blasted lawman stopped in the middle of the side street to exchange words with one of those bothersome volunteer deputies. The whole town was swarming with 'em.

The sheriff's words bugged him. That hoity-toity Aumaleigh McPhee had said in that superior voice of hers, *that glint in your eye tells me you have a good idea who it is.*

I'm pleading the fifth, the sheriff had answered. Junior's heart skipped a beat. Was it possible? Did Milo Gray know what he and Giddy had done?

To make matters worse, now there were three of them. Another deputy had ridden up with a serious look and a gun on his hip.

Junior's bad feeling turned worse. He crept out, staying in the shadows against the building. What were the lawmen talking about? What if they were really after him and Giddy?

"Young man?" An uppity, genteel lady's voice called out to him.

Blast it! Hatred burned fire-hot, but he managed to face her with a pleasant smile. "Good morning, Ma'am."

"Good morning. You know my nieces, don't you?" Aumaleigh McPhee might be acting friendly, but two bits said she was really looking down her nose at him. She set a big bakery box on the floor of her buggy. "Are you coming to the wedding today? I'm sure they would love to see you at the reception too."

"I was considering going." It wasn't the truth, but a good lie was a useful thing. He and Giddy had planned on replenishing their liquor supply, along with taking a few comforts from that stately Montgomery family home on the nice side of town. "Guess I'll see you there."

"The girls will be glad."

Looking at her phony smile nearly made him blow up right there. How dare she look at him like that, like she was the nicest lady in the world when she'd done what she'd done to his pa. She'd inherited the land, lock, stock and barrel, when a piece of it had been promised to Pa.

And that would have made a chunk of the Rocking M Ranch his and Giddy's. It was their inheritance, which was the same as their property. Think how hard Pa had worked for that old bat, Maureen, wearing his fingers to the bone while she lied and cheated him, keeping all that money to herself? And most of it was Aumaleigh's.

For now.

"Have a good day, Ma'am." Those words nearly killed him. He fisted his hands, staring at the tear in his boot. His sock poked through. It was getting worse.

"Say, you're walking without your crutch." Aumaleigh had turned back to him, studying him from the height of her buggy seat. "Good for you. It must be wonderful to be on the mend. Do you know Oscar? He's been in the same situation you are."

"I've seen him around," Junior frowned. Oscar had been the reason he'd feigned having a lame leg, getting the idea after seeing how Rose had taken sympathy on the man. Although it had been a mistake. He'd been wrong in thinking that gaining sympathy would be the way to get in good with the McPhees.

It never got him any closer to their money, and now he was torn. Torn up inside because of Iris.

"Oh, hi there, Wade." Aumaleigh called out to the deputy.

Junior bowed his head. The lawman offered a friendly hello as he rode by. And reminded him something was up. That bad feeling in his gut was still there.

Something wasn't right.

The uppity old McPhee woman drove away. Funny how she didn't drive a sparkling new buggy or a fine-stepping horse. No, her vehicle was in good repair but had a lot of miles on it, and her mare was old and slightly sway-backed. Certainly nothing of quality.

She's filthy rich. Giddy's words troubled him. It had to be true if she had the ranch. And just because he'd developed a soft spot for Iris didn't mean he had one for the rest of the McPhees.

He and Giddy were gonna get Pa's fair share one way or another.

That Aumaleigh was gonna regret pulling a fast one on Pa. Just you wait and see.

"What's going on there, young fellow?" A sociable voice interrupted his thoughts.

He blinked, realizing he was standing in the middle of the boardwalk in plain sight of the horde of lawmen gathering in front of an empty store front, that was in the middle of a remodel. The sheriff led the pack of a dozen men, riding fast and hard out of town.

Heading in the direction of their miserable little cabin.

Junior's blood went cold.

"Did you come by thinking we'd be open?" the chubby postman asked amiably. "We're closed for a few more hours yet. I'm just slipping out to get me some coffee. Come back closer to opening time and I'll let you in early. Mostly because I'll be heading off to Rose and Seth's wedding."

"Right, thanks," Junior said absently, walking off, staring at the tail end of the horses carrying the lawmen out of sight.

Giddy was at home alone. Junior took off, running across the street, even knowing the shortcut through the hills wouldn't get him there in time. But he had to try and save his brother.

"Hey!" The postman shouted out after him. "Your leg is healed! Good for you!"

Junior kept running.

* * *

"For a while there, I wasn't sure this day was gonna happen." Gabriel kept his voice low as they stood at the front of the church.

"Neither did I," Seth confessed, looking fine in his suit and tie. The boy didn't look nervous. No, he looked absolutely certain.

Gabe knew how that felt. He'd once stood before an altar, more than ready to take his vows and looking forward to the life to come. That was one adventure he wouldn't have missed for the world.

"You're going to do just fine, you and Rose." Gabriel knew it beyond all doubt. "From here on out and this day forward, your only job is to love her. Just love her. That's all. That's everything."

"That's my plan." Seth gave a wide grin. "Glad you could be here, Uncle Gabriel. But you didn't have to move out here and buy a place just on my account."

"Now you're teasing me, kid." Gabriel chuckled and shook his head. He caught sight of the full church behind them as folks settled into the last available spaces on the pews.

That's when the ground shifted and the sunlight falling through the stained-glass windows brightened. Aumaleigh McPhee stood behind the archway, giving the bride one last hug before making her way down the aisle.

"Wow, she's more beautiful than ever," Seth breathed. "I can't believe my eyes."

"I know how you feel." Air wedged sideways in Gabriel's chest.

How did Aumaleigh get more stunning over time? She wore a blue dress the same shade as her bluebonnet eyes. Her porcelain, heart-shaped face was dear to him, but time had changed it, drawn tiny lines around her eyes and softened the high cut of her cheekbones and the point of her chin.

Maturity looked good on her. She was more sure of herself, almost stately as she took her place in the second aisle on the bride's side of the church, next to some ladies he didn't know. Pain clutched his chest. She wouldn't look his way.

She had to have seen him. He was hard to miss standing front and center alongside the groom.

The minister cleared his throat. "Are we ready to start?"

"Yes," Seth answered and took Rose's hand in his.

Gabriel blinked. He'd missed Rose walking down the aisle, he was likely to miss more if he kept watching Aumaleigh. The past was so long ago. But was it long enough?

If he'd been able to get over her refusing to marry him, couldn't she move past it too?

He would have to figure out a way to help her do that.

* * *

Junior leaned against the rough bark of the Ponderosa pine, breathing hard. He pressed his hand against the stitch in his side. His lungs burned. Sweat rolled down his face. He hadn't pushed himself that hard in a long time, and it was all for nothing. He was too late.

Down below through the boughs of evergreens, he could see Pa's cabin. A ring of horses surrounded the building, standing patiently while two armed deputies patrolled the grounds. What were the chances Giddy had heard them coming and gotten out in time?

Maybe next to none.

There he was—that blasted sheriff strolling out the cabin door. "The fireplace is going. The cup of coffee is still steaming."

"Yep, we just missed them." A big, brawny man strolled out. It was one of the McPhee sister's husbands, the former bounty hunter. "There's only one set of tracks out the back door. I'll grab a few men and follow them."

"Take as many as you need." The sheriff frowned. "But don't you have a wife waiting for you? She'll want you to dance with her at Rose's reception."

"Dancing isn't my strong suit."

Whatever the men said next was lost on Junior. The back of his neck prickled—like he wasn't alone. His hand flew to his holstered revolver before he recognized his brother creeping through the underbrush.

"Shh!" Giddy held a finger to his lips. "I covered my tracks but one sound and it'll give us away."

"Right," Junior whispered back, so long it was less than a whisper. "Glad to see you, Giddy, I thought—"

"Shh." Giddy didn't even seem to care. His attention zeroed in on the men below. "There they are, the rats. That's our stuff now. They have no right."

Giddy's hands shook and he fisted them, like a man doing his best to stay in control. "I could just—just—"

That bad feeling was back, burrowing in Junior's guts. "C'mon, we gotta go."

Self-preservation kept him hiding in the shadows, leading the way among the ferns and moss, running while they had a head start. There was no going back. The sheriff was gonna figure out who they were, and he was going to see all the stolen stuff.

Now he was a man on the run, and Giddy too. How were they gonna make Pa proud now?

* * *

The wedding service was over and she hadn't had a single run-in with Gabriel. So far, so good. Aumaleigh grabbed the silver serving tray. There was only the meal left to go. She could do this. She just had to stay on the opposite side of the manor house from him, and she'd be fine.

"Aumaleigh!" Nora Montgomery waltzed over with the importance of a woman who was sure of her position in life. Her gown was the latest design and her jewelry ostentatious. "Goodness, you are always the little worker bee, aren't you? Then again, some women are simply made for work. I hear you bought yourself the darling little place on River Road."

Aumaleigh decided to let the insult slide by. "Yes, I moved in yesterday."

"How charming for you. Of course, with the income your ranch must make, you should have gotten something much more in line with your stature. I suppose your mother was right. You were always best suited for small things." Nora swiped a ham and cheese biscuit off the tray. "We'll be family soon. I suppose Tyler's will be the next wedding. If only your niece wasn't so pedestrian. Perhaps you could talk some sense into her. She insists on getting married in town, and as nice as this house is, it's hardly the Deer Springs Hotel."

"Nora, I'm not going to try to manipulate Magnolia for you. It's not going to happen. I'm sorry."

"You're not sorry!" Nora pushed a lock of carefully coiffed hair out of her face. Diamonds glittered as she whirled around. "I don't know what that girl did to get her hooks into my son, but I'm going to do my best to get her to let go —"

"Nora." Aumaleigh lowered her voice, surprised to hear the threat ringing there. But she wasn't sorry for it. "You have given my sweet niece a lot of grief, and if you do anything to stand in the way of Magnolia and Tyler's happiness, I will make you regret it."

"Your mother was always right about you." Nora's lovely face pruned with an ugly emotion. "No wonder you're alone at your age. You get what you deserve."

"Be careful, Nora. You just might wind up with what you deserve."

With a disdainful noise, the elite woman stalked off, perhaps in search of more upper-class and sophisticated folks to speak with.

"Don't listen to her." A familiar smoky baritone seemed to rumble through her. "She's wrong."

"I know." It took all her strength to turn around and face the one man she'd vowed to avoid. "Gabriel. Are you enjoying the party?"

"The food is tasty, and dinner hasn't even been served yet. The kids look happy, don't they?" He took a biscuit off the tray.

She wanted to fall through a hole in the floor and disappear. Where was a rotten floorboard when you needed one? "I think Rose and Seth are going to be very happy together. After all, he is the kind of good and gentle man who would never break Rose's heart."

"I agree. And Rose seems like the kind of young lady who would never hurt Seth." Gabriel's gaze pinned hers. His eyes were the same stormy gray. "I get the feeling that we aren't talking about the kids anymore."

"Of course we are," she denied. "What else would we be talking about?"

"How about the reason you seem so angry with me?"

Ooh! The calm and sincere way he spoke riled her up again. Anger welled up until she could barely breathe. The nerve of him! "I'm hardly angry with you. After all these years, why would I be?"

Any moment now a bolt of lightning was going to strike her dead. Horribly, utterly dead.

"My mistake." He took a bite of the biscuit. "Hmm, you made this, didn't you? I'd know your cooking anywhere."

He probably meant that as a compliment, so why did she have to fight off the overwhelming urge to beat him with the serving tray? A few sharp whaps upside his head would make her feel a whole lot better.

"That's my daughter." He gave a chin-jut in the direction of the parlor, where a charming young lady with ringlet curls and a stunning blue gown chatted with Rose and Verbena. "I wish my sons could have made it, but both of them are away at school. I'm a widower, you know."

"Josslyn mentioned it." Her anger wasn't really anger at all. "I'm sorry. I hope you and your wife had many happy years together."

"We did." Sorrow passed over his features, and the grief in his gray eyes reminded her of the young man she'd known, so sincere at heart.

Her eyes burned and she turned around before he could notice. "I've got to go circulate. Good seeing you again."

"You, too. Hey, Aumaleigh?"

She kept going, plowing into the parlor and knocking into someone's arm with the corner of the tray. "Excuse me."

"Aumaleigh! We've been looking for you." Rose stole the tray and set it aside. "You've got to meet my new cousin! Well, cousin by marriage. This is Gabriel's daughter."

"Yes, I know. Your father pointed you out to me." The instant she looked Gabriel's daughter in the face, emotions gripped her tight again. "You have your father's eyes."

"Yes, I do. And his chin, although the dimple in it isn't as deep, thank goodness!" Gabriel's daughter flashed a charming grin. "I've heard so much about you. Not so much before my mother passed away, but afterwards I've gotten a few stories out of Seth about you. You were his first love."

"Indeed." The anger that wasn't anger gathered in her chest, balling up into a hard fist. The pain of all she'd failed to have in her life—all that she'd failed to have with Gabriel. That loss hurt like a mortal wound. "It's lovely to meet you—"

"Leigh," the charming young lady said. "Everybody calls me Leigh, but my full name is Aumaleigh."

Aumaleigh? Shock bolted through her, wedging hard beneath her ribs. She couldn't breathe. The emotion wadding up in her chest exploded, leaving nothing but pain and shock. *Gabriel had named his only daughter Aumaleigh?*

"I see you two have met." He moved in from behind her to stand next to Rose and Leigh. Those deep, manly crinkles in the corners of his eyes dug deep into his tanned skin. Quite attractively. "Leigh is only staying here to help me get settled in. I was hoping that you McPhee girls could help her change her mind."

"I wouldn't even try," Rose sparkled. The wedding dress fit her to perfection, hugging her slender shape and complimenting her creamy complexion and blond locks perfectly. Her eyes shone as she winked at Leigh. "Do you have a beau back home?"

"Yes. And he's quite wonderful." Leigh blushed prettily. The girl was charming and likable and Aumaleigh could feel her heart opening, softening toward Gabriel's daughter.

Her hand shook as she picked up the tray. "Look at the time. Dinner is almost ready. I'd better go check on how the cooks are doing in the kitchen. Excuse me."

"Nice to meet you, Aumaleigh!" Gabriel's daughter called out sweetly.

If anyone else called out after her, she couldn't hear it. It took all her strength to walk away and stop the stinging behind her eyes.

Why had he named his daughter after her? It wasn't as if Aumaleigh was a common name. Had it been out of guilt? Out of nostalgia?

Or had it been out of love?

CHAPTER FIVE

Gabriel couldn't take his eyes off Aumaleigh. He sat next to his daughter at a large oak table among many tucked into the large and luxurious dining room. He hardly tasted the seasoned beef and scalloped potatoes on the plate in front of him. The rise and fall of conversations, the *clink* and *clang* of silverware and china, it was all background.

Aumaleigh sat at the table closest to the kitchen. The lamplight brought out copper highlights in her hair and caressed the side of her sweet face the way he once had.

Maybe the old love he'd held for her had never fully died, but he was no longer that young man so earnestly in love. Neither was she that gentle, sheltered girl. Life and time had changed them. They were strangers now.

How did he cross that divide between them? Could love, once lost, be captured again?

"Pa?" Leigh tugged on his sleeve. "Oh, I see what's got your attention."

"You do?" He blinked, whipping his gaze away from the molasses-haired beauty across the room. "I'm contemplating that cake over there. It looks tasty."

"Don't even try and fool me." She lifted her chin defiantly, eyes twinkling, sure she had him all figured out. "I really liked meeting her, you know."

"Meeting who?" It was best to play innocent.

"Aumaleigh." She waggled her eyebrows. "My namesake."

"I suppose you had to meet her sometime. Later would have been better."

"Seth says she was your first love. It's hard to imagine you were sweet on anyone besides Ma." Leigh took a casual sip from her water glass.

But he wasn't fooled. She was digging for as much information as she could get her hands on. "You're wrong. I didn't have a life before your mother. I just came into existence out of thin air one minute before we met."

"Okay, you don't want to tell me. I understand. Don't worry. I can get more details out of Seth." She winked, sweet as pie. As sweet as her namesake.

And his traitorous gaze zipped straight back to her. Aumaleigh rose from her chair, as tall and slim as ever, and twice as elegant. It was strange how deeply you could know another human being. So much of her had stayed the same—her smile, the way she moved, the gentle way she treated those around her.

And yet, there was so much about this Aumaleigh he didn't know. How did she spend her time? What had happened to her over the years? What did she want out of life now? She didn't seem to be aware of several older bachelors keeping an eye on her or moving in to ask her a question, just for the chance to speak with her.

"I hear from Rose and her sisters that their aunt never married. Imagine that." Leigh bit the corners of her mouth to hide her mischievous smile. "After you, she never married. Ever. If you ask me, that's romantic."

"I don't think I was the reason." That sadness haunted him. He watched as she bent to the task of clearing plates, and the humility she showed, a woman of means serving others, made his breath hitch. That was the Aumaleigh he'd once loved with all his soul.

"I hope you all enjoyed the meal." Rose McPhee Daniels stood up at the head of the largest table, and the crowd silenced.

"It was tasty, Rose!" a chubby, amiable man in the back called out.

"Thanks, Fred. I'll give your compliment to the cooks."

"Oh, I'll be happy to do that myself." Fred lifted his wine goblet in a toast and took a sip.

Smiling, Seth rose to his feet and took his wife's hand. Happiness radiated from them. You could see that they were a good match. That they were going to figure out marriage and wind up one of the very happy ones.

"Rose and I want to thank you all for being here to help us celebrate. If you'd like to head into the sunroom, there will be drinks and music for dancing. I have two left feet, but I promised Rose I'd give it a try."

Folks were laughing as they stood and moseyed from the dining room. Already several ladies and the McPhee girls were at work clearing the tables.

"Aumaleigh used to live here." Leigh stayed back with him, waiting for the crowd to thin. "I know because I asked. This is a beautiful manor, isn't it? It had to have been expensive to build. We've never lived in anything like this."

"That was Aumaleigh's mother. Her parents had money." He glanced around at the expensive things in the room, the quality construction— all that used to intimidate him.

"Ah! So you *did* tell me something about her. How did you meet her? Did Aunt Josslyn introduce you? Did you fall in love with her at first sight? Oh, maybe she was wise to your type and refused to talk to you. That's what I'd do."

He laughed, shaking his head. "It was exactly like that. She sent me packing."

"I knew it. Any smart woman would. Why Ma married you, I'll never know."

"It was a moment of weakness on her part. Or maybe just plain bad judgment."

"Everyone makes mistakes in life." Leigh sparkled up at him, far too young and perfect to ever have made a real mistake.

He draped an arm around her, full of pure, one-hundred-percent love for his little girl. "Why don't you go make more friends? And promise me you won't go digging for any old stories about me."

"Why make a promise I can't keep? That would just be wrong." Leigh bobbed away, leaving him standing in the emptying dining room.

Music started up, echoing through the house. Clearly Aumaleigh was doing her best to avoid him. She'd retreated to the kitchen where, judging by the number of voices and clanking of dishes, she was surrounded by a half dozen women. Way too many to try and talk to her. And she wasn't stepping foot back into the dining room. Other ladies were clearing the rest of the tables.

He was a patient man. He could wait.

* * *

"I bet you've never been so glad to have so many dishes to wash." Josslyn hustled over and stole the dishtowel right out of Aumaleigh's hands. "Am I right?"

"More than you know." She couldn't deny it, so she didn't even try. "Thanks for letting me hide here."

"It was tempting to toss you out, but I can't imagine what you're going through. He didn't even tell me that he was coming until he was here."

"You seem a little mad about that."

"I don't think he should move here, acting like everything is fine." Josslyn twisted the dishtowel in her hands, hopefully not as if it were Gabriel's neck. "He acts as if you were to blame, as if everything was your fault."

"I can't say he's entirely wrong." That truth cost her. It was hard to admit aloud, turning around to catch a glimpse of him down the length of the hallway, talking seriously with the apparently newly arriving sheriff. She closed her eyes for a moment, fighting resentment and that pesky anger. "I did refuse to marry him."

"He should have forgiven you." Josslyn threw the dishtowel onto the counter. "He and I get along so long as we don't talk about you."

"Then don't talk about me." Aumaleigh thought of her parents, dead. Her brothers, dead. "You never know how long you have with someone. Don't throw away another second with him. Promise me."

"Okay, but I know why you're saying that. You don't think you're worth it, but you are. I'm always on your side, Aumaleigh."

"And I'm always on yours. That's why I'm going to finish up here. You need to go and spend time with your family." Aumaleigh gave her lifelong friend a hug. "Go on. This is your son's wedding day. You've put enough time in the kitchen."

"It's my job and my pleasure." Josslyn glanced toward the archway, clearly looking past the crowd where her brother stood, still talking to Milo. "I hope you plan on sharing Rose, because I've always wanted a daughter. My son couldn't have found a better wife. I already love her so much."

"Lucky Rose." Aumaleigh shooed Josslyn out of the kitchen, but not before she caught Gabriel watching her. Fortunately she turned her back on him, blotted any thought of him right out of her mind. "Dottie, why are you still in here?"

"I want to help." The young woman was just the sweetest. She'd been as quiet as a mouse industriously lending a hand behind the scenes. "The sisters have been so good to me, offering me a job and taking me in. I want to treat them right. Let me finish setting up for dessert. I don't mind."

"Okay, I'd like the company." She shot a glance past dear Dottie to the far end of the hall, but Gabriel was no longer there.

Why did her heart give a pang of disappointment? She was angry at the man. She didn't want to see him.

"There you are!" Rose rustled in, resplendent in her wedding gown. "Dottie, I've been looking all over for you."

"For me?"

"There's someone I've been wanting you to meet. Come with me." Rose grabbed Dottie's hand. "Aumaleigh, is it okay if I steal her?"

"Only if you make sure she has some fun."

"I promise. C'mon, Dottie. You haven't met one of our neighbors yet. Lawrence Latimer has a sheep farm—" Rose's words were drown out by the crowd as she darted between people in the hallway, dragging Dottie in her wake.

Lawrence Latimer, huh? This she had to see. Aumaleigh went up on tiptoe, spying as Rose pulled Dottie to a stop in front of the odd little fellow who'd moved to town a few years ago.

Poor Lawrence. He looked terribly nervous, rubbing a hand over the balding spot in the middle of his head. His second-hand suit was carefully pressed and patched, and his handlebar mustaches bobbed as he took Dottie's hand in his and theatrically lifted it to his lips in what he likely thought was a gentlemanly kiss of greeting.

"He's not nearly as suave as he thinks he is, poor fellow," a familiar baritone rumbled behind her. Gabriel. "Is that the little man I've seen driving around with an old donkey and a homemade cart?"

"Yes. The cart is a little rickety."

"I'll say. The two of them seem to be getting along well."

"Dottie looks charmed." Aumaleigh's heart tugged, watching the shy young lady nervously push a lock of dark hair out of her eyes.

She blushed strawberry red and stared at the floor, looking terribly awkward. The poor girl. "That's exactly how I felt on our first date."

Realizing what she'd said, she gasped. The confession had rolled off her tongue without thought. She'd brought up the one thing she could not stand to talk about with Gabriel—the past. Not ever.

"I felt as out of place as that Lawrence fellow looks, too." Gabriel's deep voice warmed. "I didn't see what a beautiful lady like you wanted with a farmhand like me."

"I thought it was rather obvious." She could have lied, she could have said something glib or breezy, but she didn't. If Gabriel could be honest, then she could be too. "I counted myself lucky that you wanted to beau me."

"Which is proof that even the finest of ladies can have a flaw." His words dipped low, full of an old affection that was gone now, and it ached to remember.

Did he feel that way too?

"Dance with me." His hand caught hers. His touch was as familiar as dream, as real as a wish, and moved through her like a much-loved song. She was turning toward him before his arm came around her, anchoring her to him. His boot nudged her shoe in the first step of a waltz.

"I'm not the finest of ladies," she argued breathlessly.

"You are to me."

Did he know what he was doing to her? How could he torture her with what might-have-been? She tried to step back and break his hold on her but he held on tight, doggedly keeping her waltzing in time with the music and with him.

If she closed her eyes, she could feel time roll back. The girl within her remembered the thrill of being in his arms just like this, so close she could see black threads in his stormy gray eyes. He smelled the same—of leather, wood smoke and hay and it was somehow such a cozy scent, reminding her of laughing with him, of being in his arms in the sunshine, of the joy of simply resting her cheek against his chest.

He came to a stop in the middle of the kitchen, although the sweet strains of the music continued on. "Remember the first time we waltzed under the stars?" he asked.

"It would be better if I could forget." She tilted her head to meet his gaze. "I don't want to do this, Gabriel."

"It was just a waltz, that's all."

"No, this is far more. It's like you want to make peace or you think that I'm too quiet, like I used to be, and you can push me around—"

"Hey, wait, I don't think that—"

"You do," she argued. "You can't act as if everything between us is okay. It isn't. It never will be. You broke my heart. That might not mean much to you, but it did to me."

"No, you've got it wrong. I never meant to hurt you." Sincerity shone in his eyes. "Not you."

"What did you think would happen? I risked everything I loved for you—"

"That's not the way I remember it." He looked sorry. So, so sorry. "I shouldn't have brought up the past. I don't want to upset you."

"It's too late."

"I see that." He blew out a frustrated sigh and raked his fingers through his hair. "Maybe we should make a pact."

"I'm not sure I should make any deals with you. Gabriel, it's one thing for you to come to your nephew's wedding, but did you have to buy the house next door to me?"

"Travis Montgomery told me you had put an offer on the house. How could I refuse the chance to make things right with you?"

"Make things right? How are you going to do that?" She whirled away, pain raw in her voice. She walked away from him, leaving him standing like a fool in the middle of the kitchen.

Thankfully no one was around to see the charming way he had with the lady.

She reached the kitchen door and turned to face him. She must have gotten her emotions under control because she was staring at him like an Army general about to sentence an enemy for treason.

"I don't want to make a pact with you." She said it like she meant every word. "I don't want to call a truce. I want you to go back where you came from and stay there. Permanently."

"Sorry. No." He slid his hands into his trouser pockets, giving time for his words to sink in. "I'm not going anywhere. My life is over in Ohio. My wife is gone. My sons have moved away. When Leigh marries her beau, I'll be alone."

"That's really not my problem." Her eyes filled, pain hovering in the form of tears just behind her lashes. "I don't want you here, Gabe."

"I'm starting to understand that."

"Would you stop sounding so reasonable? You're standing there so logical, like everything is better because decades have passed. But that's not true."

"No, Aumaleigh, that's not—"

"Do you know how hard it is to look at you?" she interrupted. "To know it wasn't me you loved? It wasn't me you married, it wasn't me you raised a family with. It wasn't me. I'm just so angry at you for that. It's irrational, I know, and unreasonable. I gave your engagement ring back. I broke off the wedding, and I just—"

She covered her face with her hands. Standing perfectly still, she didn't move a muscle. It didn't look as if she was even breathing. The air grew heavy with the depth of her pain.

The back of his throat ached. He swallowed hard, trying to master his emotions. He couldn't run to her. He couldn't comfort her. He didn't have the right to hold her.

Time had rendered them strangers.

"We're different people than we used to be." It was the only thing he could offer her. "Life has changed me. I'm not the same young man who was wet behind the ears. Back then I didn't know much about life and even less about loving a woman."

"You'll get no arguments from me." She lowered her hands. Her mouth curved up in a ghost of a grin, but there was still sadness there. Still pain. "I never should have given you back the ring. I'm sorry I broke your heart."

"I'm sorry too."

"Maybe you've got your truce after all." She swallowed hard, trying to get past the emotion lodged in her throat. "But things are never going to be easy between us. It hurts to see you. I don't think that is ever going to go away."

"Okay. Good to know." He bobbed his head once in acknowledgement, studying her as if he was trying to see deeply into her heart. "This isn't easy for me either."

"Then why move here?"

"Because I had to." He said nothing more, leaving her in the silence of the kitchen, feeling more alone than she'd been in a long while.

She wrapped her arms around her middle, maybe for comfort, maybe to try to hold everything still inside her heart. No good could come from letting what he'd said have any effect on her.

"There you are." Daisy swept in with a rustle of her dress and joy on her face. "We're ready for the cake. Oh, good. You have the dessert plates ready. Did you and Gabriel have a chance to catch up?"

"In the few moments before I sent him out of the kitchen." She whisked a high stack of plates off the counter.

It had been supremely easy for Gabriel to move on and marry someone else. Proof she was never the love of his life.

She set the stack of dishes on the cloth draped table holding the wedding cake. Iris had gone all out on the design. She'd made a horse and sleigh out of cake, decorating it with colorful frosting, depicting Rose's horse, Wally, and Seth's jingle-bell sleigh to perfection.

"Did you see Dottie and Lawrence?" Magnolia rushed up, pink-cheeked from her hurry to spread the latest news. "Rose was right. The two of them are adorable. They haven't stepped away from each other. He's talking a mile a minute, and she's actually charmed by him. I didn't think such a thing was possible."

"It only goes to prove there's a perfect match for everyone." Daisy fussed with the cake server, making sure the silk ribbon on its handle was tied just right. "Everyone deserves to be really loved."

"Even Lawrence," Magnolia agreed, watching the young couple with satisfaction.

True love and happy marriages were all around her. Aumaleigh knew better than to let herself get caught up in the dream. Her time for that had passed her by. Besides, she was happy being a great aunt. She laughed as Sally and Hailie pranced by with their imaginary baby dragons.

CHAPTER SIX

Iris McPhee hummed to herself in the sparkling new kitchen of the Bluebell Bakery. She whipped up a bowl of chocolate fudge frosting, listening to the bell over the front door ring through the store and the thump of the oven door as Wynne took loaves of bread from the heat. Life was good. So, so good.

"Maebry is here for Gil's birthday cake." Dottie looked professional with her blueberry blue apron over her light blue calico dress, but it was the ear-to-ear grin that was uncharacteristic. She bounced to a stop. "I didn't know if you wanted to say hi to her. I know you two are family."

"Yes, she is." Iris gave the frosting in the bowl another stir before relinquishing her hold on the wooden spoon. "Remember, don't say a word about her surprise shower."

"My lips are sealed." Dottie rocked back on her heels, looking like a woman who couldn't contain her happiness. Remembering seeing Dottie and Lawrence in rapt conversation at Rose's wedding, Iris smiled to herself. She followed Dottie through the swinging doors and into the front of the store.

"Iris!" Maebry looked luminous, sporting a round belly and glowing with happiness. Her blond hair tumbled down from her blue knit hat. She rushed over for a hug. It was a little awkward with her stomach, but Maebry only laughed. "I feel enormous. Gil had to help me with my shoes this morning."

"It's getting close now. You must be sewing and knitting up a storm."

"It's crazy everything a baby needs, but I think we're almost there. Gil is making a cradle for our room. It's just the sweetest thing." Maebry happily rubbed the curve of her belly. "I can't wait."

"Gil must be over the moon."

"He's going to be a proud papa. I just never thought this kind of happiness would happen for me."

"I know just what you mean." Iris's chest tightened, remembering how she'd broken things off with Milo. That seemed a lifetime ago, but now her world had changed for the better too. She twisted the beautiful engagement ring on her left hand. "There's nothing like living your dream."

"Exactly." Maebry blinked the emotion from her eyes. "What about you and Milo? Any word on a date yet?"

Iris stared down at the beautiful amethyst sparkling on her left ring finger, surrounded by diamonds. The girls had picked it out for her with Milo's help. "Are you and Gil doing anything next weekend?"

"What? So soon? Oh, we'll be there. Absolutely. Iris, this is so exciting. How can you stand there looking so calm?"

"I'm jumping for joy inside." That was the truth. She couldn't believe it either. She was going to be a wife and mother, and one day she would be expecting a baby of her own. Sadie and Sally needed a little brother or sister, right?

"Here's your cake, Maebry." Dottie slid a bakery box across the counter. "On second thought, it'll probably be pretty awkward for you to carry. Let me do it for you, when you're ready to go."

"Thanks, Dottie. That's really nice of you." Maebry smiled. "Say, you look happy. You have something exciting going on in your life."

"I do!" Dottie bent over the ledger, adding Maebry's purchase to her account. "I finally have my own place. I'm so excited. I don't have to take advantage of the McPhee sisters anymore—"

"You aren't taking advantage," Iris interrupted her, because no way did she want Dottie to feel like that.

"But staying with you and your sisters was only temporary. I've rented rooms that are close to the bakery. I can walk over, which is good because I don't have a horse."

"I wasn't talking about that news." Maebry waggled her eyebrows. "I meant something much more romantic. I saw you spending some time with Lawrence. You two seemed to be getting along."

"Oh, yes! We talked for nearly an hour, and then he had to go and take care of his baby lambs." Dottie set down the pencil and closed the account book. "But I don't think it was romantic. I mean, Lawrence was just being nice to me. You've probably noticed I'm kind of homely, and it's not like a handsome man like him would be interested."

Iris bit her lip at the word *handsome*. Beauty truly was in the eye of the beholder. "So, you like Lawrence?"

"Who wouldn't?" Dottie's dark eyes lit up. "I mean, he's so thoughtful and courteous. That's hard to find in a man these days. And I've always liked a man with a handlebar mustache."

"We've all known Lawrence for quite a while." Maebry smiled, looking genuinely happy for Dottie. "He's a good, honest and hardworking man and I think he would treat a lady right."

"I do too." Iris was sure about that. Could there be a happy ending in the future for Dottie too? That was something to hope for. "Lawrence comes in now and then for a loaf of bread. Maybe you'll get a chance to treat him to a cup of coffee and talk with him for a bit."

"Really? I mean, I wouldn't if it were busy or something." Dottie brightened, giving her lopsided, adorable smile. "Okay, I'll do it. I mean, not because he likes me or anything, but maybe we could at least be friends."

"Dottie, I think he likes you." Iris studied the younger woman who was so sweet, she felt like a little sister. Someone you would always want to know. "I don't want to hear you call yourself homely ever again. Got it? You are adorable, and Lawrence would be lucky to have someone like you."

"I know you're just saying that, but thanks." Dottie's lower lip trembled. "Thanks a lot."

The bell on the door chimed merrily as Magnolia tromped in. Sunshine spilled in the door with her as she bounded to a stop, slammed the door and unbuttoned her spring coat. "Ooh, I'm so mad. Just spitting, hitting mad."

"Not again." Iris rolled her eyes. "What is it this time? Not more wedding stuff?"

"No, Travis's mother has stopped talking to me and says she isn't coming to the wedding, which is actually a relief. That's not why I'm, ooh, I'm just furious. Just ready to grab my snake stick and just—oh, I don't know what I'd do with it, but something! You know the building that's being renovated just down the block and across the street?"

"Yes, we've all been wondering what business is coming to town." Iris went straight to the window to take a peek. A wagon was parked out front, if she squinted she could just make out a newly hung sign, but the angle was wrong and she was too far away. "I can't read it."

"Dobson's Bakery!" Magnolia fisted her hands. "That woman, that Fanny Dobson, is opening up a store right here in town to compete with us. Can you believe it?"

"Oh, I hate her." Dottie circled the counter and marched up to the window. "She's coming after your business. What are we going to do?"

"I'll never order a cake from there." Maebry's chin went up. "I don't know this Fanny Dobson, but she doesn't sound like a very nice businesswoman."

"She's not," Dottie assured everyone. "I know it for a fact. What do you think, Iris? You're very quiet."

"I'm just shocked." Iris bit her bottom lip, thinking. "This town can't support two bakeries. There just isn't enough business for both of us."

The front door swung open and Rhoda marched in, hugging a bag of sugar. "Everyone is talking about it over at the mercantile. You're going to stay open, aren't you, Iris? Are we going to fight this?"

All eyes turned to her. She read the need in Dottie's and the desperation in Rhoda's. Magnolia arched her brows in a silent question, likely thinking the same thing she was. This bakery had always been her dream, back in their Chicago days when she'd been working hard hours for little pay. Her sisters had taken on her vision as their own and they'd built this business together. But now that she'd found Milo, she had a different future than they'd all imagined back then.

What were they going to do with the bakery?

"We didn't come this far just to close up shop." She knew it was the right decision the instant she spoke the words. They just felt right. "Fanny Dobson can do what she wants. It's a free country. But we are going to stay right here and bake the best cakes and cookies in the territory. We aren't going anywhere."

Dottie blew out a relieved sigh. Rhoda mouthed a silent thank you. They weren't the only two employees who needed their jobs. Iris remembered what that was like. She would never forget. A familiar

Stetson caught her attention, and joy moved through her, silent and deep. *Milo*. He spotted her and lifted a gloved hand in recognition. She waved back, watching as he ambled out of sight.

Her impossible dreams were coming true. It was time to help someone else with theirs. Dottie's dream of independence from her parents. Rhoda's dream of supporting her children, Oscar and Clint Redmond's dreams of being self-sufficient again. Leaving gift boxes of day old bread and cookies on the doorsteps of the needy families in town. That's what this bakery was going to be all about from this moment on. Fannie Dobson didn't stand a chance.

* * *

Aumaleigh pulled Buttons to a stop in the middle of the road, staring at the sign swinging above the boardwalk. *Dobson's Bakery*. She had to blink twice to make sure she wasn't seeing things. This wasn't a good development. Not good at all.

"Howdy there, Aumaleigh." Clint Redmond drew the bakery's horse and delivery wagon to a stop on the opposite side of the street. "Guess you're thinkin' the same thing I am. Maybe you don't know all the businesses Dobson's has closed down over in Deer Springs."

"I've heard rumors about it. I can't say I'm pleased to see them here." Aumaleigh squinted against the spring sunshine. Clint looked much improved these days, now that he was working for the girls. He had an easy smile and a relaxed manner. It was nice to see, since his family had a long struggle with hardship. "On the other hand, I don't doubt my nieces will rise to the challenge."

"Good to hear. I like my job." Clint's deep voice cracked and he gave his reins a shake. "Good day to you, Aumaleigh."

"Take care, Clint." Aumaleigh did the same, guiding Buttons down the street. Town was quiet, almost empty feeling. This time of year so many farmers were busy with planting their fields or tending their herds of new cow/calf pairs. Women all over the country were out working in their gardens on a day like this. Which is what she was going to do once she finished this very important meeting.

Buttons stopped obediently in front of the hitching post, and Aumaleigh hopped down. The past few days had been uneventful, and she hadn't come across Gabriel once. But that didn't stop her from glancing up and down the boardwalk before climbing onto it and tapping up the steps to the mercantile.

"Aumaleigh!" Gemma Gunderson looked up from the front counter. She was such a dear with her dark locks and ready smile. "Welcome. How are you today?"

"Just coming in to order supplies for the ranch." She closed the door behind her and pulled a list out of her reticule. "You know it's never ending. Keeping enough on hand to feed the horde of cowboys isn't easy."

"I'm here to help." Gemma closed the account book she was working on and came around the end of the counter. "Give me what you need and I'll get right on it. I can have it delivered before suppertime."

"Perfect." She handed over the long list. "What do you think about your new neighbors?"

"Oh, I'm fuming mad. I can see their sign from here." Gemma glanced at the list before setting it on the counter. "She's already been in here to try and get her products back in here. Father wasn't in, so I asked her to leave. I don't like the way she does business."

"From what I've heard, neither do I. I've got to get back to the ranch and see if I can't get some garden work done. Have a good afternoon, Gemma and thanks." She took a step backwards and bumped into someone.

"Oops! Sorry." Leigh Daniels, Gabriel's daughter, grabbed the skein of glossy white crochet thread she'd dropped. "I did kind of sneak up on you. Can we talk?"

"I—" Aumaleigh searched desperately through her head, trying to find the exact right excuse—any excuse—to escape. Her brain failed her. Not a single excuse came.

"Great! Gemma, could you please put this on my pa's account? Thanks." Leigh breathlessly bobbed toward the door and yanked it open. "I had wanted to ask you a few things at the wedding, but you didn't get out of the kitchen very much."

"There was a lot to do behind the scenes, to keep everything running smoothly."

"Sure. That's why I'm so glad we have this time now." Leigh leaned against the railing. "I didn't know I was named after someone until I met you. You must have been pretty important to my pa."

"At one time." Her throat felt tight. "Maybe not important enough."

"You were in love with him, weren't you? I can tell by your face."

Leigh played with her bonnet ribbons. "I think he loved you with all his heart."

"I hope so, since he once proposed to me." Her voice sounded squeaky, not at all like her own. She stared off down the street where a sturdy, mannish woman came out onto the boardwalk to angrily shout at the workman who was straightening up the Dobson's Bakery sign.

"I can't believe that. It's hard to imagine Pa had a life before he met my ma." Leigh shook her head, scattering her dark curls. "I've been trying to figure out why Pa would want me named after you. I mean, it's not like it's a common name and if he loved you enough to want to marry you—" The girl stopped, falling silent. "Was it painful, what happened between you? I won't go on if it is."

"It was a long time ago. Water under the bridge." Aumaleigh wished she didn't like Gabriel's daughter so much. "I'm sorry you lost your mother."

"Thanks. It was hard. It's been five years and I still miss her every single day." Leigh pulled at a thread in her bonnet ribbon, fraying it. For an instant she looked heartbroken, but shrugged it off. "Pa took such good care of Ma, especially after she got sick. Losing her was hard for him too. I think it's nice that he's found you again."

Aumaleigh felt her jaw drop even farther. The back of her neck itched, and she shivered as footsteps came to a stop behind her. She didn't need to turn around to know it was him. Her entire being sensed him, soul deep.

"Leigh, that's enough." Humor layered his voice. "What are you doing now?"

"Nothing. Just talking with Miss Aumaleigh. You know me. I'm curious."

"Yes, well, go be curious somewhere else." Gabriel planted his hand on his hips. "Go on."

"Oh, Pa." Leigh rolled her eyes. "Fine. I'll go look at yarn in the dry goods store, and I'm going to buy a lot of it. The expensive stuff too. Serves you right for wanting to get rid of me."

"I'll survive." Humor made his eyes a warm, tender gray as he watched his daughter cross the street. "I don't know where I went wrong. She was so sweet when she was little."

"She's adorable." That was the plain truth. Aumaleigh took a deep breath. She was over the pain, over the past, but was she over the anger? No, as it was brewing. "What do I have to do to get rid of you?"

"Good question. Maybe beat me with a long stick. Throw a cow pie at me. Kick me in the shin?"

"If only that would work." Aumaleigh noticed Gemma watching through the window. She glanced down the boardwalk and there was her niece, Annie, standing in front of the Bluebell Bakery openly staring. Any moment now Fred was going to step foot outside the post office and rumors would start to fly. "When is your daughter going back to Ohio?"

"Soon. I'm keeping her for a little longer. She's determined to get my house set up before she goes." He stared down the street, when all he wanted to do was to soak up the sight of her. To memorize all the little things about her he needed to learn anew. "Seth and Rose seem happy. They had me and Leigh over to supper last night."

"Oh? I hadn't heard a thing about it. Yet. I've got to go. I have a ranch to run."

"I heard you inherited quite a spread. Ranching is in your blood."

"Yours too." She smoothed a wrinkle in her skirt self-consciously. "Did you ever build that ranch you hoped for?"

"I sure did." The land he'd bought in the same small town in Ohio had never been the ranch he'd dreamed of having for her. The young man he'd been had been so sure that he needed money and standing to truly win her and keep her. He'd wised up, and in life his hard work had paid off. "I've retired now. I can enjoy the good life."

"Here in Bluebell? Maybe you'd be happier somewhere with more things to do. Like New York."

"That's nice and far away. I'm sure you'd like that. Can I ask you a favor?"

"I don't know." She arched a slender brow, studying him warily. "We've reached a truce, but I don't think that entitles you to favors."

"I know Leigh was asking questions about our past. Don't feel obligated to answer. You can tell her no."

"That's your favor?"

"Yes. Let's leave the past alone." Time may have passed, but Aumaleigh had never been one who could easily hide everything. Her heart was still tender.

"All right." Her gaze met his, and there was no smile there, no twinkle. He missed the way she used to look up at him full of humor and alive with love.

Would she ever look at him that way again?

He didn't know. But he was determined.

"Here, let me help you up into your buggy." He held out his hand, palm up, not wanting to give away how much this chance meant to him. "It's the gentlemanly thing to do. Any man worth his salt would do the same."

"Is that so?" A smile touched her soft lips, but sadness stole the life from her eyes. "I don't think there's one man in this town I've let help me into my buggy, who wasn't an employee or a nephew-in-law."

"Don't try to use that against me." He moved in, took her hand in his since she wasn't being agreeable. The instant they touched, his chest cinched tight. A mix of old emotions, both good and bad, haunted him.

But so did new ones.

If they'd never met, if they'd never loved, he still would be standing here just like this, caught in the moment between taking her hand and helping her up into her buggy. When their gazes met, he could see into her, see the lonely heart some stupid young man had broken long ago.

If he'd never known her, this moment would still have changed his life. His pulse came to a stop at the silken warmth of her hand in his. He breathed in her faint roses scent. As she lowered her foot onto the running board, he caught hold of her elbow with his other hand to help her up.

Sweet emotion rushed into him—all brand new. His feelings weren't coming back for her. This was a new love coming to life.

"Next time, promise me you aren't going to make such a spectacle." She gathered the reins in her hands, unaware of the way the sunlight glinted in her dark, rich hair and kissed the side of her creamy cheek. A pretend frown curved her mouth. "You've done it now, Gabriel. Fred has seen us. He's the biggest gossip I've ever met."

"Good." Gabriel tipped his hat so he could get a better view of her sitting up with the wind in her hair.

"*Good?*" She snapped the reins, backing the old mare away from the hitching post. "How can you say such a thing? It's not good at all."

"Sure it is." He tossed her a grin. "It's been a while since I've been gossiped about. I'm going to enjoy it."

"If I had a whip I'd hit you with it. What a thing to say." She tugged on the reins, turning the horse around in the road, apparently eager to get away from him. "Don't tease me like that."

"Who's teasing?" He had to call out because she was driving away and he didn't know if she'd heard him, but it didn't matter. This wasn't over yet. He'd caught sight of that smile she tried to hide.

Once, their love had been meant to be.

And it could be again.

Whistling to himself, he went in search of his daughter. Heaven knew what she was charging to his account.

CHAPTER SEVEN

It's been a while since I've been gossiped about. I'm going to enjoy it. Gabriel's words had her fuming and she couldn't stop. Aumaleigh jammed the trowel into the earth and dirt went flying. He wanted to be the center of attention, did he? Well, she did not.

"Is everything all right?" Louisa asked. The sweet kitchen helper had traded her apron for gardening gloves on this fine, warm spring afternoon. "You seem troubled. Can I do anything for you?"

"No, there's no cure I'm afraid." Not as along as Gabriel was alive and in this town.

No, she thought wistfully. Even dead, he'd still be trouble if he was buried in this town. *Wait, had she really thought that?* She tilted her head, frowning and then laughing at herself. She, of course, wouldn't wish death on anyone, just like she wouldn't actually want to shove someone into the mud. Or chase them with a snake stick.

But thinking about it did make her chuckle.

"Now she's laughing to herself," a different voice whispered. "Should we worry?"

"I heard that, Orla." Aumaleigh slid a couple seeds into the earth and covered them gently. "You know I'm perfectly fine."

"Right. You just have a lot on your mind." Orla lumbered up, driving a wheelbarrow full of mulch and manure. "I heard all about it."

"All about what?" Louisa wanted to know.

Aumaleigh's stomach knotted. "You weren't in town, were you,

Orla?"

"Sure I was. I mixed up a good batch of fertilizer and took it in for my mama. Gonna help with her garden when I get off work." Orla maneuvered the wheelbarrow over to the end of the acre-sized garden patch and swiped her brow with the back of her glove. "Do you know what I saw from the side street next to that new bakery going in?"

"What?" Louisa wanted to know. "What did you see? Was it something good?"

Aumaleigh cringed. "I'm surprised you haven't heard the rumors. Fred is falling down on the job."

"Oh, I'm sure he's gossiping at full speed." Orla's words were laced with amusement. "I never thought the day would come. Just goes to show you can never give up hope."

"Hope for what?" Louisa asked. "Why isn't anyone telling me anything? I'm dying to know!"

"It's nothing." Aumaleigh spread her trowel into the row, neatly turning the earth this time. "Let's change the subject."

"Let's not." Orla picked up her shovel and stabbed it into the soft loam of tilled soil. "I saw Aumaleigh sharing a moment with a handsome man."

Aumaleigh grimaced. "It wasn't a moment."

"Aumaleigh!" Louisa clapped her gloved hands, delighted. Tiny bits of dirt flew everywhere. "I'm so excited for you. There are several men in town who have been watching you for a while. How long has this been going on? Do you have a beau now?"

"No!" Aumaleigh patted more seeds into the earth. "I have nothing of the sort."

"That's not what I saw." Orla added a shovelful of fertilizer into the garden row. "Gabriel Daniels looked pretty amorous, if you ask me. The way he helped you into your buggy, there was something serious about it. He's a courting man, mark my words."

"Ooh!" Louisa brightened. "Are you talking about Josslyn's brother? He is terribly handsome. Much too old for me, but even then, he sort of stops your heart. Do you know what I mean, Orla?"

"Oh, I do, and I'm old enough for him." Orla winked, mixing manure into the dirt. "Maybe I'll knock Aumaleigh aside and take him for myself."

"Be my guest." She scooted down the row and dug in with her

trowel. "He's all yours, Orla."

"Oh, I doubt he'd want anything to do with me, when he can't seem to see anyone else but you."

"It's not like that." Was it anger burning behind her sternum? Or something else?

"Then what is it like?" Louisa wanted to know, pausing her work planting the radish seeds to frown with concern. "You look upset, Aumaleigh. Why? You must be like me, not a spinster by choice. If a handsome and nice man likes you, what's wrong with that?"

"Nothing." She stared at the seeds in her hand. Neither Orla nor Louisa knew about her past love affair and its catastrophic failure. Did she finally open up and talk about that old wound? Or would it be better just to get back to work and let it blow over?

Fortunately, the mercantile delivery wagon pulled up and Aumaleigh left her employees to go deal with it. By the time she had everything unloaded and packed away in the pantry, it was time to start supper. Since the horde of cowboys would be frothing at the mouth if their meal was one minute late, it was best to get right to work.

With so much to do, there was no time to talk about men, handsome or not, until the cowboys were fed and the dishes washed. Everyone was so tired by then, it was all Aumaleigh could do to utter a farewell and stagger out the door.

"Hey, Aumaleigh." Kellan greeted her in the barn. He'd been on the ranch a long time, first working hard for her mother and now for her. A man in his mid-thirties, he carried himself with that cowboy inbred sense of honor and might. "I got your mare hitched and ready to go."

"Thanks, Kellan. You're a wonder."

"That I am." He blushed, holding out his hand to help her into the buggy.

Always such a gentleman. She accepted his help, slipping onto the cushioned seat.

"I hear I'm not the first man to lend you a hand up today." He tipped his Stetson, grinning from ear to ear. "News travels fast."

"It's all lies. It never happened." She winked, taking the reins from him. "That Fred got it wrong again."

"Nice try, but trying to derail the rumor's not going to work. Everyone knows Fred gets the gossip right before he repeats it."

"More's the pity." Aumaleigh gave a soft chuckle. The sun had set, painting a purple glow on the underbellies of the few clouds overhead. "I suppose it's too late to stop the rumors?"

"They've likely set the countryside on fire by now." Kellan strolled over to open the double barn doors. "I can see the flames from here."

"Too bad there isn't a way to put it out."

"There's no chance of that, believe me. Everyone will be talking about this for a while. A longtime spinster like you and a widower like Gabriel? You deserve happiness. I hope it works out for you."

"I'll drop dead first." She laughed, although she wasn't entirely joking and took charge of the reins, urging Buttons forward. "Good night, Kellan, and thanks."

"Any time." He gave her a farewell salute as she rolled through the door.

Goodness! Did everyone have to know her business? And why did Fred feel compelled to tell everyone about it? Perplexed, she guided Buttons down the long sloping driveway, beneath the sign that said *Rocking M Ranch,* and onto the road to town.

"Good evening, fair madam." Lawrence called out in the dark. He was heading up the road as she headed down. He pulled his donkey to a stop. "I hope you are well."

"Very much so." She pulled Buttons to a stop too. She rather liked her odd little neighbor. "How are your new lambs doing?"

"Very well." Lawrence's handlebar mustache quivered with excitement. "I have fifty little ones now, and every one is as cute as could be. They don't survive very well, you have to take extra good care of them, you know. This is my first lambing and I haven't lost a single one."

"You have a gift, Lawrence." She felt rather motherly toward the strange little fellow. She wondered if he had any family of his own. He'd spent Christmas Eve at the ranch, when she'd thrown a big party for her family and the cowboys. "I saw you and a certain young lady spending time together at Rose and Seth's reception."

"Oh, you noticed, did you?" He bowed his head, self-conscious. "I was fortunate enough to enjoy Miss Dottie's company. Not only is she lovely, but she's quite the conversationalist. I'm sure she'll be an excellent manager of your nieces' bakery."

"Yes, I think so too." Wasn't it funny that Lawrence, who'd been so bold and gallant, seemed shy and unsure of himself when he talked about Dottie. "Perhaps you'll want to drop by and pay a visit to her at the bakery. She's new in town, and I'm sure it would mean a lot to her to make a friend of you."

"Do you think so?" Lawrence leaned forward in his seat. "I mean, if she's in need of a friend, I suppose I could step in."

"Yes, or perhaps she needs more than a friend. You never know until you try." She just liked the idea of Dottie and Lawrence together. Were they made for each other? Only time would tell.

"Thanks for the advice, Aumaleigh. I hear you have a bit of a romance going on with that new widower in town."

"Not a romance," she corrected, because it was only the truth. She was proud of herself for not even sounding defensive. "He simply helped me into my buggy. That's all."

"I hope he is interested in you." Lawrence snapped his reins, and his donkey stepped forward. "Maybe he's in need of more than a friend too."

She chose not to argue. What good would it do? Besides, Lawrence meant well. She waved goodbye and sent Buttons trotting down the lane. The road was dark and empty up ahead (thank goodness). Luck was with her. She didn't come across anyone else. When she saw the lights of town, she let out a relieved sigh. In hardly any time at all she would be home.

"Hi, Aumaleigh!" A friendly male voice called out in the gathering darkness. "You must be on your way home."

"Yes, thanks, Tyler." She drew Buttons to a stop to wait for the horse and buckboard to approach. "I hardly saw you at the wedding."

"I was there for the meal but left right after." Harnessing jingled as he pulled his horse, Clancy, to a stop. "Father had this big deal he had to put together. He's not one to put off making money for any reason."

"True. I've known Lance for a long time." She stared down the road, where the lights of town gleamed like a beacon. She could make out Fred stepping out onto the boardwalk and locking the post office door behind him. "Why didn't you tell me about Gabriel Daniels moving in next door? You could have warned me. Surely you know the history."

"I do, but it wasn't my story to tell. Mr. Daniels asked me to keep it confidential, so I did." Tyler's tone rang sincere. "After hearing about you two dancing at the wedding—"

"The wedding?" she interrupted, heart rat-tat-tatting in her chest.

What was he talking about? The waltz in the kitchen when she'd been breathlessly, horribly in his arms? Did people know about that too?

"And after your romantic moment in town with him today, or so I hear." His voice warmed. "I guess things are going well after all with you two. I'm off to have supper with Magnolia and the girls. Do you want to come? I'm sure they'd love to have you."

"I'd love it too, but I have things to do at my new house. It takes a lot of work to settle in."

"All right. Have a good evening."

"You, too." She waved, continuing on her way.

How many people knew about the dance in the kitchen? What about her nieces? Of course they'd probably heard it all by now. How was she ever going to be able to face them? They knew far too much about her old mistakes.

"Howdy there, Aumaleigh." Milo pulled his horse to a stop, faintly outlined by the lights from the remaining stores still open in town. "Guess you've heard the news."

"About Dobson's Bakery coming to town?" The best defense was a good offense. If she could keep the sheriff from mentioning those troublesome Gabriel rumors, then perhaps she could get home without having to discuss it again.

"No, we found the hideout of our local robbers. Just missed nabbing them. Don't worry, we're on their trail. Those boys won't be free for long."

"That's great news. That means people around here are going to be safer. It was scary not knowing where those robbers would strike next. You know how concerned I was about my nieces."

"You weren't alone," he assured her. "We'll be able to return the furniture in a few days. Just waiting for a sketch artist from the county to come and document everything."

"The girls will be relieved, I'm sure." She thought of other victims of the robbers. "Can I ask, who were they? Escaped convicts or outlaws on the run?"

"We think they're George Klemp's sons." Milo shrugged those dependable shoulders of his. "We won't know for sure until a telegram I sent comes back with an answer. Beckett said Klemp sometimes talked about his two sons when he was employed at the Rocking M. No one around here had ever met them when George lived here."

"George Klemp." Her stomach turned cold. He was the man who'd aided and abetted Ernest, Verbena's former stalker. He might be in jail now, but she'd never be able to understand how coldly and ruthlessly he'd turned against her nieces. "It's scary to think how much we used to trust him on the ranch. I guess you never really know what's inside a person."

"I think that's largely true," Milo agreed. "But sometimes, if you look deep enough, you find what's really there. Maybe that's true with you and Gabriel Daniels."

"What? I—" She'd been blindsided, she hadn't seen that coming.

But Milo mercifully moved on, tipping his hat to her. "Have a good night, Aumaleigh."

Honestly. It was a sad day when the news of the captured robbers was nothing compared to a man (Gabriel) helping her (an uninterested Aumaleigh) into a buggy. Next time she just might push him into the mud and get into the buggy by herself.

No, that would just cause more rumors and speculation.

She shook her head. That's what she got for living in a small town. She snapped the reins, sending Buttons into a fast walk.

Dottie stepped out of the bakery, locked the door and lifted a hand in greeting. "Hi, Aumaleigh!"

"Hi, Dottie." Aumaleigh waved and offered the girl a friendly smile, but no way was she stopping. That would only give the sweet girl a chance to ask about Gabriel. She did the same thing with Elise Hutchinson, one of the girls' friends, who looked startled at being caught in the dark side street.

Whew. Almost home. She turned down the residential street, listening to the squish of the wheels in the muddy lane. Houses sat back on the tree-lined street, windows brightly lit showing scenes of the families inside—Ma cooking supper, kids running around in the parlor, Pa taking off his coat, home from a long day's work.

She'd never had the chance at a domestic life like that. Perhaps that's why her heart always warmed, squeezing with longing. In truth, she was angry with herself, not Gabriel. He'd been able to move on, and as much as she wanted to blame him for that too, that wasn't fair.

The squeak of the buggy wheels and the jangle of the harness took her back. Memories gripped her, hurling her back through the decades to a night just like this.

Stars winked to life in a black velvet sky. Streams of clouds blotted out the crescent moon, allowing only glimpses. Aumaleigh's joy drained away like water from a leaky bucket the moment they rounded the corner. This, their second date, was at an end.

"I didn't mean to get you back so late." Gabriel's baritone dipped, low and caring.

Caring. She would give up the world to have him continue feeling that way for her. Never had she thought she would be sitting on a buckboard seat next to a good and handsome man—a man interested in her, Aumaleigh McPhee. "It's all right. We were just having fun. We lost track of time."

"That was my fault. I should have kept an eye on my pocket watch." He pulled Sully and Stu to a stop. "We were having fun with all the animals."

"I loved it." She'd always been a sucker for animals, and being introduced to the barn cats, the dogs, the goat, the baby calves and the horses on the ranch where Gabriel worked had been great fun. "I'm a country girl at heart."

"So I see." Tender those words. He turned toward her in the dark, leaning in, blotting out her view of the sky. There was only him—wonderful, funny, kind, great Gabriel. She tilted her head toward him, her lips ready for the sweet caress of his kiss.

"Aumaleigh!" Mother's sharp, scolding voice shattered the moment, coming out of nowhere.

Aumaleigh jumped, startled, and hopped onto her feet. Guilt battered her. She stood there—standing in his buckboard—like an idiot, not knowing what to do as Mother and Father bounded out of the dark driveway and onto the road.

"Get down here right this minute, young lady!" Maureen charged toward her, angrily pointing at the ground. She radiated fury. "What do you think you're doing? You're supposed to be in your room. Winston, take her back to the house."

Aumaleigh found herself on the ground. She didn't remember jumping down. Shame kept her eyes lowered as Father grabbed her by the back of the collar and dragged her up the road. She stumbled alongside him, hot tears burning her eyes. Mother's shrill voice rose and fell, but she couldn't hear the words because her heart was beating in her ears so loud she couldn't hear anything but her own heartbreak.

What was Gabriel thinking? Probably withering under the blistering tongue of her mother, taking it like a gentleman but thinking, whew, glad I'm rid of that Aumaleigh. *Or was he feeling sorry for her?*

That was worse. It would be unbearable for him to know the truth, to feel pity for her, so desperate to love him, to have a romance of her own, that she'd defied her parents, disobeyed their authority and snuck away like the liar she was just to go out with him.

"When I tell you to do something, you do it." Father's temper rose with each pounding step. "Now get back to the house and get to work in the kitchen. No supper, no sleep. You'll be cleaning all night. No daughter of mine is going to act like a whore right under my nose. Do you hear me?"

"Aumaleigh. Aumaleigh." A voice broke into her thoughts. "Are you okay?"

She blinked, realizing she'd been driving without really seeing where she was going. Clint Redmond was in the bakery's delivery wagon, clearly finishing up his route for the day. She blushed. "Yes, I'm fine. Guess I have a lot on my mind."

"That's obvious." The kindly man tipped his hat. "Is there anything I can do to help?"

"No, thank you." She could have hugged him for not bringing up the rumors about her and Gabriel. Clint merely wished her a good evening and drove on, the empty wagon rattling as he went down the dark road.

She drove past the Montgomery's grand, sprawling home, wondering how things were going to work out between Magnolia and her mother-in-law-to-be. Aumaleigh remembered all that her own mother had put Gabriel through during their engagement. It was a wonder he'd wanted her at all.

She turned down the winding road, following the river for a spell. The warm night smelled like growing grass and spring. Cherry blossoms sifted over her as she pulled up her drive. There, in the break between the trees, she caught a glimpse of light—of Gabriel's home.

Was it wrong that she pulled Buttons to a stop and stared? If she squinted, she could just make out a man's silhouette moving in the corral. Gabriel, backlit by the lantern inside the barn, walked with the same lumbering, unhurried strides as he had as a young man—his shoulders squared, his back straight, his limbs relaxed.

Her fingertips buzzed, remembering the feel of his hand in hers. Against her will, caring sparked to life in her chest. Just a small spark, a momentary flicker, but she couldn't pretend it hadn't existed.

She snapped the reins and sent Buttons trotting up the drive.

CHAPTER EIGHT

"Good night, Pa." Leigh poked her head into his den. "You aren't going to stay up late, are you?"

"I'll be right up." He dragged his attention away from the novel he was reading and shifted in his new leather chair. "You seem awful happy, considering you are so far away from your beloved beau."

"I know! I moaned through half the trip here."

"Only half?" He arched a brow, chuckling when she did.

"Okay, it's true. I miss him, but it's more important that I'm here with you. You know nothing about setting up a household, Pa. It's a good thing you have me."

"Yes, it surely is. What would I do without you?" A father's love burned hard in his chest. She'd always had him wrapped around her little finger. "Go on up. I just want to finish this chapter. I'm almost done."

"Okay, but I know you. You get caught up in those books." Leigh flashed her smile. "You want your beauty sleep. I saw what went on with you and Miss Aumaleigh."

"Oh, you did? That wasn't any of your business, young lady. Didn't I give you explicit instructions to go away?"

"Yes, but you know me. I'm nosy and I'm a bad daughter." And not even a wink of remorse. She leaned against the door frame and waggled her brows. "Everyone was talking about it. All the ladies in the dry goods store were practically plastered against the window watching you help Aumaleigh into her buggy. They said it was about time she let someone romance her."

"I see." *Let.* That one word stabbed at him, sharp as a knife, hitting his conscience. "Did the ladies say why she hasn't let anyone close?"

"Well, one lady, who looked very miserable, by the way, said Aumaleigh was a man hater. But I don't think that's true. Do you?"

"No." His voice cracked, betraying him. Aumaleigh had never been the type to hate anyone, even when they deserved it.

"Another lady said that it was Miss Aumaleigh's mother's fault. That she drove away any possible suitor even before he could try to beau Miss Aumaleigh." Leigh paused, scrunching up her face as she contemplated that. "Do you suppose that could be true? Why would a mother do that to her own daughter?"

"Why, indeed." Guilt twisted hard, making it difficult to breathe. "Not all mothers are like yours was."

"Ma was the best lady on earth." Leigh smiled and looked ready to cry in the same moment. "I still miss her so much."

"Me too, baby." Grief hit him too. Full of emotions, none of which he wanted to feel, he stared into the fire. The flames had gone down, licking low and lazy over the charred remains of wood. "Go on up to bed. You need your rest if you want to have enough energy to run me ragged tomorrow."

"Yes, I have plans that involve shopping, spending your money and doing something about your nearly bare kitchen. If Aunt Josslyn hadn't donated a few old pots and pans, you'd be eating cold gruel and bread."

"Glad you're here to fix that for me."

"Me, too! Good night, Pa." She whirled away, her skirt swishing, her petticoats rustling. She left brightness behind her that stuck in his heart.

He returned his attention to his book, but the words made no sense. They were just letters on the page. He sighed because he knew the reason why. Now Aumaleigh was back in his mind, thanks to Leigh, and his conscience wouldn't let go.

He stared out the window into the dark. He couldn't see her house from here because of the trees but that didn't stop his mind from conjuring up the memory of her this afternoon. No longer the young girl she'd been with the bubbling laughter and the quiet hope in her eyes. He didn't like seeing her so changed. He didn't much like what life—and likely her mother—had done to her.

Memory pulled him back. How miserable he'd been after her mother had sent him on his way, giving him a tongue lashing he would never forget. What he'd taken away from it was that Aumaleigh's parents were not going to let their only daughter waste herself on a humble, simple man like him.

Fine, so he hadn't been wealthy. He wasn't finely educated. But no one would have cared for her more. He was sure about that. Even after a few dates, his heart had already been hers.

It had been a physical blow being separated from her. He spotted her in town a few days later, catching sight of her across the street when she'd been sitting quietly beside one of her family's household workers in a wagon.

She hadn't seen him. Everything about her posture—head down, shoulders slightly slumped, motionless—spoke of her misery too. Had he made her situation at home worse? That troubled him greatly.

He'd considered then that maybe the best thing for her would be to let his affection go. Then she wouldn't be in conflict with her family or looking so unhappy he couldn't stand it.

Even the memory still troubled him. Gabriel snapped his book shut. Well, it didn't look like he was going to get any more reading done tonight.

After banking the fire, he made his way through the house, turning out lights as he went. Leigh's bedroom door was closed, a thin bar of light shone around the door. She was likely up reading. Wishing he could concentrate enough to do the same, he shut his door behind him and stood in the silence, in the dark.

And there, like a sign from above, was the smallest flicker of light. It flashed through his window as the wind outside stirred the trees. Aumaleigh. Alone in her house, was she thinking of him?

His hand tingled from when they'd touched. And he remembered, how sweetly he remembered...*the whisper of her footstep in the grass, the faint scent of roses on the breeze, the hot puff of summer air as she walked beneath the starry sky.*

"Josslyn gave me your note." She stopped in the meadow. Somewhere an owl hooted and another owl answered. *"You wanted to talk to me?"*

"Yes. Thanks for coming."

"I don't know what there is to say." She bowed her head, nothing but platinum

and shadows in the starlight. "Maybe you're looking for an apology."

"For what?"

"My mother. For agreeing to go out with you." She reminded him of an injured deer he'd seen once, too afraid to come close to the cow feeder but hungry enough to want to try.

Maybe it was then that he'd first started to really love her. Not the blush of falling in love with someone, of that thrill in your veins and the rush in your heart of first love, but of something deeper. This was his first glimpse of her heart, of the wounds there.

He thought of her mother's acid tongue. "I wanted to apologize to you."

"To me?" Surprised, she raised her slender shoulders in a confused sort of shrug.

"For getting you in trouble like that. I didn't know about your parents. It never occurred to me to ask for their permission."

"Oh." She stood still and never moved a muscle. Did she know how lost she looked? That the hope he'd once seen in her eyes was gone. It was breaking his heart.

Josslyn had told him a few things. About how the McPhees treated their only daughter, viewing her more as property to be owned and controlled than a gift to love. She was valued more for the work she could do and the savings in labor for the family than for the joy she could bring them.

Maureen and Winston McPhee had plans for their daughter, to marry well enough to bring money into their lives, or for her not to marry at all.

What must it be like to be loved so little?

"I got the idea they don't approve of me," he quipped. Maybe he could try humor to reach her.

"I'm so sorry." Her face crumpled. "Really, I am. I know how they can be. I can't believe you'd even want to look at me after that."

"The way your mother chose to behave is not your fault." He wanted her to be clear on that. "My feelings haven't changed."

"They haven't?" Her head came up. Disbelief lined her dear face. "I don't understand. How could you want me?"

Thin and tremulous her voice, as genuine as could be. She couldn't understand what lived in his heart, and that's when he knew the truth about Aumaleigh McPhee. She may have grown up in the finest house he'd ever seen, but she'd never had the one thing that mattered most—the only thing that mattered at all.

And he was going to give it to her. He was going to love her all the way, every day for the rest of his life.

No matter what.

Gabriel blinked, leaving the memory behind. He stood in silence, watching the light blink on and off as the trees swayed and then suddenly there was only darkness, only the sound of the lonely night, but the hope in his heart burned.

It burned bright.

* * *

"*Go on," Josslyn whispered. "Your mother is asleep. I'll keep an eye on her."*

"What if she asks for me? You know how she gets." Aumaleigh wrung her hands, torn between what she wanted and what she knew was her duty. "If they find out, I'll be sent to live with my great aunt. She's scary, Joss. You've never met her, but trust me. She makes my mother look like a sweet little kitten."

"I believe you." Joss crossed the sunroom, glancing over her shoulder to check for any maids that might be lurking around, loyal to Mother. "It's one of her migraines. She won't be getting up for days, not to mention I dosed her tea with extra laudanum. She'll sleep until tomorrow. Go now, while you can. I'll tell everyone you are upstairs. No one will know. I'll guard the door and your mother with my life. Now, hurry. Gabriel is waiting."

Gabriel. Her heart soared at the name. "Thanks, Joss. I owe you."

"No you don't. I can't wait until the day you're my sister." Joss gave her a hug, opened the window and waited for Aumaleigh to climb through.

She hit the ground with both feet. It wasn't a far drop. She slipped out from between the lilac bushes and made a beeline straight for her brother's cottage.

"He's inside." Laura, her brother's wife, met her on the porch. She scanned the grounds as if checking to make sure no one had spotted Aumaleigh and was dashing up from the manor house after her. "Gabriel is such a sweetheart, Aumaleigh. And so handsome. I can see why you like him."

"Thanks for doing this." She gave her sister-in-law a hug. Laura and Ely had only just married, and she glowed in her sweet, pretty way, so happy as a newlywed.

"He's in the kitchen," Laura told her. "I'll just stay out here on the porch and crochet. That way I'll be able to keep an eye out to make sure you two aren't discovered."

"I can't believe you're doing this." Aumaleigh pulled open the screen door, feeling as incandescent as the flawless summer day. "I mean, if Mother knew, it would ruin your relationship with her."

"Don't you worry about that. You deserve to find your own happiness, Aumaleigh. This is your chance."

Thankful, she waltzed into the little vestibule, listening to the sounds of Laura settling into the porch swing.

Her footsteps echoed in the front room, and her pulse thrummed crazily as she threaded her way to the back of the house. The moment she set eyes on him, she came alive. Her heart opened. Her soul brightened. She'd never been more herself than she was when Gabriel came toward her with love on his face and took her hand in his.

Aumaleigh blinked, waking up from the dream. It had been so real, the warmth of that hot summer day seemed to touch her skin. The scent of the chicken Gabriel had smoked for the meal he'd brought remained, slowly dissipating as she sat up in bed. The cool spring early morning air had her shivering. The sound of a hard rain on the roof overhead reminded her it had only been a memory, nothing more.

She would be wise to ignore the warm sweetness in her heart that the memory had brought to life.

Determined to make the most of the day ahead of her, she quickly washed and dressed and headed downstairs. Her to-do list today was quite long. She had to get the wedding dress back from Rose, for Iris wanted to wear it for her upcoming ceremony. She wanted to go through her things and see what she had to spare for Dottie, who was moving into the old rooms in town she'd just vacated. Not to mention the long day of work she had ahead of her at the ranch.

The instant her foot left the bottom step and touched the parlor floor, she knew she had trouble.

There was a splash, and before her brain could register what was wrong, her foot lost contact with the wood floor and she was falling backward. Her hands shot out, she grabbed the railing and stopped most of her momentum before she landed on her behind on the wooden lip of one of the stairs.

Pain charged through her tailbone. She sat there, breathing through the pain and looked in shock at the puddle of water on the floor.

Her roof was leaking. *Drip, drip, drip.* Leaking, when it hadn't bothered to do it before. This wasn't the way she wanted to start her day. Was that her trunk sitting in a pool of water?

Up she went, more carefully this time and padded delicately across the wet floor. She heaved and pulled the heavy hope chest out of the puddle. Defeat hit her like a falling tree. She stared at the damage to her trunk. Inside were all the things she'd once made with such love, the things she hadn't been able to let go of all these years.

She hung her head. No, this wasn't a good way to start the day.

Afraid of what she would find, she opened the lid and drew it back. She caught sight of the folded fabric on top, safe and dry. She carefully lifted out the quilt she'd made for her wedding bed, the one the girls had found. As she carried it across the room to the sofa, sweetness tugged at her. The memory of making every stitch, of being that young lady so crazy in love and blissfully imagining her life to come made her smile. It made her sad.

It was definitely time to get rid of these things. Maybe the leaky roof was a sign.

She returned to dig out an armful of stuff—pillows, embroidered pillow cases and sheets, a length of lace, a lace tablecloth she'd tatted. She left her armload on the sofa cushion and returned to the trunk. She didn't let herself look or feel as she scooped up a water-logged armload and padded across the room. Not having the emotional energy to deal with it now, she left everything on the hearth.

Drip, drip, drip. First she'd better see to the roof.

The good thing about being a homeowner was that she had the power to do something about it. She grabbed a mop bucket from the kitchen, put it below the drip and went in search of her coat.

There was a lot in her life she couldn't do anything about. Gabriel, who was living next door. The rumors that everyone was going to repeat about him. The fact that she felt ready to leave the ranch. But her roof, now that was going to be trouble easily solved. She'd climb up there and fix it. It'll be as simple as pie.

* * *

"Pa, there's a lady up on the roof on the house next door." Leigh took the stairs two at a time and landed at the bottom of the staircase, skirts belling around her like a princess. "I could see her from my room. I think it's Miss Aumaleigh."

"On the roof?" He frowned. Some things apparently hadn't changed. Apparently time could only do so much work on an individual. He set down his coffee cup and gaged the force of the storm through the window. It looked cold and wet, but he wasn't one to let a little rain keep him from this opportunity.

"She had a hammer in her hand and everything." Leigh's pretty face scrunched up with concern. "I don't think she ought to be up there. You'd never let Ma do such a thing."

"That's true." He didn't miss the secret smile as Leigh turned on her charm.

"I think you must rush right over there to help her. Pa, she could slip and fall. She's such a nice lady, I'd hate for her to get hurt. Since she's my namesake and all."

"Sure, you had to get that in." He rolled his eyes, snatching his duster from the wall peg by the kitchen door. "And no, I see that look. I'm not going to tell you any stories about Aumaleigh. It's private."

"Hmm. I have gotten a little out of Seth. I suppose I'll just have to get much, much more."

"Good luck with that. The boy only knows so much." He winked at his girl. "Do I want to know every detail about you and your beau?"

"As if I would tell you!"

"There, now we understand each other." He stepped out into the cool spring rain. The rancher in him missed being out in the dirt and planting. The man firmly entrenched in middle age was glad he could spend the rest of the day reading by the fire. "I'll be back."

"Don't hurry! You clearly need to spend enough time with Miss Aumaleigh to make sure you get everything fixed."

"You're talking about the roof, right?"

"Among other things." Leigh swept across the kitchen in her rose-colored dress, dark curls bouncing with her gait. "Maybe you and Miss Aumaleigh have a second chance."

He rolled his eyes and closed the door. The last thing he wanted was Leigh involved. She would get her hopes up for his sake, and he didn't want her disappointed if this didn't work out.

His own disappointment would be enough to handle.

He knew better than to take the time to saddle up Barney. Aumaleigh was a fast worker. If he wanted to get there and save the day, then he'd better hurry. Which is why he rode through the fields, jumping fences and a bubbling creek.

"I saw you coming." Aumaleigh was still on the roof, her drenched coat and skirts clinging to her. Her hat was waterlogged, right along with her dark hair. "You can do us both a favor, turn right around and go back the way you came."

"We called a truce, remember?" He halted Barney at the porch and tied him to the rail. "Or aren't you a woman of your word?"

"Don't even try using that on me. I'm in no mood this morning."

"So I see." A ladder leaned against the side of the house, so he climbed it. "Then just think of me as a neighbor, some fellow you don't know who just stopped by to help you with your roof. It's the kind of thing neighbors do."

"Is there any way to get rid of you?"

"Not until the roof is fixed." With a grin, he set foot on the wet roof. A shingle crumbled beneath his boot. "You had someone look at this roof before you bought, didn't you?"

"Yes, but a tree limb came down in the night. I rolled it off—" She gestured toward the edge of the roof.

He glanced over to see a rather large bough on the ground. That had to have done some damage when it hit, and it was big enough that she had to have really worked to get it off the roof.

His ribs constricted with a suffocating sadness. The impact of her life hit him hard. As Josslyn had told him, she'd been alone ever since, with no one to take care of her and no one to love her.

All the things he'd wished for her had never happened. Not one.

With a mix of sympathy, maybe some pity, and definitely some love, he held out his hand. "Give me the hammer. I'll take care of this."

"If I do, will you go away?"

"Eventually." He watched the hint of a smile play along the corners of her mouth. That sweet, soft mouth he'd spent more hours than he could count kissing tenderly.

And he wanted to again.

"All right, if it will get rid of you. But that's the only reason. I want to make it perfectly clear." She held out the hammer, handle first, as if she didn't want to get too close to him.

But he saw everything she didn't say, perhaps the things she never could. His soul came to life as she left him standing in the rain.

CHAPTER NINE

Aumaleigh listened to the pound of the hammer overhead, wishing she hadn't given in. But he *did* want a truce between them, and he was her neighbor now. Not to mention Rose's uncle by marriage. That meant Gabriel would be at certain family functions and events.

She would have to figure out a way to get along with him. Might as well try now.

Not that she liked it. She added cream and sugar to her coffee cup and took a sip, keeping an eye on the bacon sizzling in the pan. *Thump, thump, thump* went his footsteps high over her head. At least the hammering had stopped. Was he done? More importantly, would he leave?

She could have predicted he'd show up at her back door. Rain dripped off his black Stetson and sluiced down his black duster. The spark of that old caring flared to life within her, a ghost of what had once been.

She set down her cup and crossed the room, aware of that faint brightness within that remembered, that would always remember the man who'd gone to such trouble to court her. The man who'd made her feel special and valued like a new and improved Aumaleigh McPhee, not like her mother's daughter at all.

"I'm done." He opened the door and propped one brawny shoulder against the frame. "You're going to need some new shingles up there, but the patch job should hold for a while."

"Yes, the dripping has stopped." She tried not to care that he looked cold and wet. She wanted to have no sympathy at all for him. "The least I can do is send you home with a hot cup of coffee. I'll fetch you one."

"I'd appreciate that." His baritone moved over her like a caress.

She shivered, and the little hairs on her arms stood on end.

Do not let yourself be attracted to him, not again.

She whirled around and paced to the cook stove, but her hand shook as she reached a cup off the shelf.

"Here, let me." His large hand settled over hers, male-hot and familiar.

He stood behind her, his big body just a breath away. Heat radiated off him, and she went rigid, fighting an attraction she had to deny.

"I don't remember inviting you into my kitchen." She tried to be bold and self-confident, a woman utterly unaffected by him, but her voice wobbled. She couldn't pull it off. Not even when she sidestepped away from him, just to escape the magnetic pull of his closeness.

He knew it too. The corners of his mouth tipped up. The storm gray of his eyes gentled. He had to know how hard this was for her, and that upset her most of all. He knew this was upsetting her and yet he was here anyway, wanting—well, she didn't know what he wanted. Certainly he didn't want to try again. It was impossible. They were no longer young. He was no longer the man of her dreams.

"The c-coffee is on the trivet." She gestured toward the stove. No way was she stepping around him to get to the coffeepot. "Help yourself."

"All right." Good-natured, he left her standing at the counter. His gait was slow and relaxed. "Your bacon is starting to burn. Let me flip it."

The bacon! She silently groaned. How had she forgotten the bacon? See what the man did to her? He turned everything topsy-turvy, especially her common sense. There was only one solution. She had to get him out of her house as quickly as possible.

"Stop that." Really, it infuriated her to see him casually turning the bacon as if he belonged in her kitchen and in her life. "You can't come in here and make yourself at home."

"I'm just trying to help, that's all." The low tones booming in his voice were different from the Gabriel she'd once known. That Gabriel had been like a note in a song, steady and true. Now he was harmony—a multifaceted sound, one of depth and light.

She remembered the letter he'd written to her she'd found in her mother's things, a letter that had never reached her back in the day. Leave it to Mother to steal her daughter's mail. Gabriel had written about being a solider in the war, fighting for the Union. He'd talked about being happy with a wife and children. She remembered that now, that he'd been to war, and he'd also buried a wife. Those honors and hardships, sorrows and strengths had changed him.

"Leigh would be shooing me out of her kitchen, maybe beating me with the business end of a dishtowel if I refused to leave." Deep crinkles cut in around his eyes, showing his age.

They were attractive, and she hated that she noticed.

Honestly, why did the man have to be more handsome in his fifties than he'd been as a young man? It wasn't fair.

And here she was, looking like a mess. Her hand went to her hair, which was hanging in wet shanks. Her dress was soaked, her petticoats dripping on the floor. She was an eyesore.

And exactly why was her appearance bothering her?

She lifted her chin. Time to take charge of the situation. "I like Leigh. Especially since you said she beats you."

"I've got to be honest. I deserve it."

"I'm not surprised."

"Don't worry, I'll be done soon." He forked the strips onto the awaiting plate.

"You're pretty good with a fry pan."

"When Victoria was ill, I did a lot of the cooking."

"Victoria." She repeated the name, not liking the catch she heard in her voice. "Your wife."

The woman who'd been smart enough to say yes to him.

"Yes. Leigh looks a lot like her."

"She must have been beautiful."

"Very." Gabriel stole an egg from the bowl on the counter and cracked it on the edge of the fry pan. "She fell sick when Leigh was still so little. It was especially hard on our daughter. She was close to her mother."

"I can see that." She felt like she was strangling, but it was impossible to feel anything but sorrow for the woman. "I'm glad you were happy. Gabriel."

"It didn't come easy." He cracked another egg. "I was a mess after you. You have to know that."

"I'm sorry." The words she'd saved up over the years, the truths she'd had to face, they all disappeared now that she was at the moment to talk about them. At a loss, she grabbed the sugar bowl. "I always regretted giving you back that ring."

"I know that now." Was that pity in his voice? She couldn't tell. He'd seen her life, he'd seen the spinster she'd become. What did he think of her? Did he think she was deserving of pity? Her pride smarting, she dipped a teaspoon into the sugar and dumped it into his steaming cup.

"I take my coffee black these days." He grabbed the spatula from the counter, holding it capably in one hand.

"Oh. I hadn't even thought." How foolish. She stared down at the teaspoon. "There's no way to undo the sugar. Let me get you a new cup."

"No, it's okay." He flipped the eggs one at a time. "I could use a little sweetening up."

"No argument here. Maybe I'd better put in another teaspoon?"

"Funny." Deep brackets outlined his smile, made from a lifetime of laughter.

She could see that too. "How did you meet Victoria?"

The question surprised her.

Gabriel looked surprised too as he poked the white of the cooking eggs with the tip of the spatula. "I sold the land I had back when we were courting, so I had cash to get my own place up in Deer Lake. Land was cheaper there, so I wound up with a bigger spread."

"Good for you. I always knew you would do well ranching."

He didn't say anything for a second. A muscle in his jaw worked. "With more land to farm, I needed a second team. My hired hand knew of a good team for sale. I went to see about the horses and rather liked the owner's daughter."

"I see." She concentrated very hard on putting the lid back on the sugar bowl. Did she really want to hear about Gabriel's love for another woman?

"It was five years after you. Just so you know." He turned his back to her as he scooped the eggs out of the pan and set it on a trivet. "Five long years. I didn't know if I could risk trying to court anyone again. That's how bad you broke my heart. Just so you know. I didn't get over you easy."

"But you did get over me."

"Eventually."

His admission felt like a fatal blow. She'd already known it, but it hurt anyway. She swallowed, forcing out the words that she meant from the bottom of her heart. "I'm glad you were happy, Gabe."

"Me, too. I've had a good life. I got lucky."

She read the gratitude in his eyes. "Yes, you did. I caught sight of your son, and I've met Leigh. What about your other sons?"

"The oldest is back East finishing up his medical schooling. Liam just joined him. Both of them are going to be doctors."

"You must be proud."

"I am proud of my family." He gave a humble shrug. "They've made my life."

"I can see. It is everything I've wanted for you."

"I'm sorry you never found that for yourself." He loaded her plate and carried it to the small oak table in the corner. "I heard you had your hands full with your mother. I'm sorry to hear she had a debilitating disease."

"She required complete care for many years." She sat in the chair he held out for her.

He breathed in the familiar, faint scent of roses from her hair and skin. "That had to have been hard."

"Don't you feel sorry for me, Gabriel Daniels. Don't you do it."

"As you wish." He retreated to the counter where she'd left his coffee cup, a strategic distance away. "Why did you take care of her for all those years? She wasn't a nice mother to you."

"But she was my mother." Aumaleigh stared down at her plate but didn't touch the food he'd cooked for her.

Her hair had begun to dry, curling adorably in the dry heat from the stove. Those fragile curls reminded him of when she'd been his, with her hair down as she chased butterflies in the meadow.

That time seemed so long ago now, and farther away than it had been. Almost out of reach.

"She wasn't always like that." She sounded wistful as she picked up her fork. "It's probably hard for you to imagine Mother any other way."

"True." He paced toward her, cradling the cup in one hand. "She gave me more than one tongue lashing. Remember when I proposed to you?"

"Yes. She came marching out of the house after you'd slipped the ring on my finger and ordered you off the property. That was the happiest day of my life." Aumaleigh smiled, sad and sweet at the same time. "Why didn't you answer my letter? Why didn't you come to me?"

Gabriel blinked. He pulled out the chair across from her and sat down at the table. "What letter? I don't know what you mean."

"The one I wrote to you, asking you to marry me." Aumaleigh poked her fork into one of the fried eggs. "I know it was years later, I know I was wrong to ask, but I had hoped you loved me as much as I had loved you."

He shook his head, not registering. None of this made sense. It was news to him. What stuck out to him was her use of the past tense. She *had* loved him. Had, as in no more, as in it was over. As in she could sit across the table from him and feel nothing.

He cleared his throat. "I never received any letter, Aumaleigh. You handed me back my ring, told me you didn't want to marry me anymore and didn't want to see me again. I told you not to be such a doormat for your parents and we argued. When I left, that was the last I ever heard from you."

"Oh." A tear rolled down her cheek, hot and slow, the last piece of her heart breaking.

She sat there for a moment in silence, going back over the memory of that day. Of not being able to take the yearning in her heart for him or the pain of missing him. Mother had been particularly hard that morning, her father distant, and she'd sat down in her room and scratched out a quick letter. She'd taken the letter to town and slipped away to the post office when her mother wasn't looking.

Or maybe her mother *had* noticed.

"Are you telling me you proposed to me?" Emotions worked across his angled, handsome face. "How long ago was this?"

"A couple years after you left town." She set her fork on her plate.

She felt numb, in shock from the realization of what her mother must have done. Mother had been good friends with the postmaster's wife. It would have been just like her to make sure that letter was never sent.

After all, the letter Gabriel had written to her when he fought in the War Between the States had been hidden away in Mother's things. The depth of that betrayal hit her hard. She squeezed her eyes shut, trying to keep that fresh wash of grief inside.

"Maureen intercepted that letter, didn't she?" He sounded bitter. "It's something she would do. I don't know how many times she let me know I wasn't good enough for her family. For you."

"That was never true." She opened her eyes, seeing nothing but the blur of him through her tears. They slid down her cheeks and dripped off her chin, and still they kept coming. "There was no one better for me than you."

"Our lives would have turned out different if I'd gotten that letter." Regret filled his voice. "I would have come back for you."

"Good to know." She clamored out of the chair, knocked her knee against the table leg and almost tripped over her own feet. She scrubbed the tears from her eyes but they blinded her, hampering her as she tried to get away from him.

She did not want him feeling sorry for being duped by her mother. She felt his gaze on her. Her pride got the best of her. She stood in the archway and tried to catch her breath. Tried to get her tears under control. "I guess it's too late now."

"I see." His chair scraped against the floor. His measured steps came her way. "I guess our lives have gone in different directions. We're strangers."

"Strangers," she agreed. A sob caught in her throat, and she hoped it sounded like a gasp. "It's odd how you can know someone so well that they are like a song in your heart, and then here we are again and I hardly know you."

"Strangers." He repeated the word as if he was weighing it with care. "I guess the only question that remains is this. Do we want to stay strangers?"

"Yes." She didn't turn around, she couldn't face him. "When I look at you, it's the past I remember. But the past is gone, and so are what we were. There is no more Aumaleigh and Gabriel."

"True. It's a lot of water that's gone under that bridge."

"Yes. What we had is gone."

"I know." Gabriel held out his hands helplessly, at a loss because her gently-spoken confession was a fact.

At least now he knew the answer to his question. You couldn't rekindle a love that had died. It had burned out, and those ashes had blown away, scattering to the wind long ago.

Love, once lost, could not be captured again.

He fisted his hands, wishing he had someone he could fight, something he could do to make things right. But at least he knew that she'd wanted him and had tried to reach him. That healed the ancient wounds in his heart.

The move here had been worth that.

"Thanks for fixing my leaky roof." When she turned to him, her face was a tight mask. "I know your daughter is getting you settled in. That must be a big job."

"She thinks so, but I don't need as much settling as she thinks." He gave a wry grin. "I don't need much to get by."

"I'll bring your supper tonight." She didn't meet his gaze as she ushered him toward the door.

"Don't go to any trouble, Aumaleigh. You're trying to repay me for the roof, aren't you? And you don't need to. It was a couple of nails and a few bangs of a hammer."

"Nonsense, it's no trouble. Think of it as returning a favor. I'll have the girls at the ranch's kitchen whip up an extra casserole. All you'll need to do is warm it. I'll even throw in some dinner rolls from my niece's bakery. They're quite tasty."

He wanted to argue with her, but she had that stubborn look to her. Not to mention he suspected she was holding on by a thread, the same way he was. The revelation that they could have been together, that she had taken a risk and wrote a proposal rocked him.

And he would have married her. He would have dropped everything, stole her away from her abusive parents and loved her with all he had for the rest of his days.

But that hadn't happened. He took his hat from the hook and plopped it on his head. And if he had never married Victoria instead, then he wouldn't have his sons and his daughter.

Yet that was a thought he could not bear. Not at all. Not for a second.

"Goodbye, Aumaleigh." His voice cracked as he stepped out into the rain. "Let me know if you need help with that roof again. I want to be a good neighbor."

"Yes. A good neighbor." She lifted her chin, no longer that vulnerable, sheltered girl he'd once known. Life had changed her too.

She'd grown up into a strong, mature lady who still seemed far too fine for the likes of him.

Sadness filled her eyes, as if the impact was not lost on her either. Neighbors, that's what they were now. Strangers and neighbors.

That didn't seem good enough, but it was simply the truth. A truth he couldn't deny as he stuck his hands in his pocket and walked away from her.

CHAPTER TEN

Junior had troubles. Right now his biggest one was hunger. He sorely missed the big store of fine foods they'd had at Pa's cabin, but that was gone now. So was the whiskey and the comfortable chairs and the wood crackling in the fireplace.

The sheriff and his men had taken care of that. They'd hauled away everything for evidence. Curses sat on his tongue and burned in his heart at those lawmen. They had no right to burst in and ruin things.

And just when life had been getting better. Just when he and Giddy were starting to live the way they deserved.

Now they were worse off than ever. He was crouching in the woods on the wet earth, hungry. It didn't get much worse than that.

The tarp over his head was puddling with rain. He reached up to bat the water off. They were lucky to have stole it.

That newcomer's curly-haired daughter had strolled into the barn without warning and almost caught them. She'd come to give the horses a few carrots.

Too bad they hadn't taken the carrots too.

Footsteps rose above the steady tapping of the rain on the tarp. "Psst, Junior. It's me."

"Giddy. It's about time." He pushed out the side of the tarp. "Did you get anything to eat?"

"There was nothing to kill. No game is out in this weather." Giddy crawled into the low-ceilinged shelter and pulled something out of his pocket. "I tried to chase the pigs from of the farmer's trough, but he came back to check on the pigs and I had to run. But I got some old gunnysacks."

"Great!" Junior grabbed the bundle, greedy. "These will feel pretty nice after sleeping without blankets."

Giddy frowned, not looking pleased about the gunnysack blankets. He gestured toward the doorway. The pieces of tarp hadn't properly come back together, giving them a view of the farm below.

"If we're lucky," he said, "those folks will finally leave their house and go into town. Then I can slip in and take just a few things so they wouldn't notice 'em missing. We'll sit tight and keep watch."

Junior bit his lip. He didn't want to point out that so far Giddy's plans hadn't worked out so well. They'd been sitting here waiting for a long while already, which is why they were cold and hungry. To make matters worse, Giddy had a bad temper when he'd been drinking, and a worse one when he wasn't.

Junior's stomach rumbled again, squeezing tight like a fist and hurting. Just hurting. Food was all he could think about. Baked chicken, hot straight from the oven, slathered with Ma's gravy. Hot, buttermilk biscuits all crumbly and flaky with melted butter dripping down the sides. Mashed potatoes, soft and fluffy, full of butter and cheese and onions. Green beans, tossed with bacon and more butter. All washed down with a cup of rich, fresh coffee.

Great. Now his stomach was hurting worse. He wanted those things more than ever.

"I can't take it no more, Giddy. Maybe we can leave and come back. Go to Deer Springs and set up in a line shack on one of those ranches nearby. No one knows us there."

"The sheriff, that Milo Gray, will have told them." Giddy nodded knowledgably. "That's how these things work, Junior. The lawmen are all connected. They're buddies out to get folks like us. It's enough to make you angry. They had no right comin' after us. How did they find us? That's what I want to know. Did you do it? Did you make a mistake and lead 'em back?"

"I told you, it wasn't me." At least he hoped not. He'd been careful. And he was angry too. He missed his comfortable chair. He missed his fireplace. He hated being hungry.

His stomach growled again and he thought of Iris McPhee. He bet she would give him a gunnysack full of food if he asked her to. She was just that kind. His chest felt achy in a way it had never felt before.

Going to see Miss Iris was wrong. Of course, he couldn't show his face in town. Giddy was right. The sheriff had figured out who they were by now. If the lawman spotted him, he'd arrest him for the things he'd done (through no real fault of his own). It wasn't as if he'd done anything to hurt nobody. He'd taken things from people who could afford it. It hadn't caused no harm.

But the stupid sheriff wouldn't see it that way. That's where the law was wrong. It didn't take into account that sometimes life wasn't fair and you had to even things up. Isn't that what Pa always said? Isn't that what Pa was counting on them to do?

"Look, there." Giddy's voice had a strange sound to it.

Junior leaned forward, gazing out the crack in the tarp.

Two little boys ran into sight on the road, their lunch pails swinging. School must be out. The kids splashed through mud puddles and dashed into the yard, the faint call of their voices carried on the wind. "Pa!"

A man appeared from the barn. Something inside Junior tugged hard, making his chest ache. The father knelt down, the boys ran into his arms and he hugged them tight.

It was too far away to be sure, but Junior thought he saw love on the father's face. The man held his sons for a long moment before loosening his hold. He stayed patiently down on one knee, listening intently to the boys as they chattered on. In fact he looked rapt.

Junior's throat felt tight, longing for what he'd never had. He'd always wanted his own pa to look at him like that.

Maybe it wasn't too late.

Giddy didn't say anything either for a long while. When he cleared his throat and tried to speak, his voice came out gruff. "We can't just sit here. Come on."

"What are we gonna do, Giddy?" Junior had a bad feeling. He crawled out into the rain after his brother. "You can't go off all het up and emotional. We gotta think things through."

"We've been thinking for awhile, and doin' too much of it." Giddy charged again, plowing through the trees and knocking rainwater off branches. "Thinking don't even up scores. Thinking don't make people pay for what they've done."

Neither did sitting around drinking, but Junior didn't want to mention that. Giddy might not take that so well. He had to hurry to keep up. "What are we gonna do?"

"I'm finding something to eat. I can't sit up on the hill and look at that Aumaleigh McPhee's house anymore. I know she's got food in there—" Giddy had reached the side of the road. He froze, fell silent and pulled his revolver from his gun belt. "Shh. Someone's coming."

"Don't do anything, Giddy." That bad feeling in his stomach grew. He wasn't comfortable, and he didn't know why. "We'd better go back."

Giddy ignored him. Tucked behind a row of cedars, they were hidden by the thick branches. Between the evergreen boughs, they could peek out at the road. Hooves splashed on the road, coming closer, and Junior held his breath. Was it Aumaleigh McPhee coming home? Was Giddy going to grab her and scare all her money out of her?

What if it was Miss Iris coming to visit her aunt's house for some reason? Maybe she was leaving some stew. Junior fisted his hands, worried. It felt wrong to worry about some woman, especially a rich woman. But he couldn't help it.

"It's that sheriff." Giddy aimed his revolved and fired, just like that.

With no warning. With no provocation. Just *bang*, and the sheriff fell from his horse. He lay face down in the mud. Blood puddled on the road.

"Got him!" Giddy's triumph would have been contagious.

Except for the fact that this was the man Miss Iris was going to marry. Junior stood frozen, staring at the motionless sheriff. Sure, he'd once had the notion of trying to court Miss Iris for her money, but he'd never had a chance. Now, because of her kindness to him, he liked her. For real.

This was gonna hurt her bad.

"What are you standing there for?" Giddy shouted at him, glaring at him like he was the biggest fool on earth.

That's when Junior realized he hadn't bounded into the road to help his brother. "You shouldn't have shot him, Giddy."

"He deserved it. Look what he did to me. I'm cold and hungry. Sleeping in the mud." Giddy raced up to the lawman and stepped on his arm, pinning it to the ground so he couldn't get up. "Look at that. The rat is trying to shoot me. You're gonna pay that for, Sheriff. Who's in charge now?"

Junior didn't know what to do. A quiet plea for help shone in Milo Gray's eyes.

Giddy aimed his gun at the lawman's head.

"Don't do it!" Junior grabbed the revolver with both hands. "We don't need to kill him. Um, um, um, it'll just waste a bullet, that's it. It's that ranch we've got to worry about."

"And that thievin' old lady McPhee." Giddy spit out the words, his temper red in his face. He was so mad, he shook with the force of it. "You're right. This piece of filth ain't worth wasting another bullet. I've got plans for my bullets."

Giddy kicked the sheriff in the side of the skull. The sheriff's head jerked, and his body went slack. Unconscious, he lay there strewn in the mud, his coat growing red with blood.

He wasn't gonna die, was he? Junior didn't know what to do. He stood there, trying to think, but thinking wasn't his strong point.

Giddy stole the lawman's service revolver and the box of bullets from his pocket. He pulled money from a billfold and tossed it into the road. "Let's go. Maybe we'll get lucky and he'll be dead soon."

All Junior could think about was Miss Iris. She looked so happy these days, working in her bakery and driving around with her horse and buggy. He didn't want to see her sad.

But there wasn't nothing he could do. Giddy grabbed him by the arm and yanked him up the road.

* * *

Verbena McPhee Reed shook the rain off her hat, brushed it off her coat and opened the bakery's front door. The bell overhead chimed a merry welcome as she hurried into the warmth. Hmm, it smelled good, like fresh baked cinnamon rolls and chocolate cake.

"I hope that's for Maebry's shower." She shrugged out of her coat and hung her things up on the wall pegs. "I forgot to remind Magnolia that I would be coming by early."

"Oops. Magnolia must have forgotten." Rhoda offered a cheerful smile from behind the gleaming front counter. "But no worries. All that's missing is the frosting. I'll see if Iris can take care of that now. How about a cup of tea while you wait?"

"Excellent idea, and I'll get it myself. Don't you dare even think about waiting on me." Verbena set down her bag and her reticule on a free table and headed over to the stove. She loved her life, she loved being married to Zane and adored the little life growing inside her. She couldn't wait to be a mother.

She also loved this bakery. They had built it together, the five of them. They had made it something larger than themselves, and it felt satisfying. Even if Fanny Dobson had a big sign in her window across the street that read, *Opening Soon!*

"Verbena!" Dottie came in from the back, carrying a tray of past-date dinner rolls. "We didn't expect to see you yet. The cake isn't ready. Wait, don't pour that tea. I'll do it. It's my job."

"I'm not a customer," Verbena argued, setting down the teapot. "Don't you dare wait on me, Dottie. How are the new living arrangements working out?"

"Wonderful. I like Aumaleigh's old rooms. They're comfortable. Except I miss all the fun at McPhee Manor, who wouldn't? But it's really something to have my own place. I'm really happy. I never thought so many good things would happen to me." The sweet girl set down the tray and began carefully placing handfuls of the rolls into each of the waiting bakery boxes they would be leaving on the doorsteps of the needy families in town. "It's like a dream."

"I'm so happy for you." Verbena bypassed her teacup for the bulky bag she'd brought. "In fact, I had some extra things. Maybe you can use them in your new home."

"You mean it?" Dottie blinked, surprised. "Seriously?"

Before Verbena could answer, Magnolia stumbled in the front door, looking windblown. She took one look at the bag and shook rainwater out of her blond hair. "Ooh! What did you bring? I want to see."

"Well, I had some extra pillow cases." Verbena pulled out a lovely embroidered pair, snowy-white with roses embroidered in different shades of pink and yellow around the edges.

Dottie gasped in appreciation. "They're too beautiful to use."

"And a tablecloth with matching curtains." Verbena didn't mention she'd made them expressly for Dottie. "You mentioned how you like pink, and I remembered I had this fabric."

"Pink calico." Dottie's jaw dropped. "It's so pretty and cheerful. I'll be too afraid to eat at the table from now on."

"Oh, and here's this extra afghan." Verbena sighed, unfolding the light wool throw, crocheted in an open rose and leaf pattern. "It's too small to use when Zane and I cuddle on the sofa, but it is the perfect size for one person."

"It's so soft and warm." Dottie blinked grateful tears from her eyes. "Oh, it's too much, but thank you. It will go well with the chairs."

When Milo had offered to return the furniture that had been stolen by George Klemp's sons, Iris suggested giving everything to Dottie, who didn't have a stick of furniture to call her own. Besides, they'd already replaced what was stolen from McPhee Manor, and it seemed fitting.

The door gusted open, the bell overhead jangled and a man came in with the cool spring wind. Lawrence Latimer swept off his Bowler hat and smiled so broadly, his handlebar mustache twitched comically.

"Good afternoon, fair ladies." He bowed low, showing the bald spot on the top of his head. His comb over flopped back into place as he straightened. "It's so lovely to see you all, especially you, fairest Dottie."

Dottie sighed, transfixed, staring hopefully at the bachelor who closed the door and strutted over to her.

"Perhaps I'd better go check on Iris." Verbena grabbed her cup of tea and headed toward the kitchen door. "I need to make sure she's frosting the cake right."

"I'll go with you." Magnolia rushed after her, perhaps eager to escape the ardent Mr. Latimer, but there was really no need.

Lawrence's full attention stayed riveted on Dottie.

Verbena hesitated at the swinging door, watching the young couple.

"Oh, aren't they sweet?" Magnolia sidled up to her, watching too. "Look how charmed she is by him."

"So I see." Amazing. Maybe Lawrence had finally found his perfect match.

He was blushing bright red, perhaps from the pressure of talking to a lady who was truly interested. He straightened his stooped shoulders and puffed out his narrow chest, talking away to Dottie about the fine art of bottle feeding his newborn lambs. Dottie gazed up at him, eyes bright with adoration.

They were adorable. Somehow, between the two of them, they just...well, matched.

"Get in here, you two." Iris opened the door to whisper and scowl at them. "Nosy Rosies, that's what you are."

"I can't deny it." Verbena led the way into the kitchen. "Are they adorable, or what?"

"I say it's about time." Wynne, the new baker, set a pan in the sink. "If I have to cross the street one more time to avoid that man's courting, I'm going to explode one day like a tornado. All that will be left of him is a scorch in the ground and five decimated buildings."

"I know the feeling," Verbena agreed, and they all stifled their laughter.

"Still I've grown fond of him." Iris spooned a blob of frosting onto the cake and smoothed it around with a narrow spatula. "He's so lonely, and really a good man. He's kind to his donkey and lambs."

"I heard he grew up in an orphanage." Rhoda offered, joining the group and keeping her voice low too. "He's done well for himself, considering he started with nothing. Not one single advantage. Nor anyone to care about him."

"Poor Lawrence." Magnolia crept over to the door and pushed it open an inch so she could peer out with one eye to the crack.

"Why do I have the sudden desire to push her?" Verbena asked, and everyone burst out laughing.

Yeah, they all may be married or about to be, but some things never changed. And that is sisters' love for one another—one of the truest and strongest loves there is.

* * *

The day was ticking away as Aumaleigh reined Buttons into town, wishing she had been able to keep her wits about her this morning when she'd spoken to Gabriel. She really did. Because if she had, she'd have remembered that they were having Maebry's baby shower later and no one from the kitchen staff could be spared for the supper delivery—because they were feeding the cowboys early and going to the festivities too.

"Ho there, Aumaleigh!" Fred called out. He must have spotted her coming down the road and had rushed out onto the boardwalk. "You look lovely today. You have a certain glow to you."

"It's from all the rain." She didn't dare stop or Fred would do his best to get as much information out of her as he could. "Have a great afternoon, Fred!"

"You, too!" He frowned, as if he was not at all pleased with the exchange. Likely he still had questions he wanted answers to—answers which he would share with everyone in town.

Not that she wasn't being stared at. Oh, she could feel the speculation in the gazes as Carl from the feed store lifted his hat to her, and Kent from the newspaper waved to her from the boardwalk. Nora Montgomery stopped her carriage in the road and waved, clearly wanting to chat.

Aumaleigh kept on going. Maybe, if she was terribly lucky something else newsworthy would happen and happen quick. It would give folks in town something else to talk about. Really, why did folks think that a spinster was in need of a husband? Or if any man who showed her the least bit of courtesy, she was desperate enough to have him?

Well, she wasn't desperate. Absolutely not.

The minute she turned the corner by the river, she knew something was wrong. Buttons shied and gave a sharp whinny. There were shadows in the road. Aumaleigh squinted to bring them into focus. It was horse standing protectively over a man—Milo Gray.

CHAPTER ELEVEN

She didn't remember leaping out of her buggy, she was on her knees in the mud, terror ripping through her. There was so much blood. His chest rose and fell, and his hand reached up for hers. She grabbed hold. He felt so cold.

"Hold on, I'm going to help you." She looked in his eyes and saw the pain and worry. As hurt as he was, she could tell his only thought was for Iris and his girls. "You had to go and cause all this trouble, didn't you?"

A corner of his mouth twitched. His eyes warmed at her attempt at humor. "Every time I try to sit up on my own, I black out."

"Then it's a good thing I came along to help you." Her pulse lurched to a stop as she took in the blood. "I don't know how to tell you this, but you look awful."

"I've been better. And if you make me laugh, it's gonna hurt." He stopped, swallowing hard. Cords stood up in his neck. He went ashen. "You're gonna have to go for help. There's no way you can carry me, and I know I can't stand."

"I'm not leaving you." Her stomach dropped, thinking of the pain he must be in. What was she going to do? She had to leave him to get help.

And then an approaching vehicle rattled on the road behind her. Her spirits both fell and leapt at the sight of a pair of perfectly matched black horses.

Gabriel.

He seemed so tall sitting on the seat, with the disappearing clouds behind him and the gray sky framing him. Her heart shone like the sun fighting its way through the clouds. She fought that brightness, that light.

Her breath hitched as he swung down from his buckboard. Somehow the worry and fear for Milo vanished as Gabriel hiked over. Calm, capable, shoulders straight, he towered over her. Awesome, just awesome.

"Sheriff." Gabriel planted both hands on his hips. "It looks like you got yourself into some trouble."

"That's what I was just telling Aumaleigh." Milo coughed, grimacing in pain. "This time I wasn't even trying. Trouble found me."

"That happens when you're a sheriff." Gabriel knelt down, studying the injured man with care.

Was it the compassion on his face that got to her? Or was it the steady, solid strength emanating from him? As if no matter what, he was prepared. He could handle anything.

"Looks like you got lucky with that bullet wound." Gabriel didn't look her way as he pushed back the lapel of Milo's duster to reveal the small round hole in his lower chest oozing blood. Slow but steady.

She took in a deep breath. "I've mended my share of wounded cowboys on the ranch. Let me get some pressure on that."

"Aumaleigh." Gabriel's voice warmed, and held a hint of a warning too. "Let me handle this."

She opened her mouth to argue but his gaze stopped her. Steady. Authentic. Understanding. Something whispered from out of the past, words he'd once told her so often they seemed emblazoned on her brain. *You're not alone anymore. You have me. Depend on me, Aumaleigh. You'll see I won't let you down.*

Her head was nodding before she realized it. How had he been able to reach down deep, to the old wound inside she tried so hard to ignore?

Gabriel knelt down and offered Milo his hand. "Aumaleigh, how close is the doctor?"

"He's in town, so he's close. If he isn't out on his rounds." Aumaleigh watched as Gabriel wedged a hand behind the sheriff's shoulder blades and levered him up with care.

"We'll take him in my buckboard." Gabriel crossed the road to his vehicle. "My horses are faster."

Hard to argue with that. She climbed into the back of the buckboard, on the opposite side from Gabriel and helped ease the injured Milo onto the seat.

"You're treating me like I'm half dead." Milo managed to sit up on the seat before his head began to wobble. "I can do this—well, maybe not."

"You're a stubborn man, Sheriff." Gabriel deftly eased the man all the way back onto the seat. Every movement was slow and measured, confident, as if he'd done it a hundred times before.

"Stubborn, yep. I can't deny it." Milo groaned, blinking fresh blood out of his eyes.

Aumaleigh whipped out a clean handkerchief from her pocket and dabbed that bothersome blood away. The knot on his head was the size of a walnut, and the cut running down the middle of it looked deep. She told herself that was not bone she could see. Not at all.

"Just close your eyes," she told him as Gabriel moved in again, this time with a blanket he must have found beneath the front seat. "You'll be in a warm bed before you know it."

"Thanks for finding me, Aumaleigh." Milo blinked rapidly, like a man struggling to hold onto consciousness. "Thanks, Gabriel."

"No problem." Gabriel tucked the blanket in around the sheriff, swift and sure. "Aumaleigh, stay with him. I'm going to tie up the horses."

"Give Buttons plenty of rein. She'll want to graze." She turned her attention back to Milo, but he'd passed out. His eyes were shut, he was breathing, shallow and unsteady, but he was breathing. He was strong. That was what mattered.

The sun came out in full, throwing rays of light from sky to earth and surrounding Gabriel with that golden, rare light. Her heart threatened to tug, to fill with caring that had no end, but she was its master. She was in control.

Besides, wasn't it just that old caring she'd once felt for him? Like a ghost, a trace of a memory, that could never be real. Just a shadow of something that had once been so great and so strong. That's all.

But a part of her wasn't so sure.

The buckboard wobbled a bit as Gabriel hopped onto the front seat. "I'm going to need directions," was all he said as he turned his horses around and pushed them into an all-out gallop toward town.

* * *

The board creaked beneath his boot as he made his way down the hallway of the doctor's house. Voices rose in the back room where he'd carried Milo, leaving him to the medical man's care. He didn't much like doctors.

Muffled footsteps rushed toward him. The front door swung open. A woman appeared, her face twisted with fear and wet with tears. He stepped against the wall, giving enough room so that Iris McPhee could rush past him.

"He'll be okay," he felt compelled to tell her.

Her sob of relief was her only answer as she disappeared around the doorway.

Yeah, he knew how that felt too. Knowing your loved one was hurting, knowing there was nothing you could do. Wanting them out of pain and whole again and ready to trade your life so that could happen.

"Gabriel." Aumaleigh's pinched face was pale with worry. "I heard what you said. I was afraid about his head wound."

"I know the doc's worried, but he's lucid. That's important. Not that I know much about medicine, I've just been an observer."

"You're right. I've seen it too. Cowboys tend to get thrown when they're breaking horses and hit their heads now and again." She wrapped her arms around her middle, looking uncomfortable with being alone with him.

Remembering their last, pivotal conversation, he could see why. She thought they were strangers—and in a way, they were. But in another way, he knew her like no one had—or maybe ever would.

"You were pretty calm when I found you with Milo." He pushed away from the wall, moving slow, hoping she would come along with him. "You did a good job keeping pressure on his bullet wound on the ride here. It was pretty jostling."

"The cowboys have wound up with a few of those over the years too."

"Your voice warms when you mention them. The cowboys." He remembered every sparse but important detail he'd been able to wring out of Seth and Josslyn. "I hear you've known some of them for decades."

"Yes. John came with us from Ohio." Aumaleigh shuffled forward, coming with him as if reluctantly. Her dark hair had slipped down from its bun, and his finger itched from wanting to push it out of her eyes.

Old habit, he realized.

"They were my parent's employees first, so I got to know them from cooking for them."

"I guess some things never changed for you. You never got out of your mother's kitchen."

Her face fell. She came to a stop in the hallway. "I always hoped to. Anyway, the cowboys were friends. Some of them feel like brothers, others like sons. I'm terribly fond of them all. I don't know what I'd do without them."

"They're lucky to have you. You must feel more responsible for them now that you own the ranch."

"True. What about you?" She eyed him assessingly. "You knew exactly how to lift and carry Milo without hurting him. You've done a lot of home care, haven't you?"

"I took care of Victoria for years." His voice cracked. He didn't like the show of emotion, not when it was overwhelming. "I worked hard all my life, trying to make something of myself. Long hours, longer days, day in and day out. I was in the dirt, in the barn, working with the animals, raising crops. And when a crop failed, I was in town working a night job to make sure my family was provided for."

"I'm not surprised to hear that. I always knew you would be a successful rancher." Her voice thinned and she stared out the window again. "I always believed in you, Gabriel."

"Good to know." He ignored the ache in his chest. It mattered. A lot. "Yet all that meant nothing when Victoria fell ill."

"You did everything you could for her."

"Yes." It mattered too, that she could see that. "I found the best doctors. I hired the kindest and most competent nurses. But the one thing I could not do was leave her side."

Aumaleigh said nothing. She turned away from him. She took as long as she needed to blink the tears from her eyes. "That's the kind of man you are, Gabriel. I'm not surprised. You took care of her through everything."

"Until the end."

"I'm glad she had you." Emotion made her words thick.

He knew how she felt. "Even now, grief can still bring me to my knees. I was better until I stepped foot inside this place. Doctors make me remember."

"It's not something you should forget." It was illuminating to see this side of Gabriel. His tender, tender heart hidden inside that iron-tough man. "I wish I'd been able to love like that."

He looked like a man who didn't know what to say.

Not that she could blame him. She didn't know what to say after that either. An uncomfortable silence settled between them. She stared out at the waning daylight, wishing she could take back the words. She'd confessed too much.

The front door burst open and Hazel Gray blew in with the wind. "Where's my son? Where's Milo?"

"He's in the back. I'll show you." Aumaleigh jumped at the opportunity to leave. Wanting to help Hazel, she escorted her down the hallway and into back room.

"Milo? I feared the worst." Hazel buried her face in her hands. "Your deputy said you'd be all right, but I had to see it with my own eyes. Oh, Iris. You must be feeling this too."

"Exactly." Sweet Iris slipped an arm around her future mother-in-law. "A part of me died when Fred came into the bakery and said he saw Milo bleeding in the back of Gabriel's buckboard, that he'd been shot. All I thought was, he's dead. Even now, I can't stop shaking."

"I'm not worth all this carrying on." Milo tried to grin but wound up grimacing as the doctor stitched up his wound. Stretched out on the treatment bed with his shirt off and a bandage over his head, he looked worse off than he was. "It's just a little gunshot wound."

"A *little* gunshot wound?" Iris looked faint. So did poor Hazel.

I don't belong here. This was family business. Aumaleigh backtracked into the hall and nearly bumped into Gabriel.

"C'mon." He gave a chin-jut toward the back door. "I'll give you a ride back to your horse and buggy."

"No, need. I'll get a ride with one of my nieces."

"I'm going that way anyway. You might as well go with me. If it's adding fuel to those rumors about us, you can lay down in the back and we'll cover you with a blanket. No one will even know you're there."

She smiled. Then she chuckled. Then she laughed. "I'd feel better if I drove and we covered you with the blanket."

"Sorry, can't be done. My feet will stick out. It's a short blanket." He unhooked her coat from the wall peg and shook it open for her.

"Excuses. I expected more from you, Gabriel. You could bend your knees."

"True, but then my bent knees would stick out. I have long legs." He moved in behind her, and his nearness buzzed through her, sending little tingles into her bloodstream. He held the sleeve for her as she slipped her arms in and settled the garment on her shoulders. "Maybe I was wrong about the blanket. It's exactly five o'clock. Fred is off duty. We're safe."

She rolled her eyes as the mantel clock struck five. "Fred is never off duty when it comes to gossip."

"Maybe we can wait ten minutes and he'll be at home?"

"We'd be smarter to take the back way and stay out of town completely."

"Come to think of it, it's almost dark, so that will work." He opened the door. "The good news is, you won't have to hide under the blanket for long."

"Me?" She rolled her eyes, not able to say exactly why she was laughing. She crossed the porch. "Why do I remember that time we fell asleep in the back of your wagon?"

"We were stretched out, looking up, watching the clouds float by."

"And the horses startled, the wagon jerked and you rolled out all tangled up in the blanket. You hit the ground and rolled downhill. Snoring."

"You would have thought the impact would have jolted me awake."

"No, but the cold water did when you rolled into the pond."

"That was a shock," he agreed, and then they were laughing, and his hand found hers and he helped her up into the buckboard as naturally as if he'd been doing it for the last twenty years.

She gazed down at him from the seat, laughing, before she realized what they'd done. The humor died from her lips and the amusement faded from his eyes and in the faint light from the house's window, they let the silence—and the distance—settle back between them.

Gabriel strode away, circling around the vehicle. He stopped to talk with someone (Walt the deputy who'd come to check on his boss). By the time he joined her on the front seat, things were back to normal.

JILLIAN HART | 103

Or, at least, they could pretend they were.

"Do you like running a ranch?" he asked when they were on the road.

"It's in my blood." That was all she said. Did she want to share the truth with him? Not exactly. That would make Gabriel her confidante and honestly, she would rather pick someone else for that. "How about you?"

"Oh, I'm done with all that. I'm retired. I bought this acreage to raise horses and a few cattle. I figure I'll raise and train horses to fill my time."

"You love animals so much." She ignored the image of him in the corral with his horses, and the memories from the past of him with his animals. "You've always had a gift with them."

"A gift I've been grateful for." He reined his team through the twilight. "I remember you had a way with them too."

"It's been a while. Mostly I spend my time with Buttons. She's my only animal contact these days." The cool air breezed across her face, tangling her hair, and she remembered the days before Mother began to keep her assigned to work in the kitchen. As a young girl, she'd been her happiest—running around the barn, tending the animals, sneaking in a few snuggles and kisses. She shrugged, coming back to the present. "There's so much kitchen work to do."

"How long have you been stuck in the kitchen?" He arched a brow, watching her intently, almost eerily, as if he could look too deep into her.

And see too much. See more than she was willing to share. She pushed a strand of dark hair out of her eyes. "All of my adult life, that's for sure. Mother banished me to the kitchen when I was fourteen and the neighbors criticized her for letting a girl do a boy's work in the barn and fields."

"Frankly, the neighbors should have criticized her before that." A harsh tone rumbled in Gabriel's words, and as they slid past a thick copse of trees and fell into full shadow, she lost sight of him.

But she felt his disapproval and contempt of her mother. A feeling she knew all too well. "I've left that behind me. Mother's dead. Whatever she's done, I've just had to let go."

"It's that easy?"

"N-no." She stared down at her hands. They'd rounded a corner and the weak daylight was waning, slipping behind the high, close peaks of the Rockies, painting the world in a faint dusty-rose light. "There's simply no way to fix it. I'm not going to carry it around anymore."

"That's why you said no to me, wasn't it? Why you gave me back my ring? Because she was pressuring you so hard not to leave her." Understanding, no accusation lined his face, gave life and heart to his words.

That was worse. His anger or disapproval would be much easier to face. Instead, she felt his spirit tugging at her, his empathy drawing her closer. Miserably, she stared out at the thickening shadows in the road ahead. "No. I mean, yes, Mother and Father were pressuring me. You weren't the right man, you didn't make enough, what would people think if I married beneath my means. They needed me, I was wrong to leave them."

"I should have been there for you, understanding they might be doing that. I should have helped you, Aumaleigh, even if you hadn't said a word."

Oh, he was killing her, breaking her apart into tiny, inconsolable pieces. Why did Gabriel have to be such a good man? A man of her wildest dreams—still? "There was nothing you could have done or said. It was the other things that got to me."

"Like what?"

"Hearing over and over again from them that you were too handsome for me. That I was too homely to hold you. That I wasn't good enough inside, that I wasn't lovable. That I would run off and hurt the family who did love me only to find out that you didn't love me at all. That you were just u-using me, trying to get to their money." She bit her lip, mad at herself. She'd said too much.

The problem was that she'd gotten confused in space and time. This wasn't Ohio. And Gabriel wasn't her intended.

"There's Buttons, poor girl." She hopped down before the buckboard stopped rolling, rushing toward her woebegone old mare who looked confused, not understanding what she'd done to be left beside the road in the dark.

In truth, she just needed to escape Gabriel. To stay far, far away from him. After how honest she'd been, how could she ever look him in the eyes again?

She fumbled with the reins, breaking a bunch of needles off the cedar bough in her haste. Once she had the leather straps free, she darted around into the buggy, pushed back the rain curtains and the aroma of chicken and dumpling hit her. Gabriel's supper! How was she going to find the courage to go back and give this to him?

His boots splashed on the road behind her. "I'll take Milo's horse back to his place and tuck him in for the night."

She wasn't surprised by that. Not at all. That was Gabriel, doing what he could for others. That had never changed. The backs of her eyes burned as she scooped the baking dish off the floor of her buggy. It was carefully wrapped in towels to keep the heat in, and the lid clanked as she handed it over to him.

"That smells good." His fingers brushed hers as he took the dish.

She closed her eyes at the snap that zapped through her system—both physical and emotional. Longing filled her with a bitter sweetness she did not examine. She took a step back, climbing into the buggy. "It's your favorite."

"It's nice you remembered after all this time." That was all he said—but in his tone, in the layers of warmth in his words, she heard something else.

That he knew she'd told him the ranch cooks would make the dish, but she'd been the one to do it. That she'd made this with her own hands for him, the way she used to. The way a part of her wished she could again.

She hated that about herself, that she was that weak. And it wasn't easy knowing he understood.

"Good night, Gabriel." She lifted the reins and snapped them, sending Buttons on her way.

"Good night, Aumaleigh," his voice called after her, carried by a temperate wind.

CHAPTER TWELVE

"It's Aumaleigh!" Verbena opened the door. "You're late. We were just starting to worry, after what happened to Milo."

"I know. I'm grateful he's going to be fine." Aumaleigh crossed the threshold, her arms full of gifts. "Once he heals up, that is."

"Fred told us all he knew, but he didn't know much." Daisy rose from a chair by the fire and waved Aumaleigh over. "Does Milo know who shot him?"

"He didn't say." Aumaleigh shrugged off her coat. Magnolia bounced up to grab it and hang it up. Verbena took her gifts to the pile next to Maebry, and a couple dozen people tucked in the cozy and comfortable parlor smiled and called out welcomes as she made her way to the chair by the fire.

Oh, the heat felt good. Real good. Aumaleigh held her hands to the leaping flames, but the radiant warmth couldn't begin to touch the cold places inside her.

"Miss Aumaleigh?" Little Sally Gray, Milo's youngest girl, sidled up to her. What a cutie with her light blond hair and button face, not to mention that touch of mischief sparkling in her eyes. "Is it true you're gonna be my new grandma when Iris marries Pa? Is it? Cuz I like grandmas."

"Well, I can be exactly like a grandma." She knelt down, unable to resist brushing a loving hand against that sweet, sweet face. "Would that make you happy?"

"Oh, yes! Mitsy too. We especially love frosting on our cookies. Oh, and we love presents." Sally held up her hands, which sported a fetching pair of colorful knit gloves.

"I like how the fingers are bright pink and the rest is purple." Aumaleigh took note of the yarn, remembering seeing the exact skeins in the mercantile. "Do you know what you need? A hat to go with those gloves."

"I do!" Sally agreed, eyes bright as she gave a little hop. "That's what I need, Grandma Aumaleigh!"

Laughter rang out. Several of the party guests had been watching. Annie rose from her seat, made her way around the coffee table. "I'm watching the girls tonight while Hazel is with Milo. Sally, how did you get so cute?"

"I was made this way." Her hands shot in the air. "Oh no! Mitsy's stuck on the ceiling again. She's just a baby, you know. She needs help."

And off Sally went, dashing around the room and disappearing into the kitchen. Judging by the ruckus in there, she wasn't alone with her Mitsy problem. Daisy's stepdaughter Hailie, and Rhoda's youngest, Ida, could be spotted through the doorway, pointing dramatically to the ceiling. Apparently there was a lot of imaginary baby dragon trouble tonight.

"Are you all settled into your house?" Annie asked. "I've been meaning to come over and pay you a visit, maybe lend a hand, but I've been babysitting Sally and Sadie. Just until the wedding. But are they going to have to postpone?"

Worry for Milo dug into Annie's pretty face. She was such a dear thing, and Aumaleigh couldn't help giving her a little hug. Love for her niece warmed her right up. "Something tells me Milo is so determined to marry Iris, nothing will stop him."

"Good. We just don't know a lot about what happened, so it's easy to fear the worst." Annie shrugged, looking relieved. "There is a good side to living in a small town. If Fred had been on the ball, we wouldn't all have been worrying."

"Yes, good old Fred." Aumaleigh laughed, just so glad to see Annie relaxed and at peace, being loved the way she deserved to be by her good, wonderful Adam. "Bea must be here. Is she in the kitchen?"

"She's somewhere. Her friend Clarissa is here too."

Everyone is here." And it made Aumaleigh's heart full. After what had happened to Milo, both the fear and the relief, it felt important to be reminded of the good things in life, of what mattered most.

You could have had this too, a small, forgotten voice whispered deep inside her, but she shut it down, not wanting to hear more.

"Annie! Aumaleigh!" Penelope Shalvis Denby swept up, looking radiant with happiness. "Aumaleigh, so glad you made it. You should have seen the surprise on Maebry's face when Gil brought her back from shopping. He gave us the key, you know and we had everything all set up and were waiting. Oh, it's good to see that kind of happiness."

"We're all guessing the baby will be a boy," Annie confided. "It's a big baby. She's huge."

"And waddling like a duck." Maebry came over with a smile that could light up the sky. "I'll be glad to have this wee one in my arms instead of my stomach. Sure, I can't wait to hold him, but I'd also like to get out of a chair under my own steam."

"That's why Gil has the next three weeks off," Aumaleigh told her. "It's part of my gift to you."

"Oh." Happy tears flooded Maebry's eyes. "That's good of you, Aumaleigh. I love you, you know. Gil will be delighted. He keeps saying he doesn't know how he'll leave me when the baby is so new."

"Why haven't you started opening the gifts? Look at that great pile. It's a mountain."

"I didn't want to suggest we rip right into the presents. The party has barely started." Maebry's laugh was a happy trill. It was good to see her like this, her life full of promise and brimming with love.

Aumaleigh remembered the young, shy, frightened girl who'd come to work as an indentured servant for Maureen. It was like watching a rose bloom, seeing the beauty and the magic of a life fully lived and a true love realized.

Her throat ached, but not with an old pain. She thought of Gabriel and his confession today, of how much he'd loved his wife.

"Presents!" Magnolia started the chant. "Presents! Presents!"

A chant that made Maebry laugh harder. "All right. Your wish is my command."

"Really? Then how about cake?" Elise Hutchinson called out. "I wish for cake."

"And a good man," Gemma Gunderson added.

More laughter rang through the room.

"That's what we're wishing for you, Gemma," Rose called out from the sofa next to Maebry. "I'm certain the right man will come along. Now that Dottie has snatched up Lawrence—"

"I haven't snatched him up!" Dottie protested, blushing where she stood at the back of the room. "But he is taking me driving on Sunday."

"Ooh!" several women in the crowd hooted.

"It must be love," Elise called out.

"It's going to go great for you two," Magnolia added.

"You two are the perfect match," Penelope chimed in.

Dottie turned redder, but she looked as happy as could be.

"Now that Lawrence is off the market," Rose spoke up. "Maybe some other gentleman will start making frequent visits to the mercantile. What do you think, Gemma?"

"I know too much about all the eligible bachelors to ever have romantic notions about them." Gemma took a sip from the cup of tea she held. "There's Zeke, but he's a few years younger, and once he came in to try on a new pair of boots he wanted to buy—"

"Don't say it!" Maebry broke in, giggling as she carefully unwrapped the first present she'd grabbed from the pile next to her. "I'm afraid I know where this is going."

"The odor from his feet was so bad, I gagged. My grandmother was in the store shopping in the back, and she gagged too."

"I was there! I remember that." Rhoda broke out in laughter, standing up next to Dottie. "I remember reaching up to grab something off the shelf, and I thought something had died and the smell was coming up through the floorboards."

"I ran and quickly opened the door and the windows, trying to let the tainted air out, but the smell sort of hung there like smoke. It scared customers away for a good hour."

"It would be hard to want to marry a man with a foot problem like that," Maebry agreed as she folded back the wrapping paper on her gift. "Oh, Rhoda, thank you. This is truly adorable."

Agreements chorused through the room as Maebry held up the sweet baby blanket, a background of green crochet with embroidered ducks on it with funny little duck faces.

"I hope it keeps your baby toasty warm," Rhoda said in her gentle, kind way.

"Okay, so Zeke is off the list." Rose handed Maebry another gift to unwrap. "We still have a lot of bachelors around. Who is good enough for Gemma?"

"Not Silas Meeks, the chicken farmer." Annie spoke up. "I saw him picking his nose in the reflection of the feed store window. I'll never get that picture out of my head."

"We need to disqualify all the public pickers," Daisy suggested. "Maybe that doesn't leave a lot of choice, but it must be done."

"What about Kellan?" Louisa asked. The ranch's kitchen worker looked surprised that Josslyn immediately shook her head. "What's wrong with Kellan? He's a mighty handsome cowboy."

"I think his heart is already spoken for," Josslyn explained sagely. "I've known that boy for a long time, and he admitted it to me once. Whoever the poor woman is, she's got every last piece of his heart."

"A mystery." Magnolia rubbed her hands together. "You know how I like solving mysteries. Who could the lady be that has captured that handsome cowboy's heart?"

"We may never know," Josslyn answered. "I've been trying to get it out of him for years."

"Josslyn!" Maebry held up the box of two dozen pairs of knit booties. "These are adorable."

The conversation was temporarily held up as Maebry showed off each pair of booties. Aumaleigh smiled, because this was just the first set of the matching outfits she, the kitchen staff and the McPhee girls had whipped up on their knitting needles.

"Look, each pair is a different animal's feet. Horses. A kitten. A dog. A goat. And so colorful!" Maebry looked overwhelmed. "This is just the cutest thing, Josslyn, and so much work."

Josslyn merely smiled, clearly not wanting to spoil the surprise.

"Elise needs a happy ending too." Rose handed Maebry another gift to unwrap. "Who would be a good match for her?"

"Please, you sound like my mother." Elise's eyes sparkled as she made her way through the crowd with the teapot, filling cups as she went. "According to her, I've lost my bloom. I'm approaching thirty with no real suitor. They are considering writing to a businessman friend of theirs back East for a mail-order husband for me. Can you imagine?"

"I'll take him if he isn't too ugly," Gemma quipped. "Unless he has bad smelling feet."

"Or is a public picker," Magnolia supplied helpfully.

"Would they really bring someone out for you to marry?" Daisy asked, concerned. "That would put a lot of pressure on you."

"Oh, I have no problems telling them no." Elise emptied the teapot and circled toward the kitchen. "They are dreadfully disappointed."

"They should want you to marry for love." A new voice spoke up, one that surprised Aumaleigh. She did a double take, recognizing Leigh at the back of the room, sort of hidden behind everyone. "It's the one thing my pa said to me. That there were only a few things that mattered. How I felt about him. How he felt about me. And how he treated me."

"That's the truth!" Josslyn spoke up. "Leigh is getting married in June. I haven't asked my boss for time off yet, but I'm planning on being in Ohio for the wedding."

"Your boss says it's okay," Aumaleigh called out. "Take as much time as you need."

"I love my boss." Josslyn blew a kiss across the room.

Aumaleigh blew one back.

"Look at this! Look what Aumaleigh made." *Oohs* and *ahhs* filled the room as Maebry held up the first of a dozen baby hats and caps. "This one's a little bear head. And oh, this is a little lamb. It's adorable. And this one's a duck. Wait a minute. It matches Josslyn's booties."

"It's all part of our plan," Aumaleigh explained.

"There must be a dozen hats here, maybe more." Maebry kept holding up one after another. "A horse, a kitty, a dog. Oh, they are all different and so cute."

"Glad you like them." Aumaleigh thought of the evenings in her rooms in town that she'd spent knitting or crocheting away. A labor of love.

"What about you, Aumaleigh?" Fred's wife called out from the kitchen where she'd been busy warming up the potluck dishes everyone had brought. The jovial woman waggled her brows. "I've heard some saucy things about you lately."

"None of it is true, sadly." Aumaleigh held up her hands helplessly. "I'm innocent. For once, Fred got things wrong."

"Well, that's just not like my Fred at all. I'll have to tell him to keep a sharper eye out. You're not getting any younger, Aumaleigh, and let's face it. You need family in your life."

"I have my incredible nieces." Aumaleigh braced for it. She knew exactly what was coming, but she smiled anyway. "What else would I possibly need?"

"Surely there's one bachelor in this town that might catch your fancy." Fred's wife bit her bottom lip in thought. "Wait, I know. How about that Briggs family, the two brothers who started the local newspaper. They've got a father, and he's quite fetching. He's about your age Aumaleigh."

"He's a new widower in deep mourning." Aumaleigh did feel sorry for him. "He needs his grieving time, poor man."

"Maybe you could help him with that." Fred's wife waggled her brows, and several other ladies in the room were eager to agree.

"I don't think that's a good idea," Leigh spoke up, looking quite distressed. "A new widower needs to honor his wife with his grief, not start beauing the first pretty lady who comes along. That's how it was for my pa. Aumaleigh, you're not interested in that Mr. Briggs, are you?"

The room silenced. All eyes turned to her, instead of Maebry opening her next gift. Uncomfortable with the attention and with the plea in Leigh's gray eyes, all she could do was shake her head.

"I'm way too old for that. Romance is for the young." She said the words gently, because she could see what Leigh hoped for. "That time in my life has passed. I'm happy with my life as it is."

"Oh." Leigh bowed her head, trying to hide her disappointment.

Aumaleigh did the same, because she was disappointed too.

"Oh, Daisy!" Maebry held up the little yellow sweater. "This is adorable. It's a duck. And it matches Josslyn's booties and Aumaleigh's hat, doesn't it?"

"Yes." Daisy smiled, but she looked unusually pale. Aumaleigh, thoroughly warm by the fire, stood up to fetch the poor girl some ginger tea to settle her stomach.

Maebry opened another gift, a sweater from Magnolia. "A lamb! How cute!"

The sound of happiness followed her into the kitchen. Aumaleigh smiled to herself, happy too, because she was surrounded by friends and family, by people she loved. This is what life is about.

* * *

"Good night, dear Maebry." Aumaleigh gave the mother-to-be a hug. "You sleep well now. I fear we overtired you."

"No, I'm fine." Maebry waved to the last departing guests. "Gil has been keeping an eye on me. He was pretty brave to come home in the middle of the festivities and stay."

"I'm fearless!" Gil ambled into the room and took Maebry by the hand. Tenderness shone in his eyes as he gazed upon his wife. "Let's get you to bed. No, don't even argue with me. All the clean-up is done."

"Thanks to everyone who stayed." Maebry let her husband draw her into his side, holding her close. What a happy couple they made. "And thanks again for the gifts. I am going to have the best dressed baby in town. Maybe even in all of Montana."

"It was our pleasure." She kissed Maebry's cheek and grabbed her reticule. "I'll let myself out. Get her to bed, Gil. Look at her yawning. The baby needs his rest."

"Thanks, Aumaleigh." Gil led his wife down the hallway and out of sight.

Time to go. She'd put that off as long as she could, helping with the dishes and the clean-up. Now it was time to face the solitude of the night and of the home that awaited her.

But the moment she opened the door, she could see she was wrong about the solitude—at least for now.

"Miss Aumaleigh!" Leigh Daniels stood in the shadows on the porch. "I loved how everyone coordinated the gifts. Those outfits were just about the cutest thing I've ever seen. I'm going to remember that for when I'm expecting. Well, I have to get married first."

"Your wedding will be coming up in a few months."

"Yes. It's quite thrilling." Leigh stepped forward, into the glow of light through the window. What a pretty girl she was, so full of life and charm. "Pa said that I could have any wedding I wanted, he would pay for it. He spoils me terribly, especially since my ma died. It was hard being real good and not spending too much of his money."

"You sound like a good daughter, Leigh."

"Oh, I try." When she smiled, dimples cut into her cheeks. Gabriel's dimples. "It nearly killed me to keep the guest list small, but I did it. We're just having close family and friends. I have so much to do when I get back home, but I had to come here and make sure Pa got settled. A man alone setting up a house? That is the recipe for a certain disaster."

"It's nice you take such good care of him." That was easy to see.

Aumaleigh steeled her chest, holding back her feelings. It would be so easy to come to care too much for this girl, for Gabriel's daughter.

"I hear you know something about taking care of a loved one." Leigh gripped the porch rail. "I helped take care of my ma."

"You must have loved her very much."

"She was a great mother. When I was little, she would design and make the prettiest dresses for my dolls. Then we would play together with them until it was time to fix supper for Pa and the ranch hands. She was always singing." Leigh shone with love, with the power of those memories. "When she got sick, I used to lay in bed with her and read her stories. She liked books."

"I can just picture it. She was a lucky woman to have you."

"Oh, I was the lucky one." Leigh cleared her throat, working to control her emotions. "It feels good to talk to someone about her. It's hard for Pa, and my brothers do better if they close off the past. That's a boy for you."

"Yes, male types are like that." Aumaleigh resisted the urge to inch closer. Maternal instincts told her to put her arm around the girl, who seemed vulnerable. Who looked like she needed a woman's caring. "You must feel alone with your loss sometimes."

"When I'm sewing. When I walk into the kitchen and part of me expects her to still be there, singing to herself while she was kneading bread or something." Leigh rubbed her eyes with the backs of her gloves. "I especially miss her when I'm planning my wedding."

"I bet you do. It's such a special time. I remember how excited I was, all the sewing and embroidering and getting things I would need to set up my new household. The thing I wanted most was my mother to sit down next to me and sew with me. To help me dream."

"Yes! Me, too." Leigh sniffed. "That was when you were going to marry my pa, right?"

"Right." Aumaleigh sighed.

"Pa made me promise not to badger you with questions, because I am really good at badgering and I'm terribly nosy. Everybody says so."

"Don't worry, I'm used to that. I have nosy nieces."

"I like them." Leigh sighed. "They've made me feel so welcome, and it was nice of them to invite me tonight. I had a lot of fun, plus my aunt Josslyn was there. And I've got to know you better. I mean, if things had turned out differently, you would have been my, well, sort of ma. I think you would have been a good one too."

Blindsided, that's what she was. Aumaleigh opened her mouth and nothing came out. She didn't know what to say so she simply spoke from her heart. "That's the nicest compliment I could have received. If I'd had a daughter, I would have loved her to be just like you."

A shadow moved in the road. They weren't alone.

"Is that so? You wouldn't say that if you knew her." Gabriel emerged from the darkness, and her heart tugged against her will, as if he'd put a noose around it and pulled tight.

"Pa, you're late." Leigh traipsed down the steps, her pretty skirts belling around her. "What did you tell me about men? That a beau or a husband should never make me wait on him?"

"Yeah, but your father has that prerogative." He chuckled, like a man who knew he'd already lost the argument. "All right, fine. I'm late. But what I'm really sorry about is how you badgered Aumaleigh. When I told you not to."

"I didn't badger her, Pa. Honest. I didn't bring up a single topic you forbade me to talk about. Can you believe he's that kind of a tyrant, Miss Aumaleigh? It's terrible. I'm glad I'll be rid of him when I get married." With a big grin, she looped her arm through his. "Okay, I'm done teasing you now. So, how is the sheriff doing? Is he still doing better?"

"Milo is resting and healing. He'll be fine, but he'll be sore for a while." Gabriel turned, searching in the dark.

It's a sad thing when the night can't hide you from the man you most wanted to avoid. She felt his gaze like a touch, as she untied Buttons from the hitching post. After all they'd been through, after all the opportunities they'd missed, what else was there to do? She went on her own way.

He said nothing, watching her go, as if he felt the same.

CHAPTER THIRTEEN

Junior felt sick, just plain sick to his gut. He huddled beneath the grain sacks they'd taken with them after sneaking into Aumaleigh's garbage for food scraps. It hadn't been enough. His stomach growled.

"I'm still cold, and it's your fault." Surly, that's what Giddy was, and mean-spirited too without booze. "I wanted to break into the bunkhouse and steal some blankets, but you said no."

"Do you want the law around here to know where we are?" He shivered as the wind picked up, driving the night's cold through the cracks in the line shack.

The old cabin was abandoned this time of year, but not for long. Soon as calving season was done and the calves old enough, the Rocking M's cowboys would be driving the herd to the summer pastures. But it would do for now.

Junior scowled. "After what you did to the sheriff, the law's gonna be all het up. They're gonna wanna catch who did it. You don't wanna let them know we're close."

"Then we steal from the other side of the valley, idiot." Giddy lifted his lip, sneering. "Oh, wait. We can't do that. Cuz those rotten deputies got our horse. How are we gonna make the McPhees pay if we don't got a horse?"

"I told you, it's the old lady we got to worry about. She's the one that owns the ranch now. The one Pa was promised part of." Junior heard his voice go high. Emotional.

He winced. Had Giddy noticed?

Giddy shoved off his gunnysacks and lunged off the bottom bunk. "What's it to you? You got a soft spot for them all of a sudden?"

"No!" He grimaced, mad at himself. He'd said that too fast and too high.

He'd tipped his hand for sure.

"I thought so." Giddy grabbed the edge of the top bunk and glared up at him. The single lantern burning in the corner cast an orange glow on him, making him look like a monster. "You got sweet on that old sister, didn't you? That quiet little Iris. I never should have tole you to try and beau her."

"That's not true!" Junior denied that too hard, too. He couldn't wish away the soft spot in his heart. "She was kind to me, Giddy. You weren't there. She wasn't like the rest of those rich people, lording it over the rest of us like they're so much better. She's different from 'em."

"Ooh hoo! Sounds like you're in love with Miss Iris." Giddy's laugh was cruel. "Now that the sheriff's probably dead, you'll have a shot at her again."

Junior's stomach twisted up again. It felt squishy and bad. Sick in a worried way. "I'm not in love with her."

"You're a disgrace, that's what you are. A disgrace to our Pa." Giddy stomped away, making the wick jump in the lantern so that it flickered eerily around the room. "What would he think if he was here right now? He'd be as disgusted as I am. Next thing you'll want to leave that old lady be. Let her keep makin' all that money off the ranch that by rights should be ours."

"Partly Pa's," Giddy corrected softly, knowing he'd gone too far, knowing he should have just stayed silent. But no, he'd gone and spoken his mind and now Giddy reared up like an agitated bear.

"What's Pa's is mine—I mean, ours." Giddy's fists clenched. His face turned ruddy. "Do you know what I found out? Do you know how much that ranch is worth? And here I am, living like this, like a rat in a hole, when that old witch has everything, and it don't even belong to her. It just makes me so mad. I could just—just—"

"Giddy, calm down." Junior's heart started to beat fast. "You know I didn't mean it. Don't get like that. Please."

"I ain't gonna calm down. I'm mad now." Giddy kicked the wall so hard, the window rattled in its frame. "Nothing's gonna stop me."

* * *

"Iris, sweetheart, you're hovering." Milo took a sip from the teacup she'd brought him.

"I am not." Her chin shot up in the air. She had to deny it. They weren't married yet, so she technically wasn't his wife, but if anyone thought she was going to leave and not take care of the man she loved, they had another thing coming. She grabbed a wool blanket by the quilt stand next to the door and made a beeline to his bed. "I'm exhibiting the exact right amount of not-quite-hovering behavior."

"Is there some kind of official measurement of that?" One side of his mouth quirked up in an attempt at humor.

How the man could joke when he'd been shot through the side of his chest and was suffering from a mild skull fracture was beyond her. There was nothing funny about this. Not one thing.

"I could have lost you today." She unfolded the blanket. "If that bullet had been an inch higher, we would be planning your funeral."

"Iris." The comfort in his voice, the love in it, was something that could never be measured.

But she felt it with all the pieces of her heart. Tears flooded her eyes again, those pesky tears, and she blinked hard, fighting against them.

There was a clink as he set down the teacup and his hand—large and warm, covered hers.

"Fortunately, I don't get shot at often, and I rarely get hit." Steady that voice, dear those words. "When I hit the ground after I'd been shot, I couldn't catch my breath for a minute. I was stunned. The gunman stood over me—"

"You mean, George Klemp's son." Anger flashed in her eyes.

Yeah, he knew how she felt. "The youngest son. Not Junior. It was Giddy who pinned my gun hand and pointed his weapon at me. He wanted me dead. I could see it in his eyes. And the only thing on my mind was you and the girls. All I could think about was wanting to live and be with you."

A sob caught in her throat. Hot tears scalded her eyes, and she had to blink harder.

"After the Klemp brothers left and I came to, I just wanted to get to you. Iris, I've been waiting to live my life with you. I've been looking forward to all the things we are going to share together. Easy days and hard days, sunny days and stormy days, the good and the bad. I've thought of the babies we're going to have and what it would be like if they were all girls, and what it would be like to love you through the years of my life."

Sweet, that's what it would be. She knew that beyond all doubt. "You're making my heart hurt. Those are the things I want so much."

"Me, too. All this wedding stuff is just fine with me, but when I was at the doc's house and I heard your footsteps in the hall, I knew I couldn't wait to marry you. Let's move the date up. We'll have your family and the girls and my mom. I know it's not the wedding you were probably planning—"

"No, it's not." She let the tears fall, unable to stop them. "It's better. All I want is you, Milo."

"Now, pretty lady, that's a good thing. Because all I want is you. That makes us a good pair."

"The best." Her heart melted more when he brushed the tears from her cheeks. Happy tears now, tears that kept coming as she let him pull her nearer.

He brushed her tears away with the pad of his thumb. His touch, his comfort, his caring hit her deep, just wrapped around her. Theirs was a forever, once-in-a-lifetime love. A dream come true.

His kiss was magical, like stardust and moonlight and grace. For one sweet moment. And then pounding footsteps in the hallway disrupted them.

"Sadie, give it! Pleeeeease!" Sally begged. "It's my sword."

"You poked me with it. I'm telling Iris."

"It wasn't me. It was Mitsy. She's just a baby. She can't help it if she pokes you with her horns."

"It was your sword. I saw you do it."

A dog's happy bark echoed in the hallway. Fluffy had rushed up to join in the fun.

Milo rolled his eyes. "I hope Mitsy isn't coming to the wedding. Do you think we can institute a no-dragon rule for the ceremony?"

"Sorry, I'm pro-dragon. Not only is Mitsy attending, but she's standing up with us and the girls." Iris laughed out loud. This is what she wanted, a good man who loved her and a house full of laughter.

"Iris!" Sally dashed into the room, trailed by Mitsy. "Sadie took my sword. She took it. And now I can't defend my realm from the evil dragon invaders. They're gonna come and eat *everybody.*"

"Oh, no! Not everybody." Iris opened her arms and Sally ran into them. Such sweetness, and she hugged the girl tight. "Tell you what. It's the evil dragon invaders bedtime."

"Noooo! I don't wanna go to bed." Sally snuggled against Iris. "Can we get a story instead? Here with Pa?"

"Yeah, we wanna stay with Pa," Sadie chimed in, rounding the doorframe (after she'd set the stolen sword down with a thunk) and burst in with Fluffy panting at her ankles. "Pa can tell us a story about a terrible outlaw."

"No terrible outlaws tonight," Iris decided, releasing Sally so the little girl could jump onto the bed beside her father. "There's been enough shooting for one day."

"Then you tell us a story, Iris." Sadie crawled onto the other side of Milo and snuggled in against him. "Do you know any stories?"

"There's one my ma always used to tell me and my sisters when I couldn't sleep." Iris turned down the wick on the bedside lamp so it was darker. A faint glow flicked on the wick, giving her just enough light to see her Milo, and her Sally and Sadie.

Her family.

"Tell us! Tell us!" The girls chanted.

"And sit with me!" Sally scrunched closer to Milo to make room.

"Okay, let me get settled in on this nice soft bed. Are you girls ready for a thrilling tale?"

"Yes!"

"A story with danger and excitement and true love ever after?"

"Yes!"

Iris smiled. Love from times past filled her right up, adding depth to the love she felt right now, for Milo and for their daughters. Love wasn't a place in time, and memories weren't anchored in the past. Love and time were fluid, borne on the wings of memory. For an instant, she remembered sitting in her mother's bed, cozied up against her sisters, eagerly listening to the exciting tales her mother spun.

She looked at the eager faces as Sadie wrapped an arm around Fluffy (who wanted a story too) and Sally who clasped her hands in anticipation. Her heart had never felt so full.

The secret to life was easy. No matter the hardship, love could still happen. The best of dreams could come true, and the best of dreams weren't about money, gold or fame. They were right here, in this room, the people she held in her heart.

"It all started with five little princesses..." Iris began, reciting the same words to her daughters that her mother used to say to her.

* * *

"Aumaleigh!" Fred came racing out of the post office. "How are you feeling?"

Aumaleigh hid an inward grimace. And here she'd hoped to slip into the bakery without being noticed. "I'm fine, Fred. How are you?"

"It's a fine spring morning, and I feel chipper, thank you. But concerned about poor Milo. I hear he'll be just fine, but when I heard it was George's son that shot him, I was flummoxed. I didn't even know that's who those boys were. I always thought George was a bachelor when he moved here. Why would his boy shoot our sheriff?"

"Maybe because he was the thief stealing things around here?" Aumaleigh bit her lip to keep from smiling. Fred did have a flair for the dramatic. "Have a good day, Fred, and tell your wife hi from me."

"Oh, I will. Good day to you, Aumaleigh!" With a grin, Fred ducked back into the empty post office and stood at the window, watching the street as if waiting for something exciting to happen.

The upside was that now her and Gabriel were old news. Not that there was anything between her and Gabriel—

"Aumaleigh!" Rhoda circled around the counter. "Come in. Is the day perfect enough for you? Look at the flowers blooming. Hear the birds singing. It's the perfect day for a wedding."

"Yes, it is." She'd gotten Iris's note at the ranch early in the morning and had been in the best mood since. She felt like dancing—not that she was about to break out in a waltz in the middle of the bakery.

"Magnolia is in the back dying of agony." Rhoda winked as she brought out a bakery box, sealed and ready to go. "Which means the cake isn't ready yet, but I put together some cookies for Sally and Sadie."

"That was thoughtful of you, Rhoda. With Iris gone, what are you going to do? Hire another baker?"

"And a designer." Rhoda set the box on one of the tables near the door. "We have to advertise over in Deer Springs, I think. It's large enough to have the kind of skilled people we need. That's where Dottie is right now. She went on the delivery route with Clint so she could stop by the newspaper."

"What about Dobson's Bakery down the street? Won't they be hiring too?"

"Yes, but maybe they've already done so. They're getting ready to open. I'm thinking tomorrow or the next day, by the look of things." Rhoda glanced out the window. "I've been walking by and spying on them. It feels like they're the enemy."

"They *are* the enemy." The bell rung as the door opened and Dottie stormed in, a petite fury dressed in pale pink. She untied her sunbonnet. "Back when the girls were in Deer Springs to spy on Fanny Dobson, I told them all about her. How she moves in next to another bakery, undercuts their prices, steals their employees and puts them out of business. It's terrible. They were family businesses, and those families lost everything."

"She sounds ruthless." Aumaleigh wondered what was in store for the bakery. She didn't like the notion of anyone trying to run her nieces out of business. "Hasn't anyone stopped her?"

"No." Dottie shrugged. "I'm kind of scared of her."

"I have experience with ladies like that." She thought of her mother. Maureen McPhee had grown ruthless over time, shedding the pieces of her heart and soul. "She sounds like the kind of lady who doesn't stop until she gets what she wants. She doesn't much seem to care about other people or their feelings."

"I don't know how we'll fight her, but we can't let her win." Dottie's chin jutted. "I already love this place. I love working here."

"I do too," Rhoda agreed.

The swinging doors banged open to reveal Magnolia balancing a cake box in both hands. A streak of frosting marked her cheek and a smudge of it dotted her chin. She looked a little wild as she bounded into the front of the shop, and she was breathing a little hard.

"I did it. I didn't think I could squeeze in another cake, but I did." Magnolia handed over the box. "Aumaleigh, make sure you let Iris know I suffered. Let her know she got this cake by the skin of her teeth, but I came through for her. I'm the best sister."

"Does that mean you get the biggest piece of cake?" Aumaleigh couldn't resist nudging up the lid to peek inside. The two tiered cake was frosted in a soft spring green, adorned in numerous, colorful spring frosting flowers. A riot of color and joy. "This took effort."

"Just a little bit. I've made so many frosted flowers, I'll be doing it in my sleep for weeks! But at least I've settled on a cake design for sure."

"You have been undecided," Dottie chimed in encouragingly. "Are you going to get one like this?"

"Yes! I love all the flowers. I suppose it will give Tyler's parents another reason not to come."

"I don't know, Nora looked rather pale when she walked by the other day," Rhoda teased. "Maybe she knows about the flowers. What do you think, Missy?"

Missy poked her head out of the kitchen (they'd stolen away her from Nora Montgomery's kitchen where she used to work as a maid). "I think Magnolia should get back in here and help me with all the frosting. I can't do it as well as Iris."

"Nobody can. Guess I'd better get back to work." Magnolia flashed everyone a smile before rushing away. "So many cakes, so little time."

"And I'd better get this to Iris's. There's a lot to get done if she's going to get married today." Aumaleigh held the cake box carefully. "I can't believe I am going to be a great-aunt again."

"It's cute how the girls call you grandma." Rhoda grabbed the cookie box. "I'll walk you out to your buggy. It's a lot to carry."

"Thanks, Rhoda." Aumaleigh stepped aside as a familiar face appeared on the other side of the glass door. The bell overhead chimed. "Hi Gemma."

"Hi. That must be Iris's cake. Oh, I can't wait to see it later on." Gemma held the door, waiting for Aumaleigh and Rhoda to pass through. "Is there anything I can do to help? I'd love to lend a hand."

"You're welcome to come an hour early," Aumaleigh invited. "I'll put you to work in the kitchen."

"Okay, I'll be there." Gemma slipped inside the bakery. There was something about her today. She didn't look happy.

Come to think of it, her eyes had been red-rimmed. As if she'd been crying.

"It's hard not to worry about Gemma," Rhoda confided as they crossed the boardwalk. "Her parents work her so hard."

"They surely do." Aumaleigh slipped the cake onto the floor of her buggy before hazarding a glance up at the bakery window. Gemma stood in silhouette, with a teacup in her hand and sadness shadowing her.

Aumaleigh knew what it was like to grow up working for your family. How great the expectations were, and how enormous the pressure to continue to make a difference for them. "If Gemma could do anything, I wonder what she would choose?"

"Besides slaving away in her father's store? I'd like to see her do anything else." Rhoda sounded thoughtful. "I've always wondered about you that way, Aumaleigh. You have spent how many years in your mother's kitchen?"

"I was fourteen, so that makes it over three decades." Now that was a depressing thought. The sunshine stung her eyes as she took the cookie box from Rhoda and slid it across the front seat. "That's a long time."

"And you took care of her for decades, complete care at the end." Rhoda gave her blond locks a push, looking so golden and pretty in the warm spring morning. "I hope the rumors about you and that new man to town are true. You deserve some dreams of your own."

"I won't argue there." She climbed up and settled in beside the cookies. As she waved goodbye to Rhoda, a set of matched black horses several blocks away caught her eye. Gabriel stood next to them, talking with the lumberyard owner.

Longing filled her, sweet, sweet longing. Yes, she thought to herself as Buttons turned down the side street, she had more dreams to dream.

CHAPTER FOURTEEN

Magnolia McPhee was late. Not terribly unusual for her, but no way was she missing Iris's wedding. Not Iris's. After everything her oldest sister had been through, the fear that she would never marry.

"Bye Magnolia!" Missy's shout followed her out the bakery's back door.

She didn't take time to answer. She didn't have a minute to spare!

The side street was quiet, painted with the purple shadows of dusk. The warmth of the spring day had faded, but not the smell. She drew in the scent of growing grass and pollen as she pounded around the corner, clattered up onto the boardwalk and nearly collided with Elise Hutchinson's mother. The very proper woman gasped, a dainty, lace-gloved hand fluttering to her throat.

"My goodness, Magnolia McPhee! Watch where you're going! That's no way for a lady to behave!"

"Sorry, Mrs. Hutchinson! Coming through!" She barreled around the rather wide skirts of the older woman, wove around the various members of the Dunbar family, including the troublesome twins who were punching each other, and dashed up the stairs toward the real estate office.

"Tyler!" She threw open the door, not at all shocked to see him hard at work at his desk. Either he'd lost track of time, or his workaholic father had been pressuring him again. "We've got ten minutes. *Ten*. Up on your feet. C'mon, let's go."

Tyler set down his quill, and the look in his eyes as he took in the sight of her standing there was something out of dreams. The exhaustion vanished from his face. The lines unhappiness drew on his sculpted, handsome face disappeared. Love so big and rare lit him up—bright enough to light the world.

"Magnolia." He stood, capping his ink bottle. "I lost track of time."

"Then it's a good thing that I knew you would." She ignored his father's disapproving *hrrrmph* from the corner of the room and waved at the middle Montgomery brother, Travis. He waved back. "I want to have enough time to see the bride before the ceremony."

"What's the rush?" Lance Montgomery, patriarch of the family, pushed his chair back and rose heavily. His face turned ruddier than usual. "It's a home wedding."

He said that with the same tone as you might say, *disgusting, dead snake in the road.*

"They can start the ceremony whenever they want." Lance rose heavily. "Tyler, I need you to stay and finish reconciling the business account."

"It can wait until tomorrow. I'll get on it first thing in the morning." Tyler circled his desk. He had to know his father had fisted his hands and looked angry enough to scare off an agitated, hungry grizzly. "How is Milo doing? I hear he's up and around and doing pretty well."

"We got lucky." Magnolia was grateful for that. "He still has a bad headache. Not to mention some dizziness and balance issues, which is why he'll be sitting down for the ceremony."

"I hear the deputies brought in Zane to help track down the Klemp brothers." Travis set aside his pen, the ledger in front of him forgotten. "I wanted to volunteer, but Pa wouldn't let me off work."

"You belong here," Lance growled, crossing his arms over his chest. "That's why we pay taxes. Let them do their jobs. You can stay here and do the job I pay you for."

Travis gave a good-natured shrug. His father's tough ways didn't affect him the same way they did Tyler.

Magnolia took hold of her fiancé's hand and gave it an encouraging squeeze. Strain corded in his neck as he reached for his coat with his free hand.

"Did you hear what I said, Tyler?" Lance boomed, a man used to getting his way. "I'm going to dock your pay if you leave."

"I'm leaving, Father." Tyler opened the door, holding it for Magnolia. "See you tomorrow."

Ooh, it was too bad she was outside, because she thought she heard a rather interesting and creative use of cursing, but she was too far away to make out anything more than the tone.

"I'm sorry about that." That's all Tyler said.

She didn't press him for more. She knew how hard it was for him to live up to his family's expectations. The problem was that you loved your parents, faults and all, and it was hard to disappoint them. Besides, Tyler had given his word to his father many years ago. Tyler was a man who kept his promises, no matter how difficult.

That was one of the thousands of reasons why she loved him, but she really wished he could be happier. She knew he missed working with his hands building things.

"Will Zane make it for the ceremony?" Tyler asked as he untied his horse at the hitching post.

"I think he's coming expressly for it and then leaving again." Magnolia held out her hand, palm up, hoping Clancy would acknowledge her. He gave her a distrustful look but did not turn his head from her. "Hey, I'm making progress. I'm going to win him over. You wait and see."

"You've been trying for a long time. He's stubborn."

"So am I." She gave Clancy a kiss on his cheek before he could protest and darted into the buckboard. "Your father seemed like he was in a pretty good mood today."

"Yes, it was a nice change." Tyler's dimples flashed as he settled onto her next to the seat. "This is my favorite thing. Spending time with you."

"Soon you'll get to do it every day." She snuggled against him. "Are you ready for that?"

"Are you kidding? If I get to come home to you every day for the rest of my life, it will not be enough." He reined Clancy down the street and slipped an arm around her shoulders.

The minutes were ticking by. Magnolia kept an eye on her lapel watch as Tyler pressed Clancy into a fast lope. They dashed down the side street, whizzed down the residential streets and clamored to a stop in the street in front of Milo's house. (It was already crowded with horses and buggies).

"Slow down!" Mrs. Crabtree snarled from her front porch. She stopped sweeping long enough to scold them. "What's with young people these days?"

"Hi, Mrs. Crabtree!" Magnolia gathered her skirts and leaped into the road. "Good evening to you! Come on, Tyler. Run!"

"I have to tether Clancy." Amusement rumbled in his voice as he moved in the shadows, deciding on a low hanging tree branch to use as a post. "You go on. Your sisters are waiting."

And they were. Daisy, Verbena and Rose glared at her. "Hurry!"

They charged up the stairs, and she went too, barreling down the hall and into the room where Iris stood in front of a beveled mirror.

Magnolia skidded to a stop and blinked, but she still couldn't believe her eyes. "You look like a princess. I've never seen a lovelier bride."

"Oh, you're just saying that because it's my wedding day." Iris waved off the compliment, blushing with pleasure.

"No, Iris, you're simply stunning." Magnolia wanted to remember this moment, as she had with her other sisters. The flush of excitement, the glow of happiness, that moment when her beloved sister's life changed. This was everything she'd ever wanted for Iris.

"See? It's not just us," Daisy chimed in. "You're gorgeous, Iris."

"Amazing," Rose agreed.

"Breathtaking," Verbena added.

"It's the dress." Iris smoothed her hand over the delicate lacework skirt. "It's Aumaleigh's dress. I swear I can feel the love in it."

"No one can argue that." Verbena's hand flew to her heart. "When I wore it, that's what I felt too."

"Me, too." Daisy wiped a tear from her eye. "I know you did too, Rose. And soon it will be Magnolia's turn."

"I can't wait." Magnolia took a moment just admiring the dress. The princess style cut, the softly belling skirt, the pearls sewn into the bodice, the intricate lace overskirt—it was incredible.

But that was not what made it special.

Aumaleigh stepped into the room, elegant as always with her dark curls and kindness. "Iris, you look like a dream. You are going to take Milo's breath away."

"Which is not a good thing with a gunshot wound." Iris sparkled. She shone. Her quiet beauty was mesmerizing. Then again, there was nothing more beautiful than true love.

"It's time." Aumaleigh couldn't help moving in to fuss with the bride a little. Straightening the pearls she wore around her neck, patting the girl's cheek. Oh, she loved her nieces. She wanted every happiness for them. "Are you ready to become Mrs. Milo Gray?"

"I feel as if I've been waiting a lifetime." Iris took Aumaleigh by the hand. "Walk with me."

"It would be my pleasure."

She escorted the bride along the hall and down the staircase. Family and friends had all arrived and were waiting in the parlor. Aumaleigh smiled at her nieces Annie and Bea, who were sitting with her nephews-in-law—Beckett, Tyler, Zane, Seth and Adam. She nodded at the girls' friends—Elise, Penelope, Gemma, Dottie and Leigh.

Her heart stopped at the man standing in the back, all dressed in black. It was his familiar, dimpled smile that made her miss her step. She grabbed the wall for support.

Gabriel. What was he doing here?

"You're our ma now." Sadie bounded up to take Iris's hand. "There ain't a better one."

"Mitsy loves you." Little Sally came up, solemn as a judge, and so Aumaleigh stepped aside to let the girl have the place of honor beside the bride. Sally gave a little sniffle and the purple tiara she wore slipped a bit sideways. "I love you too, Ma."

"Oh, my precious girls." Iris crouched down, dress and all, and took both girls into her arms, holding them, just holding them.

You could feel the love. Aumaleigh's throat ached, full of gratitude for the happiness her niece had found. She felt Gabriel's gaze on her, as bold as a touch. When their eyes met, her heart skipped two beats, the way it used to do when they were young.

"Are we ready?" Pastor Ammon cleared his throat and opened his bible.

"We gotta wait for Fluffy!" Sally dashed out of place beside Iris and patted her knee. "C'mon, girl."

Amused chuckles filled the room. Aumaleigh tried to keep her attention on the puppy who looked up, abandoned the piece of rope she was chewing and darted to Sally's side. But it was Gabriel who stayed at the edge of her peripheral vision, Gabriel who seemed to affect every beat of her heart.

"Dearly beloved," the pastor began, and those age-old words were the same ones she'd once looked forward to reciting.

Did Gabriel know that was the dress she'd made for him? It was the single, slight nod and the brightness in his eyes that told her he did. All she could do was to stare hard at the floor and pretend she didn't want to go back to that time—to that sweet, sweet time.

But she did.

* * *

*G*abriel *pulled his rattling wagon to a stop in the shadow of the Ohio ranch house. Actually, ranch house wasn't an accurate description of the sprawling, Tudor-inspired structure. He felt uncomfortable around such fanciness, he was a country boy born and raised, but at the sight of Aumaleigh through the big kitchen window, all other thoughts and feelings fled.*

Something tugged at his hat brim.

"Sully, knock it off." He playfully batted the gelding away, the big lug.

Aumaleigh. He couldn't take his eyes off her. She was incredible. Her lustrous, dark hair was drawn back into two long braids, framing her face in the sweetest way. Intent on her work, she gave the rolling pin a push over the dough, and the long lean line of her arms and the curve of her shoulder painted the prettiest picture— one he could look at all day, every day for the rest of his life.

He was going to marry that woman. She was going to be his wife. How he got so lucky, he didn't know, but he was grateful. One hundred percent.

She looked up, turning toward him as if by heart. The instant their gazes locked, it felt like they were one. As if when he breathed, she did too. In that still silent place, staring into one another, he could feel her there, in his soul.

She swiped her forehead with her rolled up sleeve, pushing a shock of dark hair out of her eyes. He felt brighter when she smiled, like standing in full sun. She came toward him, opening the door and stepping out into the light.

What a dear face she had. Heart-shaped. Framed by unkempt little strands of falling down locks that were adorable. Her slope of a nose, as cute as could be. Eyes the color of bluebonnets that sparkled with unassuming kindness. Sweet, unaffected, she swished toward him down the path in her plain calico dress.

A dream, that's what she was. A dream he was afraid he'd wake up from.

"Gabriel!" She ran toward him. His engagement ring sparkled on her finger. "You're early!"

"I couldn't help it. I wanted to see my special gal."

She came into his arms like a summer's dawn, filling him with her light and her softness. He wrapped his arms around her, treasuring the sensation of her against him. He breathed in the rose scent of her and smiled at the sensation of her hair catching on his whiskery jaw.

"I'm almost done with my work." She stepped back in his arms. *"I hate to make you wait."*

"I don't mind. I'll just sit here on the porch until you're done."

"I'll hurry." She went up on tiptoe and brushed her lips across his.

That was about the greatest thing he'd ever known. Letting her go wasn't easy. Watching her skip away from him about tore him apart. He stood there in the glare of the summer sun, lonely without her.

"Hey there, Daniels." John ambled by, cowboy boots kicking up dust. *"Come by to take Aumaleigh on a buggy ride? Aren't you a little early?"*

"Yep, I just couldn't wait."

"You've got it bad, don't you?" John tipped his Stetson and followed the path to the kitchen porch.

There was no denying it. He had it bad for Aumaleigh, in the best, most wonderful way. He swept off his hat and trailed up the walkway. Found a comfortable seat in the shade and watched the butterflies flutter by.

The screen door slapped open and she rushed out to him, with a streak of flour on her cheek. *"Here, it's nice and cool. I got the pies in the oven and Cook told me to mix up more bread dough."*

"No worries." He took the glass of lemonade and kept his opinion to himself. *"You're worth the wait."*

Her beaming smile was his reward. She whipped away, as sweet as a song and disappeared into the kitchen. If he leaned back in his chair, he could just see her through the window, rushing around the work table to disappear into the pantry.

"You're back." The chill in that voice could turn the Great Plains into a glacier field. Maureen McPhee limped around the corner of the porch, with a handful of roses from her prized garden. *"Guess you're holding out for more money than the thousand dollars we offered you."*

"You've got it wrong, Mrs. McPhee." He swept off his hat respectfully, although it wasn't easy to keep calm or respectful. Not with all that had happened and all he knew about the woman. *"I'm not interested."*

"There isn't a single reason why you'd want that homely girl in there, and you know it." Low that voice, carefully pitched so no one inside the kitchen could hear. *"Trust me when I say you aren't getting your hands on my money. Aumaleigh has been cut off. Disinherited. We took her name off the will the moment we found out she'd been sneaking around with you."*

"I don't care. That doesn't matter to me." That was simply the truth.

Too bad Maureen McPhee wasn't a lady who cared much about truth. *"You and I make a deal right now. Two thousand dollars, that's a fortune to someone like you. You can outfit a ranch with that. Buy all the livestock you need. Two thousand dollars, you walk away and we never see you again."*

"I feel sorry for you." That was the truth too. "Money isn't the be all and end all in this life."

"Boy, it's the only thing that matters. You can count on money. Money never lets you down. But love." Maureen's face pruned up, full of disdain. "Love is a lie. It dies, and what do you have then? Nothing, you fool."

He watched her walk away, but he wasn't thinking about the money. He glanced over his shoulder, catching sight of Aumaleigh emerging from the large pantry, with a flour canister in her arms. She was moving like lightning, rushing here and there, grabbing a mixing bowl and accidentally dropping a handful of wooden spoons on the table.

He imagined there would be a few more last minute tasks assigned to her, designed to keep her from having her Sunday afternoon off, thereby leaving him waiting for her. But he didn't care. Nothing and no one was going to separate him from his Aumaleigh. His love was stronger than that.

"Pa?" Leigh elbowed him in the side, pulling him out of his thoughts. "Isn't this a nice wedding?"

He blinked, glancing around, realizing the bride and groom had just finished their first kiss as man and wife. Poor Milo sat propped up in an armchair by the hearth, looking ashen and wobbly. It was hard not to have sympathy for the fellow.

"I heard a little rumor." Leigh leaned in, going up on tiptoe. "The dress Iris is wearing? That's Aumaleigh's. It's the one she made to marry you."

His jaw dropped. Words failed him. It was a beautiful dress, and so her. Simple but lacy, sweet and garnished with pearls. His ribs cinched up tight, making it hard to breathe.

"Although I completely understand why she would give your ring back." Leigh's smile sparkled. "Ma always talked about what a mess you were. How she had to train you up right. You were a disaster."

"Can't deny that." He'd been a wreck for a long time. His heart in pieces, disillusioned and disenchanted. He'd given his heart to her.

"Your mother loved me in spite of it." His voice cracked, because he was grateful for that. "Your ma made my life."

"So did I. Admit it. You need me, Pa."

"That I do." A father's love filled his heart, too great to measure.

The ceremony was done, the party started and his gaze drifted over to Aumaleigh. He wished he knew what to say.

CHAPTER FIFTEEN

"Aumaleigh, away from that sink right now!" Hazel bustled into the kitchen, looking healthier than she had in a while. "You're a guest and I won't have you touching one single dish."

"Too late. I've touched more than one." Aumaleigh plunged her hands into the steaming wash water and began scrubbing the glassware. "Go back in the dining room, Hazel. Spend time with your son and new daughter-in-law."

"Forget the in-law part. She's a daughter. My daughter." Hazel teared up, her chin wobbling with the strength of her emotions. "I love that niece of yours. Just love her."

"Which is why you're going to turn back around and leave me to do the clean-up." She used the no-nonsense tone she reserved for bossing the cowboys around. "You're Iris's mother now. Go celebrate with her."

"When you put it like that, how can I say no?" Hazel wrung her hands. "You're a wily one, Aumaleigh."

"I try. Now I'm right, and you know it. Go on. Leave."

"We're family now." Hazel waggled her finger, a woman not to be ignored. "I'll get you back for this. The next family get-together, I'm doing the dishes."

"If that makes you happy." Family. That word mattered to her. Big time. "Save me a piece of cake, would you?"

"I'll make sure it's one with lots of frosting flowers!" Hazel disappeared through the archway and Aumaleigh returned to washing the glasses.

The click, click, click of dog paws padded across the kitchen. Fluffy cocked her head, lifting her fuzzy, floppy ears and studying Aumaleigh with melty-chocolate eyes.

"Begging for food? Really?" She wiped her hands on a dishtowel. "Didn't you get enough from the girls feeding you under the table? Don't think I didn't see that."

"Are you still talking to animals?" Gabriel ambled in. "That brings back memories."

"Yes, of you talking to your horses." Aumaleigh braced herself. Maybe, if she were lucky, her heart would turn to stone and she wouldn't feel anything for him. Not one thing. "Don't act as if I'm the only one around here who does it."

"Oh, I reckon it's a family trait. I saw your Rose chattering away to her horse—"

"Wally," Aumaleigh supplied, slipping the sparkling clean glass into the rinse water.

"And then there was Daisy whispering to her horse while her husband tethered him out front." He sauntered over, closing the distance between them.

"That would be Marlowe." Aumaleigh plunged the dishcloth into the depths of the glass she was scrubbing and swished it around. "The girls rented Marvin and his brother Marlowe when they first got here. The animals were so sad and downtrodden, they didn't have the heart to turn them back."

"And so they kept them and spoiled them." He grabbed the dishtowel from the counter and sidled up next to her. "That sounds familiar too."

"You're thinking of Primrose." She yanked the dishcloth out of the glass, aching at the loss of that sweet mare. "She died of old age, dear thing."

"She had a good life, thanks to you." He plucked the clean glass out of the rinse water and started drying it. "You saved her from a life of abuse from that neighbor of yours."

"He charged me three times what she was worth. It was my entire savings, but she was worth every penny." She steeled herself against the memories that rose up—of petting Primrose on the street that day, realizing the handsome new man in town was watching her across the street, of feeding the mare carrots with Gabriel at her side, of racing the horse barebacked through the field, with tears in her eyes, upset by her parents—

No more memories, Aumaleigh. Maybe if she didn't remember, then she wouldn't start wanting him now.

"You've done a pretty good job drying that glass." She plopped another clean one into the rinse water, changing the subject. "Can't say I've seen a man do better."

"It's a gift." He shrugged, feigning humility. "Folks tell me I'm great, but really it's a skill that comes naturally."

Don't laugh, Aumaleigh. She bit her bottom lip. "Good. Maybe I should leave you to do the dishes and go have a piece of cake."

"Maybe. It's good cake." He took the glass she was washing and slipped it into the rinse water. "But stay here and talk with me."

That was the last thing she wanted—and the thing she wanted most. "Tell me again why you're here?"

"I'm family. But mostly because Rose insisted. She said it would be good for Leigh to come and spend more time with their friends. And she's right, Leigh is a social butterfly. It's not good for her to be isolated on my farm."

"Surely you knew I would be here." She worked the dishcloth around the tines of several forks, refusing to look at him.

"That's why I spent so much time outside watching everyone else arrive." He took the forks from her. They were clean enough.

She just didn't want to let go. "You were trying to avoid me."

"I heard you were already inside, helping with the set-up and the dress."

The dress. Her chest seized up. It was impossible not to remember, not to stop the memories. The lace he'd bought for her, that adorned the bodice. The pearls she'd saved for, each stitch she'd made. The lace she'd tatted late at night when she should have been sleeping, imagining her life as Gabriel's wife.

She cleared her throat, but her voice sounded scratchy, not at all like her own. "I had to make a few alterations. Iris is a little taller than me, so I had to sew on a ruffle on the skirt and lace on the sleeves."

"You would have been beautiful in it. Just so you know." He said nothing more, drying the forks with practiced ease as if he knew his words got to her, just pierced her deep inside.

What was there to say to that? She wanted to be angry at him for never forgiving her. She tried to tell herself she wanted the type of man she could trust.

But they were terribly young back then, still growing their characters, still becoming the people they were meant to be. Words from the letter she'd found in her mother's things, words he'd written to her long ago. *Falling in love with you changed me, made me the man, husband, father and now soldier I am today. I regret ending things the way we did. Neither of us deserved that hurt. I wish you a happy life. I hope you can think of me fondly and not with regret.*

Those words pulled at her now, overwhelming her. "This is hard, isn't it?" He took the wet dishcloth from her and set it aside.

His fingers were big and hot against hers, and his hands engulfed hers, cradling them, and everything vanished. The room, the floor, the conversations coming in from the dining room—until there was just him, just the two of them, hearts beating as one.

"Yes, this is quite difficult." She had to agree. With her heart this open, exposed against her will, she had no choice. "It's painful to remember."

"And impossible to forget." He nodded as if he knew. "Have you at least stopped hating me?"

"I suppose the truce you asked for has been a success." What flickered to life inside her, felt too fragile and frightening to let him see. She pulled her hands from his, and he let them go gently, but his gray gaze was shielded, hiding so much from her.

Once, she could read him like a book. Now there was too much unknown about him, that span of decades she knew little to nothing about. She cleared her throat, determined to be just as much of a mystery. "We're on neutral ground."

"I'd like something more than that." He grabbed the glasses sitting dry and clean on the counter and opened cupboard doors until he found the spot to put them away. "Can we try to be friends?"

"Friends? Isn't that a tall order?"

"Maybe." He held his feelings still, refusing to let them fall. Romancing her when they'd been young had been easy and as natural as breathing. This time around, he could see he would really have to work for it.

But he'd gotten this far.

Footsteps and voices came closer, breaking the moment. He would have liked to talk more about this with her, but he was glad he'd had this chance. Little wisps of curls had worked free from her artfully done up hair, falling in airy, dark curls that brushed against her soft skin. Tenderness dug deep, tenderness he had to hide as he yanked out drawers looking for where the forks went.

"Got to get back," Zane Reed was saying. The strapping, former bounty hunter was a likable guy, the kind that drew your instant respect.

"I'm riding out tonight, after I get my girls home." Beckett managed the ranch for Aumaleigh, and he looked good at his job. He radiated integrity and was easy to like. "Gabriel. Maybe you'd like to ride with us."

"What's going on?" He put away the forks and closed the drawer. "I heard some talk about volunteering."

"Are you a good tracker?" Zane wanted to know. He stood at the kitchen door, pulling on his duster. "If so, then grab your coat and come with me."

Aumaleigh nodded at him, as if she were eager to get him out of the kitchen. "I'll take Leigh home and get her in safely."

"Okay. I'll get my coat."

Aumaleigh didn't look at him again, standing at the counter, meticulously washing the spoons over and over. He'd gotten to her, he could see that.

* * *

The stars were shining like jewels in the sky, glittering and twinkling. Junior shivered in the cool night. If only he could reach up and grab one, they'd be rich enough to afford dinner, a warm place for the night and a horse to run with. If he ran far enough, maybe then he could get away from that sick feeling inside his stomach. That, horrible, squishy feeling that he'd done something terrible.

The image of Iris haunted him—every time she smiled. The spring in her step. How her bakery always gave him free samples. He'd give anything right now to be able to walk down Main Street and open her bakery's door. She would smile and welcome him and offer him a cookie.

Well, that wasn't exactly true. Once she knew what he'd done, she would hate him as much as he used to hate her. Shame crept through him. He couldn't stand to think how Iris would look at him now.

"Junior! Are you keepin' a good watch?" Giddy strutted out of the thick shadows of the forest and into the clearing around the line shack. "I practically sneaked up on you. If I were one of those rotten deputies, I could have shot you dead and you'd never have known."

That only reminded him of the sheriff. Junior's stomach felt even worse. "Sorry, Giddy. I was keepin' an eye out, honest. I'm just too hungry."

"I got some stuff. Just wish it was more." He sat down on a stump and opened the gunnysack he carried.

There wasn't much in it, but it smelled good. Junior grabbed a half-eaten roll, a little mushy from sitting in gravy, and shoved it into his mouth.

"I went through the ranch kitchen's garbage." Giddy dug out a partly eaten roll for himself. "Snuck up in the shadows against the house. I was doin' good, too, until a woman came out with a broom thinking I was a raccoon."

Junior didn't answer. He was too busy chewing. "Next time I'll go. I'm pretty sneaky."

"I'd better do it." Giddy took a leisurely bite of his roll. "That way I can get the lay of the land. That lousy sheriff set us back. I had the route all scoped out. Figured out how to get into that old lady McPhee's house at night without making a sound. Picked out my way, so I could hide my tracks the best. Now I gotta start all over again."

"The ranch is right down there. I can see one of the barns from here." Junior swallowed and dove into the gunnysack, grabbing a handful of what felt like mashed potatoes. He stuffed it into his mouth—yep, mashed potatoes and gravy. Peppered just right, too. "We can steal some kerosene from the kitchen. Look how dark it is at night. We creep in, douse the house and barn and light 'em up."

"A fire?" Giddy took another bite of his roll. "What good will that do? They'll just rebuild."

"But it'll cost 'em. They'll lose all their horses and look at all the equipment they've got. That'll hurt them. You know it will." He dug in for another handful of mashed potato.

"It ain't enough. Did you see how fast them McPhee sisters replaced the furniture we took? I've been sniffing around. Playing poker in the feed store those few times, I asked questions. And I learned some things."

"What things?"

"There was a big inheritance. Bigger than what those barns and horses would cost."

"I don't know, Giddy. Them horses are expensive. Pa said he was promised 'em. And if he can't get his share of them, when he was the one who raised 'em, no one should. Remember when he said that? It was when we was done with our supper at the prison. He looked us both in the eye and asked for our solemn vow. He asked me to do him proud, Giddy."

Junior stared down at the glop of gravy and potato stuck to his hand. His chest ached, remembering the moment when his father had needed him, when his pa had hugged him—a *real* hug.

Tears burned behind Junior's eyes and he hated being so soft, but through his whole life, that's all he'd ever wanted. His pa to love him.

"You're not gonna get soft on me, are you?" Giddy took possession of the gunnysack, keeping it all to himself. "Pa is counting on us. I know he wanted one thing, but I've been planning a lot. This way is better. We get the money out of the old lady, and run off. We can buy men to break Pa out of jail. Then the three of us can go anywhere in style. It'll be first-class for us all the way. Just think of it, Junior."

"And Pa will be with us." Junior could picture it—they'd get a nice manor house somewhere pretty, maybe down south where the weather was hot and they'd never have to worry about getting cold. Steak to eat every day. Servants to wait on them.

Yeah, he liked that picture. But it looked even better with Pa sitting beside him, Pa playing checkers with him, and Pa going out to the stables to look at their fancy horses. Junior's eyes burned again, because it meant so much.

"Glad you agree." Giddy held open the gunnysack so Junior could get more food. "Are you paying attention? You're supposed to be our lookout."

"Sorry, Giddy." Junior grabbed a handful of something warm in the bottom of the sack—a piece of mostly eaten chicken. He shoved it in his mouth and returned to his post.

He could see a lot of the valley from here. If the deputies were out tracking, Junior would see them. He was going to keep his eyes sharp.

* * *

"You've been quiet, Aumaleigh." Daisy slipped into the kitchen, carrying a stack of dessert plates. "We've missed you out there."

"I just didn't want to leave any work for Iris, this being her wedding night." Aumaleigh finished wiping down the counter. "Let me take those. You go out with the others."

"No. I'd rather stay in here with you." Daisy looked exhausted. Dark circles bruised the delicate skin beneath her eyes. The color had drained form her cheeks. "Maybe I'll have some tea."

"I steeped some for you. Ginger tea." Aumaleigh set the plates in the wash water and fetched a clean teacup. "I made it for your mother when she was expecting you."

"The doctor confirmed it this morning, but with the shooting and the wedding, I wanted to wait." Daisy gratefully took the soothing cup of tea. "I like to think Ma would be happy to see where we've all wound up."

"I know she would love Beckett and Hailie." That Aumaleigh knew for sure. Love for her sister-in-law warmed her right up. "She was so ecstatic when she was expecting you girls. She treasured every minute."

"That sounds like Ma." Daisy leaned against the counter and took a sip of tea. "If it's a girl, we're going to name her Laura."

"After your mother. She would have been so pleased. May your baby be just as sweet."

"I know she will be. If it's a boy, we have no idea about names. I don't like Pa's first name, and Beckett doesn't like his father's first name."

"If I'd had a son, I would have named him William." She plunged her hands into the water and began cleaning the plates. "I just always liked that name. It seems strong and kind at the same time—" —*just like Gabriel.* She bit her bottom lip before the words popped out.

"I can picture you sitting sewing on your wedding dress and making up your mind about future baby names." Daisy took another sip. "Seeing Gabriel again must bring up old feelings."

"Too many." Aumaleigh sighed, slipping a couple plates into the rinse water. Maybe she should have kept that thought to herself too. "But I made my choice back then. I didn't marry him."

"And you told me you regretted it ever since. What were the exact words? Let me think. *When I had the chance, I should have said yes.* That's what you said. You also said he told you that he would love you until he drew his dying breath." Daisy set down her cup. "What if that has been true all along?"

"Gabriel stopped loving me long ago." Of that she was certain.

"He named his daughter after you. There's only one reason to do that. Believe me, I know." Her hand drifted to her stomach, a mother's pure love shone on her face. "What if this is your second chance?"

What if? It was the one question she'd fought to keep out of her head because it hurt too much. She was not the girl she used to be. She felt every wrinkle. The time for romance in her life had passed...right? She shrugged. "He wants to be friends."

"Go ahead and tell yourself that. I don't believe it. Not for one minute." Daisy's chin went up, stubborn. "Don't forget we all love you, Aumaleigh. You're part of this family now and we look out for our own. If Gabriel tries to break your heart again, he will answer to me. I'll send Magnolia with her snake stick after him."

"That would put true fear into anyone," Aumaleigh quipped, breaking the moment, and they laughed together. The conversation turned to other things, but something had crept into her heart.

It felt suspiciously like hope.

CHAPTER SIXTEEN

"Giddy! Giddy, wake up." Junior shook his brother's shoulder hard.

Giddy gave one final snore before bolting up on the bunk. "What? Huh?"

"Someone's comin'." He grabbed the gunnysacks from his bunk and stuffed them into the water bucket that had been left in the shack. "They're comin' fast. We gotta go."

"What do you mean?" Giddy grabbed his revolver and drew. "We'll sit in the woods waiting for 'em. When they come up the trail, *bang, bang*. We'll have us a few dead deputies."

He hopped from the bunk, looking eager about it.

Junior wished his brother wasn't like that. He'd seen him like this before. There had been times—more than a few—when it had been better not to ask. But now that they were living together, he had to wonder. "Have you ever killed a man before?"

"Haven't you?" Giddy looked down the nose of his .45, lining up his sites and pretending to shoot. "There was a time or two I had to even the score. Make 'em pay for what they'd done to me. This ain't about that sheriff, is it? He's dead by now. Guess that would make four notches on my belt."

Giddy buckled on his gun belt, scuffed across the floor in his boots. "I've got a spot all scouted out with a good view of the trail. How many would you say are coming? Two, three?"

"A dozen." Junior's feelings stung. He didn't appreciate his brother talking harsh about the sheriff like that. What about Iris? Was she crying? Was she sad she was never able to get married? The thought of her heartbroken broke him up inside.

Maybe he was more than a little sweet on her. Very sweet.

"You're wrong." Giddy seemed sure about it. He stalked outside to check for himself. It sure seemed like he had it all figured out.

Junior went straight into the woods, heading up into the higher foothills. It was dark, and there were wild things out here. An owl hooted overhead. Something moved quick and predatory through the undergrowth on a faint trail ahead of him. Stars flickered between the trees. His foot caught on an exposed tree root and down he went. Bam! His knee hit a rock, the bucket flew from his hand and he caught himself with his palms. Stickers dug into his flesh, into his hands, and he bit back a curse of pain.

Sound carried in the night, in the quiet. The rolling clunk, clunk, clunk of the metal bucket rolling downhill sounded as loud as cannon fire to his ears. He pushed himself up, pulled the stickers out of his skin and adrenaline spiked through him. At least the deputies weren't close enough to pounce.

"Aw, they're all the way down the road. You chicken-livered coward." Giddy grabbed him by the armpits and yanked him up. "You're running away like a little girl."

"Do you know who lives in this town?" Junior pulled a few stickers out of his arm. "Zane Reed, that's who. He's close with the sheriff. They're friends. Everyone in town knows that. Who do you think that is leading the pack?"

"So what?" Giddy sounded all brave. "I'm not afraid of no bounty hunter. Besides, we're gonna be long gone by the time he gets here. C'mon."

No argument there. Junior didn't have time to bemoan the loss of the bucket and gunnysack blankets. He followed Giddy into the dark. The forest surrounded them as they climbed and climbed some more, keeping to the shadows as they circled McPhee land. By the time he was breathing hard and the back of his throat was dry, Giddy stopped and crouched low.

"There's that stupid bounty hunter. If only we weren't so far away." Giddy carefully pushed the needles of an evergreen bough aside just enough to frame the men dismounting midway up the trail to the cabin. Giddy pointed his finger like a gun at the bounty hunter. "Bang, bang."

Junior shivered. "C'mon, let's keep going. I don't want to get caught by that man."

"Don't worry." Giddy eased the tree branch back into place. "We won't."

They headed into the hills, stopping to cover their trail before splashing through the river and into the night-swept meadows of the neighboring ranch. They kept going until dawn.

* * *

Gabriel pulled Barney to a stop and leaned back in his saddle, taking in the view. The Rocking M was an impressive ranch in the early morning light, part valley, part hillside and rimmed by an emerald forest and towering mountains. He shouldn't be surprised, knowing Aumaleigh's parents had built it. They had been two people driven by money and by appearance—and ruthless enough to succeed at all costs.

Good for Aumaleigh for winding up with all this. She deserved it. He swung down, took a moment to pat his weary horse. They'd been going all night. His mind drifted to the past, to how hard they used to work Aumaleigh. Not her brothers, just her. *A son is to carry on your name, your legacy,* Winston McPhee used to say. *But a daughter, she's only good for what you can get out of her.*

The back door of the two-story log house swung open, and Aumaleigh bustled out, whistling as she reached up to ring the dinner bell. The melody carried on the wind, rising above the chatter of birds busily building nests and the whinny of a gelding leaning over a wooden corral closest to the house.

"Oh, goodness, Phil, you are a demanding horse!" Aumaleigh called out, looked toward the whinnying horse and jumping when she saw him instead. "Gabriel! You startled me. What are you doing sneaking around my ranch?"

"I'm up to no good."

"Typical." She smiled at him, wiping her hands on her flowered apron. She looked pretty as the morning, standing in the golden-hued sunshine with the wind tousling her hair. It was sleek and dark, curling around her heart-shaped face, a face he knew so well. "It's feeding time. The cowboys are on their way."

"Feeding time? You mean for the animals?"

"Sometimes I call them that." She pulled something out of her skirt pocket—a carrot. She swished toward him, following the path the sun made as if it were shining just for her.

"Hey, I heard that, Aumaleigh!" A cowboy hollered across the way. "We've worked hard not to be animals. We've improved our ways."

"Yeah, now we wipe our feet," another cowboy called out, leading the way across the yard. "We don't spit tobacco in the house anymore."

"That's because if you do, I'll take my wooden spoon to you, John. I won't hesitate." Aumaleigh tossed him a caring smile. Her manner was easy, her nature kind. You could see how much she respected the men who worked for her.

And how much they respected her.

"Hey, Gabriel." John stopped to greet him. "It was good to have you riding with us last night."

"It was good to come along. Thought I'd get home, grab some shut eye and be ready to ride again tonight."

"We'd be glad to have you." John's gaze cut sideways to pretty Aumaleigh waltzing up to the corral, sweet talking the whinnying gelding. "It's a worry those men were hiding out here on the ranch. Makes you think they were up to no good here."

"That was my thought too." Gabriel nodded, sharing an unspoken agreement with the cowboy. The Klemp brothers were wanted, they were criminals and they were being tracked. There could be only one reason why they were hanging around. "I hear their father used to work here."

"Like Beckett." John waved across the yard to where Beckett emerged from the barn, heading toward them. "He was promised a piece of this ranch, but his sweat equity wasn't good enough. Maureen likely burned up their agreement. When she died, there was no way to prove it."

"Sounds like Maureen." He'd had plenty of dealings with that woman. She'd done her best to buy him off more times than he could count, and when that didn't work, she'd tried to scare him off. "She cheated that Klemp fellow too?"

"That's what Burton and I told Milo. We've been talking to him ever since we found out about his sons. We ain't gonna let them hurt this ranch. It's Aumaleigh's heritage, and it's our livelihood. It's our sweat and our blood. We'll defend it."

"Let me know what I can do. I'll do anything." He meant that—with everything he had and everything he was.

Aumaleigh. She was at the fence line petting the demanding gelding's nose. It was in her stance, in the humor like a bell in her voice, in the natural accord she had with animals.

"Phil, you are a nut. Here's your carrot." She held the vegetable on the flat of her palm, laughing as the horse lipped up the treat. "Oh, you're such a gentleman. What a good boy you are."

The animal preened. She had a way with animals. She still had that soft touch. Tenderness took him over, melting even more.

"I don't think the true nature of the situation has occurred to her yet." John was grim. "Aumaleigh has a gentle soul. She doesn't understand the deception of certain kinds of men." John's voice dipped with meaning, with feeling.

Gabriel tried not to bristle. It wasn't hard to see that John was being protective of Aumaleigh, the way a father might. All he could do was to reassure the cowboy. "I'll be careful with her, John."

"See that you do. Burton and I don't want to have to come knock some sense into you." John winked, belying his threat. "Not that we're violent sorts, but you'd be mighty unpopular with us."

"I don't want to risk that, believe me." Gabriel understood. He liked that she had good men looking out for her, good men who understood what she'd been through with her family. "Save me a place inside. I want to talk with her."

"Okay, but don't be long." John chuckled. "We're a hungry horde. We'll eat anything that's not nailed down. Ain't that right, Beckett?"

"That's the truth." Beckett strolled up. "C'mon, John. Let's leave the two of them be."

The younger man nodded his approval, and it felt good. It mattered a lot. Maybe her family would be behind them this time. Wouldn't that be a change?

"Sorry, Phil, there's just one." Aumaleigh's laughter was like music, and for an instant, he caught sight of the girl she'd been, full of charm and hope. "Stop that, stop kissing me right now. That's just—oh, you're tickling me."

The troublesome Phil didn't stop. He went right on nibbling Aumaleigh's ears and face, giving her a rough lick along her jaw. He swished his tail, his chocolate eyes full of mischief. The horse seemed enchanted too by the willowy woman, as good-hearted as a princess, as sweet as spring.

Gabriel didn't remember crossing the yard, only that he was near to her, that he was touching close. His fingers itched to settle on the small of her back and turn her toward him so he could capture that laughing smile of hers with a kiss.

"Gabriel. Why aren't you in eating with the cowboys?" She stepped back, safely out of reach of the kiss-prone horse. The gelding stretched his neck over the top rail as far as it would go, and when he couldn't reach her with his tongue, he put more muscle against the fence.

Yeah, he knew just how the horse felt. "I could use a bite to eat and a cup of coffee, but I just had to come see this horse."

"What? Phil? Oh, he's nothing but trouble. Look at him, trying to break down the fence." She reached out a hand, graceful and kind, and her touch made the gelding close his eyes.

Longing lodged in Gabriel's chest. He wouldn't mind being touched like that by her. Would it still be as sweet? Or would it be different? Would time have changed what once sparked between them?

"I hear the tracking went pretty well last night." Aumaleigh gave the gelding one final pat before pushing away from the corral. "It was smart of Zane and the deputies to break up and search all the different out buildings. It sounds like it paid off."

"Yep, we found tracks outside one of your line shacks up on that rise." He nodded in the direction of the emerald hills and the purple mountain peaks rising behind them. "They'd clearly been staying in there. They'd already left, they must have been nervous enough to have been watching for us. But Zane followed a clear trail through the woods. He's still at it."

"And I bet you would be too, just like John and Beckett and a few more of the cowboys, if Zane hadn't sent you home." Aumaleigh stopped in the middle of the yard, crossing her arms over her chest like a barrier. "I hear he's got men on rotating shifts."

"Yep. Zane knows what he's doing. The Klemp brothers don't have a chance."

"I'm thankful for that. If they'd shoot a sheriff in cold blood, one who'd never done them harm, what else would they do? And who would they hurt next? Women? Children? I'll be glad when this is all over."

"Me, too. At least the Klemps are safely away from here. Zane tracked them through Lawrence's land and through the valley."

"Better for us, I suppose, but not for those in their path." Aumaleigh shivered. After all her nieces had been through with Verbena's old beau Ernest, who'd tracked her down and refused to let her go, and George who'd helped him to do it, she had a new perspective about criminals. "Let's get you inside and fed."

"Those are some beautiful horses you've got." He didn't move toward the kitchen house, but turned his attention to the paddocks surrounding the barns. "You wouldn't happen to have any for sale, would you?"

"Why? You already have a team. Your horses are beautiful."

"Yes, but I thought I'd breed and raise horses. It would give me something to fill my days. I'm not sure retirement is going to sit well with me."

"Retirement. It's hard to believe that's where we are in our lives. How fast the years whip by—"

"—and I keep wondering how I got here," he finished. "It makes you realize how precious your days really are—"

"—that they can be spent so quickly." This time it was her turn to finish his sentence. She did it without thinking, simply saying what she felt. Was the accord between them so great? Or was it simply because they were so alike in their thoughts?

"Show me your horses," he asked. "I can get food and coffee later."

He had to be exhausted. He'd been up all night. "You can look at the horses later."

"I want to see them now." The pitch of his voice dipped, rumbling low and tender, meaning so much more.

Or was she hoping so? *Don't start hoping too much, Aumaleigh.* Gabriel was here about the horses. It was best to be realistic. She shoved her hands into her skirt pockets. "I'm sure Josslyn can handle things without me in the kitchen."

"Are you kidding? Josslyn loves to be in charge." He took the first steps up the hill toward the barns.

She moved with him without thought, falling in line beside him the way she always used to. But it was different. It was sad. There was no closeness between them. No connection. Time had severed that.

"Did Leigh talk your ear off on the drive last night?" He tipped his hat up a notch and their gazes met.

Once she'd gotten lost in the tenderness of his gaze. But that was gone too. "Leigh is adorable. She kept me entertained all the way home to my house. I invited her over for tea and cupcakes."

"You did?" He arched an eyebrow. "What did she want? I'm almost afraid to ask."

"She wanted to see the house. She was being nosy." Pleasure softened the delicate angles of Aumaleigh's face. Clearly she hadn't minded. "I also think she wasn't sure about coming home to an empty house. So I kept her until almost bedtime and then drove her home."

"Thanks for looking after her, Aumaleigh. She's engaged, but to me she'll always be a little girl."

"That's the way it should be." Aumaleigh paused at the paddock gate. "She spent quite a bit of the night talking about you."

"About me? Wait—maybe I don't want to know about this. I have a feeling she violated one of the laws I laid down." He moved in close to her, his hand brushing hers as he grabbed the latch. "Let me do this, Aumaleigh. You've been on your own so long, and I know you're independent and capable, but this is courtesy. Let go and let me open the gate."

"You've gotten bossier over the years."

"Something I learned from my daughter," he joked and lifted the latch. "The horses know you. Look at them run to you."

"I've been known to come with treats." She breezed past him with a snap of her skirts and the faint scent of roses.

He breathed her in, wanting, just wanting. Hoping for what could be.

But Aumaleigh's attention was on the horses. She held up her hands. "See? No treats today. How are my good girls?"

The mares loped toward her, surrounding her. Some were heavily pregnant, others sporting long-legged, knobby-kneed foals by their sides.

Just like old times, Gabriel thought, watching Aumaleigh rub a nose there, pat a cheek there, stroke her fingers down another mare's neck. She snuggled foals, chatting to the animals all the while. They clearly loved her. Mares pressed closer, eager for her touch. Foals lipped her skirt and apron.

This was the life she'd built. Admiration beat through him. Animals had always flocked to her, and over the years her tenderness to them had not changed. The notes of her voice, the kindness, the melody of her laughter were the same, but the woman was not. She possessed an inner strength that neither diminished nor outshone her beauty. He could not look away.

"Miss Ginger, I didn't mean to ignore you." Aumaleigh turned her attention to another mare. "You are looking very pretty today, you good girl."

The mare lifted her chin to give Aumaleigh better access and her eyes drifted shut, enjoying the attention.

"Gabriel, don't stand back there. Come and take a look," she invited, and he moved without thinking, drawn to her like she was his destiny, like they'd never been apart.

But the way she turned from him reminded him that they had. She spun around, bending down, to take a foal's muzzle in her hand and give it a kiss on the nose. The little filly preened, brown eyes warm with adoration.

Yeah, he knew how she felt.

"This is Petunia. Her dam is Angie. She's the sorrel with the three white socks." Aumaleigh laughed when another foal nosed in and knocked little Petunia out of the way. "Hey, Felix! You are a bad boy. No, I'm not going to kiss you next. No, I'm not at all."

Aumaleigh stopped herself. Not everyone thought the way she talked with animals was, well, practical or sane. But Gabriel didn't seem to mind—that much about him hadn't changed either.

He held out a hand to let the spunky colt scent him. "Hello there, little fella."

Her pulse fluttered. Just went wild in her chest like a hummingbird taking flight.

"Would you and your pretty mama like to come live with me?" He knelt down, using both hands now. Big, powerful hands, and so, so gentle. "I made my living with cattle, raising horses when I could afford to. But it's time to start living new dreams. I'm going to buy some horses from you, Aumaleigh."

"Okay. You'll want to talk to Burton about that. He's our resident wrangler. He can tell you all about the mares, their age and their lineage." The wind tangled her hair, plastered her dress against her slim shape.

Nothing could be more beautiful than her, standing among the green grasses and budding wildflowers, surrounded by the horses who loved her.

"I don't need Burton." He took a risk, took a step toward her. "I just need you."

CHAPTER SEVENTEEN

"M-me?" Her hand flew to her throat. Shock rocketed through her, and the wild fluttering in her chest grew. A quiet, vulnerable hope rose up to the surface. Was that how he felt about her? Did he feel the beginnings of real tenderness for her too?

He swept off his Stetson, looking strong and vital in his blue muslin shirt and denims. The wind tousled his thick, dark hair. It was a friendly smile he tossed her, bracketed by his charming dimples.

Friendly. Not the intimate, loving smile she'd once lived to see.

"Sure, you used to be the best judge of a horse's temperament I knew. Or has that changed?" He arched an eyebrow at her, good-natured, unaffected.

So, no tenderness then. Disappointment, as heavy as lead, settled over her heart. Disappointment she had to hide. "Burton certainly would be better."

"But if you love a horse, than I know I will." He took a step closer and a few of the foals moved with him. Curious, they nibbled his trouser leg and licked his boots. "This isn't a business I'm starting. This is all for me. I love horses, I want to spend my time with them."

"I understand." She didn't trust her voice for a moment, so she stood there, with the sun in her eyes and a vast hollowness filling her.

"What are your dreams?" He reached down to ruffle Felix's bottlebrush mane. "You've spent your entire adult life in a kitchen. I know you're not happy there. I remember the dreams you used to have."

"Some dreams aren't meant to come true. They're just dreams." She smiled as if he wasn't one of those dreams, lost forever. She lifted her chin, going toward him like a woman who was too strong to let foolish emotions into her heart. "There are more important things in life than chasing after what you don't have."

"And every once in a while, something—or someone—is worth anything to have." His eyes darkened, stormy gray, and in them she could not guess what he was feeling.

Another reminder that the man in the past, and what they'd had, was gone forever.

"Spending my time with horses, raising and training them, now that's a nice thing to have." Gabriel knelt down to check out another foal who'd bounded up to him and ran his big, capable hands along her back. "Aren't you a fine filly? Something tells me you're Aumaleigh's favorite. I saw you nuzzling up to her earlier."

"That's Libby." Her step faltered, so she stayed where she was, hit hard because Gabriel had read her so well. What else had he seen?

Here's hoping he hadn't seen her weakness for him, her feelings that were starting anew. Gabriel would always hold a spot in her heart. Perhaps it was time to accept it.

"My dreams are practical ones these days." She wanted him to be clear about what she expected and what she wanted in life. "Can you keep a secret?"

"You know I can."

"I've decided to sell this place." A mare came up to her and she wrapped an arm around the animal's neck. "Mother's illness dictated my life for so long. I don't want the responsibility of this ranch to do the same thing."

"You've put in your time, Aumaleigh. Few people would have stuck it out to the end with Maureen."

"My mother was impossible, but she was my mother. I think you really do choose who you want to be in life. Which means you have to be careful with what you let into your heart. She was different when I was young. Part of me kept hoping she would be that person again."

"Is that why you chose her over me?" He gentled his tone. "Or maybe that wasn't the real issue?"

She blushed, looking down suddenly at the grass at her feet.

So, he'd hit the nail on the head. That hadn't been the real problem, not at all. "So after you sell this place, then what? Are you going to travel? Move somewhere else?"

"No, I'm staying put. I've never been one to want to see the world. I have everything I need right here in Bluebell. In my heart."

"Your nieces are here. Your best friend is here." He could see what family meant to her. Now he knew for sure how much both meant to this woman who'd never known love as a child. "You're going to retire then. You've certainly earned it. I hope you like it as much as I do."

"There's going to be so much to do. There's one more wedding to plan, and then there are babies to sew for. I hope to be the great-aunt they call when they need a baby-sitter. I missed seeing my nieces grow up. I don't want to let that happen again."

"Good for you. The hardest part for me is being away from my kids."

"You're going to have a hard time letting Leigh go. That isn't hard to see." Aumaleigh gave the mare one last pat before moving away. "What about your future grandchildren? They'll be so far away. You won't get to know them."

"That is a problem, but maybe it will solve itself over time. It's why I let Leigh talk me into bringing her out here, and why I'm glad she's staying so long. Maybe the town of Bluebell and the people in it will grow on her, and she'll bring her husband out here."

"You've got it all planned out."

"Just hoping. I don't know how it will work out, but Leigh does seem to like it here." Gabriel wished he could hold onto this moment, make it last, that it would never need to end. As they smiled together, the sun seemed to brighten and the air to change, and she felt closer. As if her heart had opened to his just a smidgeon.

Driven by the purest of wishes, he knelt to the ground and plucked a buttercup from the grass. He knew she understood it's meaning when he handed it to her. Tears stood in her eyes.

Their fingers touched as she took it from him. Without a word, she stared into his eyes, into him, and it felt like what he wanted most was within his grasp. She was the reason his heart stirred to life once again.

"Aumaleigh!" A rotund woman hollered from the back porch, cupping her hands around her mouth so her voice would carry. "We're being run ragged in here."

"I'm coming, Orla!" Aumaleigh hollered back. The sight of her clutching the buttercup healed something inside him. She filled the empty places in his soul.

Her smile dazzled as she turned to him one last time. "You're welcome to come get some grub, or stay out here and pick out your horses. I can already tell you're going to stay. You've found your next dream, haven't you?"

"Yes." But it wasn't the horses. She breezed away, leaving him behind, standing in the middle of a buttercup patch.

The sun—the world—had never been so bright.

* * *

*H*e gave me a buttercup. Aumaleigh cupped it in the palm of her hand and took one last look at Gabriel as she closed the kitchen house door. He was busy with the horses, walking among the friendly creatures, doing his best to win them over.

"Grab the toast!" Orla shouted as she disappeared down the hallway.

The loud clatter and clank of the cowboys eating filled the house like strange, discordant music.

"I saw what he gave you." Josslyn scooped slices of ham out of the fry pan and tossed them on a platter. "I know what that means."

"No, you don't." Aumaleigh grabbed a saucer and filled it with water. It was just deep enough for her buttercup. She left it floating in its saucer on the counter and grabbed the platter of toasted bread. "Gabriel was being nostalgic."

"Is that what you really think?"

"No." Aumaleigh couldn't say why her eyes teared. She blinked hard, carrying the platter across the room. It was a question that haunted her.

"Aumaleigh!" Kellan waved his fork in the air. "I'll take some toast. Is there more ham coming?"

"Because you're my favorite, I'll give you the first piece." She circled the big table where a dozen cowboys were crowded, shoving down food as fast as they could go.

"I love you too, Aumaleigh." Kellan was a cowboy through and through. That one could charm. "How about first choice with the ham, too?"

"Anything for you." She held the platter for him as several others around the table stated their opinions.

"He ain't worth the saddle he was raised on," John grumbled with a wink. "I have seniority. I ought to be served first."

"But I'm older," Burton pointed out, scooping a forkful of scrambled eggs into his mouth. "Plus I was up late last night riding with the posse."

"The poor old man is tired!" Shep teased, and a few other cowboys at one of the other tables whistled.

"Poor Burton," Pax called out. "Let me have your bacon if you wanna go to bed and rest up."

"Nobody gets my bacon," Burton joked. "Them's fightin' words."

"What about me?" Beckett asked, sitting back in his chair. "I'm family. Doesn't that count for anything?" The cowboys all shouted *no*, having their fun.

Aumaleigh looked down at the platter and it was empty. The cowboys within reach of her had helped themselves to every last piece of toast.

"What about us?" Pax asked from the next table over. "Don't we get any toast? I guess we don't rate."

"She loves them more," Shep agreed.

Oh, she was going to miss these boys. Laughing, she whirled away with her empty platter. "I think it's pretty clear who I love."

"It's me," Tiernan Montgomery called out. "I'm everyone's favorite. Admit it."

Bits of bacon flew his way, as he got plenty of comments about that.

"What is going on in here?" Josslyn demanded, coming in with the ham plate. "If you boys don't start acting mannerly, I'll take a switch to you. Starting with you first, Tiernan."

"Me? Why me? I'm innocent."

The other cowboys had plenty to say about that. Aumaleigh left the dining room in search of toast for her platter, and she felt sad for the first time. Sad, because she loved life on a ranch. She loved the people who'd become her family when she had none.

But it was time.

The instant she stepped foot in the kitchen, her gaze arrowed to the window, finding Gabriel among the horses. He'd moved on to the second paddock, which was farther away and harder to see. But that didn't stop her from stopping at the window for a better look.

He moved among the horses, powerful but patient, and intrinsically kind. His goodness still shone through—it was what made him so magnetic, it attracted her like nothing else. He'd grown more rugged, stronger, and as he walked through the yellow patches of buttercups in the paddock, she began to believe.

"He gave you a buttercup on your first date." Josslyn returned with an empty platter too and set it on the counter. "What is he still doing here? Wasn't he up all night with the posse?"

"So were a good quarter of my cowboys. Another quarter are out riding with Zane right now." Aumaleigh turned her back on the window. "And it's still calving and foaling season."

"I can run the kitchen with just me, Louisa and Orla. If you want to lend a hand with the livestock." Josslyn's voice trailed behind her, and then she was out of sight.

The kitchen door swung open and let in the spring breeze and a half-dozen cowboys.

"You looked surprised to see us." Lew whipped off his Stetson. "Don't tell us the food's already gone."

"Yeah, we're done starved!" Dale agreed. The junior wrangler sat down on the bench and shucked off his boots. "It was hard riding, both tracking with Zane and after when the Deer Springs sheriff took over."

"Yeah, he tossed us out of his jurisdiction." Lew rolled his eyes. "Whew, there's a man with a temper."

"And an ego," Burton commented, padding through the kitchen in his stocking feet. "Aumaleigh, I'm gonna head out and talk to Gabriel. Josslyn said he's looking at horses."

"Yes. Give him a good price, would you?"

"Your wish is my command." Burton tipped his hat and sat down next to Dale. "Does that mean Zane is off the job?"

"Those Klemp brothers ran. And I mean, they ran. They left a trail of stolen and abandoned horses in their wake. They used every trick in the book. Trust me, at least one of 'em has been on the run before." Burton yanked on his left boot. "Aumaleigh, rest assured the danger has passed. Those boys are on the run. They have no reason to come back."

"I hope you're right." Aumaleigh grabbed a fresh pot of coffee and began pouring cups for the newly arrived men. "Can you trust the sheriff to finish the job?"

"He's a good man. He'll bring them in." Burton pulled on his other boot. "But we'll keep an eye out just in case."

"Wise." Aumaleigh glanced out the window. Gabriel was out of sight.

But he was making her dream.

* * *

"*Gabriel, I'm so sorry.*" *The sob lodged in her throat, making her croak instead of talk. The exquisite summer heat fanned over her as she stood on the back porch.* "*You've waited all afternoon, and now Mother is making me help with supper. One of the maids went home sick.*"

"*I see.*" *He stood up slowly, thoughtfully.* "*Guess it happened again.*"

"*I don't know what to say.*" *Her heart was breaking. Any moment now he was going to say the words, the ones she could not bear to hear.* "*Don't break it off with me. Please don't ask for your ring back.*"

The tears came then—hot, swift, dripping down her face.

She took a step back, bracing for the inevitable. She'd let him down too many times, and he was going to say she wasn't worth it.

"*Hey, shh now.*" *Soothing, that voice, that touch. His hands cupped her face, rough and callused from his work but infinitely careful as he pulled her close to kiss her tear-stained cheeks.* "*I'm not going to ask for any such thing. Not on my life. You hear me?*"

"*Y-yes.*" *It was hard to believe he could still love her, but it was in his eyes, in his touch, soft in his kiss when their lips met. Nothing was more tender than that kiss.*

Nothing.

When he broke away, he wiped away every tear with the pads of his thumbs. "*Don't worry. There's always next week.*"

Next week. Her spirit fell. What if this happened again? "*Mother is determined to keep us apart.*"

"*She's just mad that everyone knew about us the second I bought that ring in town. Popular opinion will keep her from interfering.*"

If only that were true. Aumaleigh bit her bottom lip, keeping that thought to herself.

"*I'll head home now.*" *He leaned in and kissed her forehead.*

It left her feeling warm and safe inside, cozy and snuggly. She could feel his heart in hers, she could feel his love. Her fingers twined with his. She held on tight.

"*Aumaleigh!*" *Cook opened the screen door.* "*Get in here, girl!*"

Gabriel winced, but whatever his reaction was, he didn't let it show. He squeezed her fingers once before stepping back. His fingers left hers. He hopped down the stairs.

It took everything she had to watch him go.

"Get in here." Maureen marched onto the porch and grabbed Aumaleigh by the ear.

"Ow!" Her protest only seemed to make Mother madder. She was yanked into the kitchen, scolded and shamed in front of the kitchen staff. She kept her head down as she peeled potatoes for the ranch hands' supper. Defiance burned inside her, raging hot.

This was her chance for love. Her one big chance. She was never going to let it go. Mother was not going to destroy it.

Later that night after she'd been released from her chores, she spotted something sitting on the outside lip of her bedroom window sill. The warm night breeze blew in the scent of wild roses.

Flowers Gabriel had picked and left for her. It was hard to believe he could love her so much.

* * *

Gabriel smelled coffee carrying to him on the warm puff of breeze. Around him the foals frolicked, running and kicking up their heels while their mamas watched. He had hoped it was Aumaleigh, but the moment he saw Burton, Beckett and Zane coming his way, he knew he was in trouble.

And he knew why.

"Brought you some vitals." Burton handed over a tin cup and plate.

"We appreciate you helping us out last night." Beckett came to a stop next to Burton.

"It was good you stepped up to help." Zane squared his shoulders.

All three men looking at him made him dread what they were going to say next. Maybe they thought he'd let Aumaleigh down long ago and he'd come to do it again.

"The sheriff over in Deer Springs is going to let me join in on the hunt. I'm going to get home and get some rest, then head over." Zane knuckled back his hat. He had a powerful presence, like a man who always did right. "The sheriff knows Milo, and he's committed to catching the men who shot his friend."

"We all think the Klemp brothers are going to keep running," Burton added, a strong, lifelong cowboy. He radiated the honor of his trade. "But we've thought that before. The man who was after Verbena, he got away and came back. Something like that's hard to forget."

"So we and the deputies are going to keep an eye on this town." Beckett planted his hand on his hips, a natural leader, the kind of man who stood for what was right. "Seth, Adam and Tyler are in on this too. We'd like to ask you to join us."

Gabriel's hand shook, nearly spilling his coffee. That wasn't what he was expecting. Not at all. "I'd be right happy to help out."

"Good. Glad to have you with us." Beckett's grin said everything Gabriel could have hoped for.

That was one obstacle down. He had her family's approval. Now all he needed was hers.

CHAPTER EIGHTEEN

I t felt like a long day, and it wasn't over yet. Aumaleigh had spent half the day cooking ahead to help make up for the fact that she wouldn't be working that evening, and also cooking up a few extra meals for Iris's fa mily.

As she drove through town, she dodged school kids racing through the streets, freed from their prison of school. Their happy shouts and squeals put a smile on her face as she went over the errands she had yet to run—bakery, mercantile, newspaper office.

"Aumaleigh!" Fred leaning against the railing in front of the post office, sunning himself on this fine day. "Did you hear all about the Klemp brothers?"

"Yes, I did." She pulled Buttons to a stop and hopped out of her buggy.

"And here I felt sorry for the one who was limping." Fred shook his head. "Guess you never really know about folks. Wonder what they were doing in town? Aside from stealing from us, that is. Living in George's cabin. I heard the Deer Springs sheriff is furious mad. Brought in a huge posse to hunt 'em down."

"That's what I heard too." Aumaleigh grabbed a crate from the floor of her buggy and hefted it into her arms. Good old, Fred. He was always full of speculation. "My theory is that the boys wanted a new start, but couldn't leave their old ways behind them. My nieces felt sorry for Junior too. They were going to offer him a job."

"I heard that too. Don't think I'm gonna let a pretty lady like you carry something heavy. Not when I'm alive and kicking." Fred came over, took the box from her and escorted her up the steps. "What's this I hear about you and Gabriel Daniels?"

"There's no more new news to get out of me, Fred."

"Rats. Here I was hoping for a good scoop. Well, a man's gotta try." He pulled open the bakery door. "I'm hoping things work out for you. I think he's got a courting look in his eye."

"Thanks for carrying the crate for me." She laughed. "I adore you, you know."

"Everybody does." Fred winked, sliding the crate onto a nearby empty table.

"We certainly do." Dottie circled the counter with a cookie in hand. "No good deed goes unpunished around here, or at least it's rewarded with a cookie."

"That's right." Rhoda agreed from behind the counter. "I just heard some gossip about you. Your wife was in here not an hour ago for some of our cinnamon bread—"

"—it's a favorite of mine," Fred admitted.

"And she said your daughter is coming to visit." Rhoda beamed. "I'm so excited. We were friends back in school."

"I remember." The proud father flushed with pleasure. "She's a good girl, coming back because we've been begging her to see us."

"We're thrilled—oops! I see a customer. I'd better go. Thanks for the cookie!" Fred scuttled off, the bell above the door jangling in his wake.

"I love him." Dottie flushed. "If I could pick anyone for a father, I would pick him. He's so fatherly. And sort of like Santa Claus."

"Without the beard and the red suit," Rhoda agreed.

"And the spectacles," Aumaleigh chimed in. "Dottie, come over here. I've been going through the extra rooms at the kitchen house and I found some extra things we don't need. I thought they would help you out."

"You mean for my new place?" Dottie's eye widened with surprise. The shy girl lit up. "Aw, you didn't have to do that. I'm getting by just fine."

"Come take a look." Aumaleigh knew what it was like to be alienated by your family. She wished she'd made the decision Dottie had, to find a place for herself in this world.

But if she had, she wouldn't have had this life. Maybe it was one of those mid-life things, or maybe with the nieces coming to live here in Bluebell she'd spent more time thinking about young love than she used to.

The decision she'd made in her youth had long reaching consequences, but that was true for anyone. She treasured her life here because she could see everything she had. Family, friends, a community. She had a life filled with love.

"Oh, there are mixing bowls in here, and a fry pan and, oh, Aumaleigh. A set of ironware that matches!" Dottie looked overwhelmed. "I don't know what to say. Thank you seems too little."

"Why don't you think of me as your aunt. That's what I want in return." Aumaleigh had a soft spot for little Dottie, who was just as sweet as pie. "This way you have enough kitchenware to fix supper for a certain interested gentleman."

"Oh!" Dottie turned beat red, but her happiness was hard to miss.

Aumaleigh gave her a hug, and the bell above the door chimed again.

Magnolia tumbled in, wild-eyed and disheveled. "Fanny Dobson and I just had a big argument in the alley behind her store. They just opened, can you believe that? They put out a sign, she had the employees she brought in from Deer Springs standing on the boardwalk giving out samples. All our school kids are there, munching on Dobson's cookies instead of ours."

Aumaleigh had a bad feeling. "What happened with you and Fanny?"

"She backed her wagon out of the alley and rammed into my buggy." Magnolia fisted her hands. "I think she did it on purpose too. The cake for Bradley Calhoun's wife's birthday flew off the seat and hit the ground. It was a disaster. It's nothing but crumb and frosting bits."

"Are you okay?" Dottie rushed toward her.

"Magnolia, come sit down." Rhoda pulled out a chair.

Aumaleigh crossed to the stove and poured a cup of tea. "What matters is you, Magnolia. Did you fall out of the buggy too?"

"Perhaps a little." Her distress gave way as her mouth twisted into a grin. "Okay, it was funny. Maybe it was really funny. I totally flew off the seat too, but I grabbed the dashboard. Quick thinking on my part.

Honestly. So I was hanging there when Carl came out onto the loading dock."

"Wait, you were hanging on the buggy?" Dottie looked aghast. "Were you stuck?"

"No, I was just dangling there, holding onto the dashboard for dear life. I was just about to let myself down when I realized my skirt had flown up from the force of the impact and I was showing off my nice lace stocking all the way up to my knees."

"Now I can't say I'm the only one to show off my bare legs in this town." Rose blew into the shop with the sunshine. "Glad to know I'm not the only one who humiliates myself around here."

"Hi, Rose." Magnolia dropped into the chair. "Do you know what the worst part was? Fanny climbs down from her wagon and clomps over in her man boots and says real sweetly. Oh, did I do that? I didn't see you there."

"Ooh!" Dottie scrunched up her face and fisted her hands. "You know she was lying. You know she did it on purpose. She's a bully, and there's no way to stop her."

"You could get Nathaniel involved," Rhoda suggested. "He's a good attorney. She's responsible for the damages."

"That's the second time I've been in a wreck with that buggy." Magnolia rolled her eyes. "What if they hold that against me? Like I'm a bad driver or something."

"You really are kind of a bad driver," Missy came out of the kitchen to add. "Not that I'm judging, but you're more one of those near miss drivers."

"You know my motto. A miss is as good as a mile." Magnolia started laughing. "You should have seen it. Wham! The cake goes flying, I go flying and poor Marlowe, the sweetest horse in the world is like, *I didn't do anything. What's going on?* He reached around in his traces and was checking on me, lipping me with his mouth while I was hanging there off the dash with my skirts up over my hips."

"Wait. That wasn't part of the story before," Aumaleigh pointed out.

"Okay, I showed off more than my stockings." Magnolia doubled over, laughing.

So did everyone else. Peals of laughter echoed in the bakery. Wynne came out, spatula in hand, to see what the fuss was all about.

The bell above the front door chimed.

"Magnolia, are you sure you're all right?" Oscar stormed in, breathless, worry lining his chiseled face. "I took the bashed-in buggy to the livery stable. Seth said he'll fix it up for you and give Marlowe some extra loving."

"Thanks for the help, Oscar. You're a gem." Magnolia's praise was genuine.

It was easy to see they all felt the same about Oscar. He was always ready to lend a hand, always helping out. He was a good man. How were they ever going to let him go back to his logging profession?

"Is there anything I can do?" Aumaleigh offered. "I have some free time."

"No, I'm fine. All that's wounded is my pride." Magnolia patted her hair, trying to tame it. "And maybe, just maybe, my reputation, but it won't be the first time. Do we have a spare cake?"

"I made an extra for the display case." Wynne swung around, bustling back to the kitchen. "Missy, come help me with the frosting. We'll get it fixed up as good as we can. Let's move!"

"Gotta go!" Missy waved and scampered off, disappearing through the swinging doors.

"Oh, I almost forgot your order." Rhoda circled the counter and plucked two small bakery boxes off a shelf. "Cinnamon rolls for Verbena, with extra icing just the way she likes it. And dinner rolls for Iris. I threw in a cupcake for everyone. I couldn't resist."

"Thanks, Rhoda." Aumaleigh took the box, noticed that Magnolia was fully recovered, retelling the tale for Fred who had popped in for the latest scoop. She accepted Dottie's thanks one more time, gave the girl a hug, boxes and all, and headed out onto the boardwalk.

Buttons lifted her head in greeting, so good and patient as always.

"I didn't mean to be so long," she told the mare and stowed the boxes on the buggy floor. "Let's go down to the mercantile. There are other horses tethered down there. Oh, and a donkey too. Let's go, girl."

Buttons waited until Aumaleigh was seated before daintily making her way down the street. It was hard not to feel resentment when she saw the A-board on the other side of the street advertising *Now Open! Free Samples!* Several young ladies holding trays full of cookies. School children crowded around, taking as many as they could hold.

"Is Magnolia okay?" Lawrence Latimer was stowing a box of

groceries in his handmade cart. "I heard what happened in the mercantile. Everyone's talking about it. Did that Dobson woman really run into her?"

"Yes, but Magnolia's okay." Aumaleigh pulled Buttons to a stop. "You're looking happy, Lawrence."

"Why, thank you, Ma'am." He gave a humble shrug. "Guess my life's going pretty well these days. I've caught the attentions of a fair lady."

"Yes, so I've heard." She hopped down and smoothed her skirts, glad for the lost little man. It was hard not to like him. Everyone deserved love and the chance for happiness. "I'm hoping good things for you and Dottie. Have a good afternoon, Lawrence."

"You too, Aumaleigh." His handlebar mustache twitched when he smiled.

Leaving him to untie his donkey, she lifted her skirts, skipped up the steps and let the warmth of the sunshine sift over her. The world felt brighter. Better.

"Hi, Aumaleigh." Gemma greeted the instant the door swung open. "I saw you out there chatting with Lawrence. Isn't it an improvement? He hardly talked my ear off at all this afternoon. I sure hope things work out for him and Dottie."

"Me, too." She stopped to loosen her sunbonnet strings and pushed it back, letting it dangle down her back. She took a moment to study Gemma. The girl looked better today, less sad than the last time she'd seen her. Family troubles were never easy. She knew that firsthand. "Did you get the new button shipment in?"

"Yes! I just finished putting up the new display this morning. We've got some lovely mother-of-pearl ones in." Gemma opened the account book on the counter in front of her, flipping through the pages. "Is there something specific you're looking for?"

"I'll know it when I see it. Thanks, Gemma."

She wandered over to the sewing corner, her thoughts turning to her morning's conversation with Gabriel. *Every once in a while, something—or someone—is worth anything to have.*

Had he meant her? Oh, she hoped so. She wished it with her whole heart.

She moved into the kiss of the sun, streaming through the window, and made her way through the packets of buttons on display. Pink ones, red ones, blue ones, metal ones. She stopped at the card of carved ivory roses, dainty and intricate.

She used to have buttons like these, in fact they were the same buttons she was buying when—

The door whooshed open, and warm spring air breezed in. A shiver of recognition tingled down her spine, and her gaze flew upward. *Gabriel.* He stood braced in the doorway, dark-haired and handsome, so rugged he dwarfed the entire shop. A black, wide-brimmed hat shaded half his face, so all she could see was the straight blade of his nose, a masculine, sculpted mouth and an uncompromising iron-hewn jaw.

Wow. Just wow. Her jaw dropped, her soul stilled and she knew she would never be the same again.

She felt the impact of his gaze long before he tipped back his hat to reveal intense gray eyes fringed by black lashes. The force in his gaze startled her, made her heart lurch into a frantic dash. It was as if he could see inside her, past her facades and her defenses. Just the way he used to.

"Hi, Mr. Daniels," Gemma called from the counter. "How's Leigh?"

"She'll be mad when she finds out I came here without her." He may be speaking with Gemma, but his attention stayed riveted on her, standing in front of the button display.

A strange sense of déjà vu whispered over her.

Their gazes met and locked. An eternity passed in that moment. Recognition came to the innermost part of her. She knew this man down to his soul. She'd always known him.

And forever would.

"Gemma, could you get me a bucket of nails?" He called over his shoulder, breaking eye contact.

Aumaleigh grabbed the edge of the counter. She felt wobbly, dizzy. Breathless.

"Burton and I worked out a deal." He strode up to her, long, denim-encased legs, a blue shirt covering muscled arms and torso. He tipped back his hat. "I'm the proud owner of some of your best horses."

"Oh, good." Flustered, she couldn't seem to make her brain work. Words tangled on her tongue. Or maybe it was the disappointment he'd come to talk business when she'd been expecting...well, what exactly was she expecting? She shrugged. "They couldn't have a better home. This way I'll get to see them now and again. Your fields come up to my side yard."

"Yes, I know. You're welcome to climb the fence and visit them any time. I promise not to chase you off."

"Generous of you."

"Yes, I know. It's just in my nature." The corners of his chiseled mouth hooked upward, and his laughter rumbled rich and low.

"Shouldn't you be home sleeping? You were up all night."

"I'm on my way. Just stopping for some nails. I'm hoping to get in some repair work this afternoon before I'm hauled in for deputy duty."

"So you've been drafted, have you? You're already part of the community."

"It feels that way. It's nice. I'm starting to feel at home around here." He turned when Gemma called out to him, nodding in acknowledgement. "Guess I'd better head home."

"Guess so." Her voice cracked. Maybe because of the longing filling her up. She wanted more than this friendliness. Much more.

"See you later, Aumaleigh." He backed away. "You can count on it."

His gaze met hers, and the connection left her reeling. Steady eyes, radiating integrity and something more.

That wasn't desire, was it?

There was the murmur of his voice, then Gemma's answering and he was out the door, crossing the boardwalk and heading out into the street. Muscular form, impressive shoulders, iron strength. The bright rays of the sun drown him out, and he was gone.

"Aumaleigh, did you find what you were looking for?" Gemma swished over, business-like in her plain brown dress. "Aumaleigh? Are you all right."

"F-fine." She stared down, realizing she held two packets of the carved rose buttons in her hand. "I'll take these."

"I'll put them on your account. Anything else?"

"N-no." She didn't trust her voice to say more. This feeling Gabriel had left with her, this awareness of him deep in her soul—she'd felt it before.

"Okay, do you want me to wrap them up for you, or do you want to put them in your reticule?" Gemma asked.

In answer, she loosened her reticule strings and popped the buttons inside. "There."

"Great. Have a good day, Aumaleigh. Tell Iris I'm thinking of her and Milo." Gemma retreated behind the front counter.

"Iris?" Her brain refused to work. She reached for the door knob, trying to remember what she'd been planning to do with the rest of her afternoon.

"Aren't you going to see her? Tell her I'll stop by for her grocery list this evening. I do not want her leaving Milo's side."

"That's sweet of you." Aumaleigh pulled open the door, still a little dazed, touched by Gemma's thoughtfulness. "Have a good day, dear."

"You too." Gemma waved.

Aumaleigh closed the door, standing on the boardwalk. The world rushed around her—horses clomped by on the road drawing wagons, shoes struck the boards as shoppers passed by. Kids across the street shouted, racing around with cookies in their hands from Dobson's Bakery.

But it was Gabriel she saw. Across the street, he untied his team of horses from the hitching post. Her pulse fluttered frantically, knocking against the backside of her ribs.

He glanced up and spotted her. He fastened his gaze on hers with unexpected power, seeing everything, all of her to the depths of her soul.

She saw him too—a good man, a good, good heart. A touch of loneliness, someone who always did the right thing. He climbed into his wagon seat with athletic ease. Raised a leather-gloved hand to her as he drove away.

She stood mesmerized as his wagon rattled down the street and out of sight. There it was again, the powerful feeling, the soul-deep knowledge that he was the one. The one man she would love for the rest of her life.

CHAPTER NINETEEN

"Gramma Aumaleigh!" Sadie swung down from the tree in the front yard sporting a sheriff's badge and hung from her knees by a branch. Her Stetson stayed on thanks to a band at her chin. "I didn't know you were comin'!"

"That's me, full of surprises. How's the county, Sheriff? Any bad men on the loose?" Aumaleigh gave Buttons a final pat at the hitching post. "I hear there's all sorts of trouble."

"Yes, there is!" Sadie nodded vehemently, making her hat and braids bounce. "But it's our job to hunt down trouble."

A second face appeared, swinging down from the tree. Evie had a Stetson too. "We're tracking the Klemp brothers."

"Yeah, we're gonna bring them down." Sadie swung back and forth like a monkey. "Are there any cookies in there?"

"You'll have to wait until after dinner to find out." Aumaleigh balanced the two bakery boxes in her arms. "Any luck with those Klemp brothers?"

"Wait! I think I see somethin'!" Sadie pointed across the street in Mrs. McClellan's yard.

"Me, too!" Evie agreed. "Sheriff, I think it's them!"

"Let's go!" Sadie landed on her feet, already running. "We're bringing those rats in!"

"Yeah, those rats!" Evie landed on her feet and dashed after Sadie. They ducked behind the white fence that protected Mrs. McClellan's roses.

"Aumaleigh!" The front door swung open and Iris stood in the doorway, radiant.

Didn't that say everything? Milo must be doing well. Iris, dear sweet Iris, had never looked so good.

"I brought a little something for supper." Aumaleigh clomped up the steps and handed over the boxes. "Here, take these, I have more in the buggy. Josslyn and I were far too industrious in the kitchen this morning."

"You're spoiling me, Aumaleigh."

"That's the idea." She went to fetch the two dishes of food wrapped in towels on her buggy floor. "Now that I've started, don't expect me to stop."

"We should be spoiling you. You don't know how it felt being on our own in Chicago, and then to find out we had you. You're going to stay for supper, right?"

"I'd love to, but maybe another time. I have Annie and her family coming to my place for supper. Besides, you and Milo just got married. You don't need me hanging around."

"Are you kidding? It's always a treat to have you over. Mitsy loves you."

"Yes, I'm quite fond of Mitsy." Aumaleigh tucked one dish in the crook of her arm and clutched the other. "Have you heard? Dobson's Bakery is opening today."

"Yes, we're having a meeting later, the five of us, to figure out what to do. We can't let Fanny try to run us out of business." Iris held the door open and closed it after Aumaleigh passed through. "You're welcome to stay for that, but something tells me you've got other plans."

"Big plans. Lots to do." Aumaleigh thought of the newspaper advertisement she'd just placed in town for a cook for the kitchen. Tomorrow, she would be seeing Nathaniel about the ranch. She headed straight for the kitchen, where Fluffy rushed up to bark a greeting and Sally could be seen in the back yard with her tiara and her sword, fighting imaginary dragons.

"Maybe some of those big plans have to do with a certain handsome man new to town?" Iris slipped the boxes on the counter. She waggled her brows. "I heard about a romantic encounter in town."

"Not that old rumor again!"

"Oh, no, this is an entirely new one. Mrs. McClellan saw it herself through the mercantile window. She said you and Gabriel looked rather enchanted with one another. Do you deny it?"

"Adamantly. Honestly. Nosy Mrs. McClellan." And then she was laughing, just laughing. She set both dishes on the counter. "Nothing is private in this town. It's a disgrace."

"It's life in a small town, in this town. It is rather nosy, but I like to think it's because everyone cares."

"Yes, I think that's true." Everyone left a legacy behind. She had plans for hers. Life wasn't what you had, it was the people who went with you on the journey. She had some pretty great company. Some of the best. "Is Milo resting?"

"It's killing him, but I'm making sure he does it. I'm standing over him like a prison guard. He's upstairs napping right now, but it's about time for me to go and check on him. That Milo is trouble."

"I've always thought so." Laughing, Aumaleigh threaded her way through the house, retracing her steps. There would be many other times to come where she would stay, where she would visit and laugh and enjoy the Gray family's company, but today she had a few more things to do.

"What's in the back seat of your buggy?" Iris asked, stepping out onto the porch. "I thought we'd moved all your things from your rooms in town. Did we miss something?"

"No, these are from the kitchen house. I went through to make sure I'd gotten everything, only to discover there was more." Aumaleigh's heart felt heavy at the crates of old things she'd cleaned out. The last of the McPhee family things. "I'm in a spring cleaning mood. Out with the old, in with the new."

"Embrace change. I like it." Iris opened her arms for a hug. "But one thing will never change."

"That's right." Aumaleigh squeezed Iris extra tight, holding her just a second longer. Love was the true treasure in this world, and she was wealthy with it. Her friends, her cowboys, her nieces and now her grand-nieces. She let go of Iris, warm of heart. "I'll drop by tomorrow. I'll have some big news to share."

"About Gabriel?" Iris waggled her brows again.

"No. Honestly." She was laughing as she climbed up and settled on her buggy seat, and she was hopeful.

* * *

Junior had never been so tired in his life. All he wanted to do was sleep. It was shady and warm beneath the pines, soft in a bed of pine needles. A little scratchy, but he didn't mind that too much. Considering the last place he'd taken a few moments of shut eye a snake had hissed, waking him up.

"I ain't sayin' it again." Giddy spun the chamber of his .45 to check his bullets. "Get up or I'm leavin' you behind."

"I don't wanna move, Giddy. I can't go anymore."

"Do you wanna know what that possee'll do to you? They'll lynch you without a trial, and that's *after* they beat you to a bloody mess. Cuz you killed a lawman."

"*Me?*" Junior sat up, bonking his head on a low-slung branch. A few pine needles fell onto him and he batted them off. One was a spider, and he batted that off too. "I didn't do it. It was you and you know it. Don't you try and blame me."

Giddy laughed. "Just jokin' with ya. Now get up. Do you know where we are?"

"No." Warm breezes stirred the trees on the hillside. His muscles ached and burned as he moved. They'd been running and running hard.

All he wanted to do was rest. "I need more'n fifteen minutes of sleep, Giddy."

"Me too, but do you hear me bellyaching?" Giddy's sneer was mean. Cunning. The same one he had when he stood over the sheriff and pointed his loaded gun at the injured man.

"We're here. Back at Bluebell." Giddy fell to his knees, pulling himself along his belly over the rise of the hill. "Look at this view. There's the sheriff's house. He must be rotting in a grave by now."

Bluebell. Junior didn't want to look. His stomach hurt something fierce thinking of Iris. Was she crying and heartbroken? He took a step back. "We should have kept running, Giddy. We should have taken that raft we made and escaped down the river."

"That's what we wanted them to think, dummy. If Pa could hear you now, what would he think?" Giddy pulled Junior to his knees. "He'd disown you. He'd never want to see you again. Think of him penned up in that jail. He's sittin' there counting on us. Counting on you, Junior."

"I know." He so wanted his pa to be able to count on him. When they were together, and Pa was free of jail, they'd be a real family, the way they never had a chance to. That mattered so much to him. He wanted it so bad.

"That's her old mare, for sure." Giddy unsheathed a knife out of his belt and held it up to the light. The sharp edges glinted in the sun. "That old spinster and I have got a date."

Junior shivered. He crawled forward on his belly to get a better look over the rise. There, past the downward slope of the hillside lay the town. They were close enough to see kids playing in the street and Aumaleigh McPhee hugging a woman on the sheriff's front lawn.

Iris! Poor Iris. She must be hurting something fierce. He caught sight of her strawberry blond hair and then she was gone, stepping out of his line of sight. But her aunt—Aumaleigh—she reached out with a loving touch, probably patting Iris's hand in comfort.

"We don't have time to waste. The minute we can get her alone, we'll get the money out of her." Giddy studied his knife's sharp blade, as if he were imagining using it. As if he had done this before. "Then we can run. I'll give you the job of holding her down."

"Holding her down?" Junior gulped. "Maybe you otta tell me how you get money out of someone?"

"Just leave it to me." Giddy sheathed his knife and pulled out his gun. "Maybe I'll use this instead. I wonder which one she's most afraid of."

In the town below, Aumaleigh waved and climbed into her buggy. She reined her old horse down the street, disappearing among the trees. Little girls ran into the yard. The sheriff's daughters. Iris stepped out into the yard again, into the sunshine and knelt to take both girls into her arms.

His eyes burned. He had to look away. First the sheriff, then her aunt. Iris seemed awful partial to her aunt. "You ain't gonna really hurt her, are you, Giddy?"

"She's our first class ticket, Junior. Once we get the money, we can't have her telling what happened. Those men will just come after us harder." Giddy backed up, crawling until he was safely hidden. He stood, holstering his revolver. He wasn't gonna stop when he was like this. He wanted blood—and he was gonna get it. "You ain't gettin' cold feet, are you?"

"N-no." Junior's throat went dry. His knees shook because he didn't want his brother to know that was a lie. He wasn't a killer. He wouldn't never hurt anyone that bad.

And never Iris. He tried to see her again, but she was gone from the yard. Memory gripped him, and her face flashed into his mind. So pretty. In that alley that night, she hadn't looked at him like he was despicable, like he was less than anybody else.

No, she'd treated him the nicest that anyone ever had. That put a strange warmth in his chest.

In his heart.

* * *

The sun burned hot on her back. Aumaleigh reined Buttons along the road home. She'd squeezed a few more visits and errands into the afternoon, running much later than she'd planned. But Nathaniel had everything he needed to draw up the contract she wanted. Now she had the rest of the day to herself.

What was left of it, anyway. The sun tilted low in the sky. It was a beautiful world. The wind whispered, rustling through the fields where buttercups and daisies bloomed. Birds sang with merry little chirps and melodies, and almost drown out the rhythmic, *bam, bam, bam* that grew louder as she turned onto her driveway.

There, on the high slope of her house's roof, crouched a man with a hammer, his Stetson at a jaunty angle. She'd know those sturdy, impressive shoulders anywhere, that line of arm and back, the steady calm radiating from him.

Gabriel. Her palms went damp. Anticipation trilled through her. She forgot everything, just everything, drinking in the sight of him. He hitched up the brim of his Stetson and greeted her with a dimpled grin.

"Hey, there." He pulled off his work gloves, drawing her attention to his large, capable hands. "Here I was hoping you'd be a few minutes longer. I saw you coming from town, and I meant to get this done and be gone before you got here."

"What are you? A secret roof repairer? A stealthy handyman?" She hopped out of the buggy and landed in a patch of buttercups.

"No. Just didn't want you to know I was up here. Then you'd want to make me supper or something in payment, and all I wanted was to make sure you didn't have a drip in your house when the next storm blows in." He studied her so intently, as if he found her fascinating and beautiful and too captivating to look away from.

Just like he used to.

She melted. Utterly and completely. If only her heart would too.

"Don't you even think about fixing me supper for this." He grabbed his hammer and deftly walked down her roof, like a man who was born to do it. "I know how you think, Aumaleigh. It was a few nails and a couple of shingles."

"I saw you buy those nails."

"True, but I'll never miss them. I bought a whole bucket full." He climbed down the ladder propped up against the porch roof.

"Where did you get the shingles?" She arched a brow, trying to hide the tenderness rising up to shine like a summer sun at dawn. "I saw you parked at the lumberyard."

"I can't deny it." His boots touched the ground and he hefted the ladder over his shoulder, swinging it onto the back of his wagon. "When I was buying a load of fence posts, I picked up a few shingles for my roof."

"And mine." She wanted to read something into that. Oh, she wanted it so badly. She wasn't imagining the intensity in his gaze, was she? He had to know how she felt. Feeling vulnerable, she stared down at her hands, clasping them together.

"What are a few nails and shingles between us?" He finished stowing the ladder. His grin was friendly, his stance relaxed, his voice easy-going.

Afraid she was wrong, afraid she wanted this—him—too much, she didn't dare look up. She did not want to see any casual look in his eyes.

"Fine." The word came out croaky. She cleared her throat, but the lump was still there.

"I can't promise Leigh won't find an excuse to come over." His boots thumped toward her. "I'm going to head out to join the deputies tonight. She's never really been alone, especially in a new house."

"Why don't you tell her to come over for supper?" Her voice sounded all wrong, thick with emotion, high with growing disappointment. She couldn't meet his gaze. What if she saw no desire for her there? No tenderness? No love? She swallowed hard, fearing he could see everything. "I'm having Annie's family over tonight too, but I'm sure they will love her. I have cupcakes."

"That'll tempt her. I'll pass the invitation on. Thanks, Aumaleigh." He towered over her, and when he reached toward her, it was like the oxygen vanished from the air. He squeezed her hand for one brief moment, and it was like lightning striking.

White, dazzling light bolted through her—pure and life-changing. Like fate. Was he her destiny?

Before she could gather her courage to face him, he'd let go and was striding away. Fear—old and new—beat through her. She listened to the clink of horse hooves carrying him away until there was only silence.

Her heart throbbed like a wound. That's when she realized something was sitting outside her front door. The warm breeze carried the scent of roses.

Roses Gabriel had left for her.

CHAPTER TWENTY

Roses. Aumaleigh kept looking at them. She'd found a vase, trimmed the stems and set them in water. Now they were scenting up her house, reminding her of Gabriel.

Her chest tightened, aching. The contents of her hope chest were out—laundered, fully dried and folded up in a crate ready to go to Dottie's. The leaky roof had done her a favor.

She was finally ready to get rid of these things she'd once made with all her hopes and dreams. Her quilt was on top, folded neatly.

We loved with a love that was more than love. She traced her fingertips along the embroidered quotes. *Soul meets soul on lover's lips.*

Could they love like that again?

She lifted the quilt out of the box and draped it over the back of the couch, debating. Could she really give that away? Now she wasn't sure. As she circled around the coffee table, Gabriel's roses in the dining room caught her eye.

Was this really a second chance for them? He had changed. She could see that. He'd become even more strong and reliable. But something kept her heart from opening. Guards were there. She was afraid to love him—when loving him was what she wanted most.

She stared at the boxes. It was tempting to walk away, to lose herself in something that kept her from thinking. Or that kept her from facing whatever was in those boxes. But that wouldn't get the boxes out of her house. It was time to clean up the last of her parent's things. They were both gone and so were their human frailties.

Winston! Winston, you come back here and look at me. Just look at me, would you? Mother's voice, wracked with agony, echoed through Aumaleigh's memory as she walked through the house, putting out lights. She'd been a little girl then, so concerned for her crying mother.

Some loves were fragile. Others were quick to burn out. But not all of them. She would never forget the times she would run over to Mother, crumpled up on the floor, crying hard for the husband whose love had gone out like a light.

Down deep, she'd been afraid so long ago that would happen to her. That her mother was right. That she was unlovable, and Gabriel had only to discover that about her. And then she would be living the rest of her life, crying over a love that died and a husband who kept his distance. Who, over the years, couldn't stand to look at her.

And that wound would poison her with bitterness the same way it had Maureen.

But she wasn't afraid of that, not anymore. Resigned, she eased off the nearest box's lid and peered inside. Oh, there was the china doll she used to play with as a girl, as pretty as ever with her dark hair still perfectly coifed. She was accompanied by a plethora of beautiful outfits and accessories.

How cute. Aumaleigh held up a party dress in her favorite butter yellow and memory grabbed hold of her like a thief.

"You'll have a gown like this one day, Aumaleigh." Maureen worked her needle *through the hem and pulled the stitch through. "Won't that be fun? We'll have your hair up all nice, and we'll introduce you to all the right men."*

"Can my dress be yellow, just like this?" Her fingers wistfully brushed the *lace overskirt, awed by the notion she might be grown up one day and able to wear something so fashionable.*

"It must be the right color to compliment your coloring, dear." Mother knotted *the thread. "But yes, yellow is a complimentary color for you. You want to look your best to catch the right kind of husband."*

"I'll wear this dress and I'll dance and dance."

"You'll dance with the richest man in the ballroom." Maureen worked her *needle one more time, hiding the end of the thread. "There, it's all done."*

"Thank you, Mother." It was a wonder, holding something made of real silk, *even if it was a scrap from Mother's last gown. Aumaleigh smoothed out the skirt, admiring the garment. She couldn't wait to put it on her doll!*

"Remember, Aumaleigh, you can fall in love with a rich man as easy as a poor one." Maureen put the needle back in her sewing basket. *"Always marry the richest man you can. That's what I did, and now I can wear all the pretty dresses I want."*

Aumaleigh blinked, pulling herself out of her thoughts. Her mother was a tragic figure, and largely of her own making. Maybe that was one truth in life. Be careful of the choices you make. Because they determine who you become.

Sadness clung to her, and she put the dress back in the box. She secured the lid and set it aside. Tomorrow, she'd take these things to Penelope and Nathaniel's house. Maybe their little Evie would enjoy them.

Aumaleigh sighed. Well, going through that box hadn't been so bad. That only left one box to go. Braver this time, she popped off the lid and a framed charcoal sketch sat on the top of a ton of papers. A small portrait of her father.

Oh, Papa. She grabbed the frame, clutching it tight, her heart full of grief. He'd been captured in his youth, maybe before he married Mother, strapping and handsome with a chiseled face and kind eyes.

"I'm sorry I grabbed you off that Daniels' fellow's buckboard like that." Father pushed open her bedroom door, standing in the doorway uncertain. His black hair was disheveled, his eyes red-rimmed. He had a glass cupped in one hand. Whiskey. The strong scent of it filled her room.

"I know." Aumaleigh turned away from the paned glass, but stayed firmly on the cushioned window seat. Gabriel was long gone, he wasn't going to come back for any more dates after her mother's tongue lashing.

"Did I hurt you?" His lower lip trembled. Swaying, unsteady on his feet, he stared down into his glass like a man staring at temptation he wasn't strong enough to overcome. Resigned, he took a sip. Then a bigger one.

Her ear throbbed, hot and painful. Her arm where he'd also grabbed her had a bruise the size of his hand. A deep bruise. He'd practically thrown her through the doorway to get her into the house, and she'd hit her head. She had a lump from that.

"No," she lied. The truth would only make him drink more.

"Good, because you don't know what really getting hurt is like." Father stared at his empty glass. He swayed and swayed.

"Here, Father, let's get you lying down." She feared he might fall down the stairs as drunk as he was and hurt himself.

"You're my good girl, Aumaleigh."

The memory faded. Her poor father, haunted by the demons he'd never been strong enough to overcome, by a past he couldn't let go of. That didn't excuse his choices and how he'd treated her, but it was sad.

She set the frame on the coffee table, a little afraid to find out what else was inside the box. But it just looked like old papers. She pulled out a handful. Letters, she realized. From Aunt Judith. She and mother had written back and forth for many years.

Aumaleigh scanned through the first lines of several of the letters. *Winston fell down the stairs and cracked his back... The garden party meeting was a success... Thank heavens Aumaleigh gave that farmer back his ring... My new dress...*

Well, none of this was important. Out it went. Aumaleigh began tossing letter after letter, envelopes and all onto the table, when a familiar script caught her eye. Gabriel's handwriting. Gabriel's letter.

No, she realized, reaching into the box again. There were more of them. Over a dozen. Each one addressed to her. Each one unopened. They were dated through the year following their break up.

Shock hit her like an avalanche, burying her completely. She couldn't move. She couldn't think. She could only stare at the letters she'd never received.

The letters Gabriel had written her.

Her vision blurred as she grabbed the first one, ripped open the flap and pulled out a single sheet of paper.

My dearest Aumaleigh,

I know you didn't mean what you said. That was your parents talking. I know they are pressuring you hard. You are such a tender-hearted girl, and that's one of the reasons I love you so much. You care about everyone more than yourself, but trust me. It's time to do what you want. Not what I want. Not what your parents want. If you followed your heart, where would it lead? To me? If so, then please come to me. Or ask Josslyn to get word to me and I'll be there for you. I'll do anything for you. I just want you to be happy, sweetheart. I love you, and I'm never going to stop loving you.

Gabriel

A tear dripped onto the page, smudging one corner of the parchment. She let his words sink in. He had loved her enough. He'd been willing to fight for her. He hadn't walked away easily.

She put her face in her hands and wept.

G abriel was dog tired, but every thought he had as he drov was of her. The wind sweeping the meadows made him thinке the walks he wanted to take with her. The sun on his back reminded him of the summer afternoons he wanted to take her riding down to the cool river for a swim. The empty corrals by the barn reminded him of the horses he'd bought from her ranch. Her favorite horses.

Maybe one day she'd come walking out of the house, with a handful of carrots for the horses and a lunch basket for them. They'd picnic in the shade by the orchard, talking and laughing and maybe getting some kissing in. His ribs squeezed as feeling and hope rose.

"Hey, stranger!" Seth rode into sight through the field. He had a Colt Peacemaker strapped to each hip and a rifle holstered to his saddle.

He wasn't alone. Oscar and Tyler were with him, each on horseback and heavily armed.

"Glad to see the afternoon shift is bright eyed and bushy tailed." Gabriel drew his team to a halt. "Any sign of the Klemp brothers?"

"No. With the sheriff hunting them from behind and with us waiting for them, we'll get them." Tyler looked determined. "If they come this way, we're ready. After our experience with Ernest and George, we can't be too careful."

"That's the truth." Oscar lifted his binoculars and carefully scanned the hillside.

"Looks like you men have it covered." Gabriel appreciated that. He glanced up at his house to see Leigh waving at him from the porch. She'd taken her embroidery out to enjoy the warm weather. He waved back. "I'll put up my horses and get some shut-eye. Holler if you need anything."

"Will do." Seth tipped his hat, and the men moved on, all business. Moving down to patrol the road by the river.

The wind puffed warm, redolent with the scents of growing grass and mountain meadows. Gabriel felt at peace watching over the valley where he would live out the rest of his life.

He liked that idea. Very much. He squared his shoulders, sitting tall on the wagon seat. He clucked to the horses, driving them toward the barn. From his vantage point, he could see straight across the hillside to Aumaleigh's house. Sunlight glinted in the windows, and he thought of her there.

WHERF₂ress today. Was he one step closer to winning her He'd ꜀ped the connection he felt with her remained. Steadfast. hear₊ang.
ʳ Stronger than it had ever been

* * *

The river gurgled, moving swift and cold. And wet. Junior's mouth was dry as dirt and tasted like sand. He couldn't help stopping and cupping his hand into the water. Ice cold, he slurped it up. It sluiced over his tongue and ran down his throat. Oh, it was nice.

"Did I tell you to stop?" Giddy growled. Unshaven, dirty and rumpled, he looked as bad as his temper. His hands shook, quaking hard. "We're out in the open, idiot. When I tell you to move fast, you do it or I'll beat you bloody. I'm in no mood."

Junior was getting tired of his brother's moods. He shook the water droplets off his hands, plowing through the river. They came up on the other side dripping and shivering, the bank soft with grass. His stomach growled louder than a bear. "We gotta eat, Giddy."

"We'll eat when I say so." Giddy pressed his palms to the sides of his face. A sure sign he had a monster of a headache—which meant his temper was gonna stay mean.

What Giddy needed was a few bottles of whiskey, and he'd drink himself to sleep. Maybe then he'd calm down some. Giddy was on a rampage. He'd gotten things twisted up in his head, Junior could see it. He followed his brother up the bank and into the trees, winding their way up the wooded hillside until Giddy crouched down, satisfied.

"Look." He pointed across the way. "Right there's our ticket. First class all the way."

Junior squinted into the sun, already knowing what he would see. Aumaleigh McPhee's two-story log house, as pretty as a picture in a storybook. But it wasn't a mansion. It was a nice but regular home.

"Are you sure she's rich, Giddy?" His chest felt hollow, maybe because he knew deep down it was wrong. He knew Giddy was wrong.

He loved his pa, but Pa was wrong too.

"She owns that ranch, doesn't she?" Giddy licked his lips, a man yearning for his whiskey. "She's got all that land and all them animals. Do you know how much money a place like that makes in a year?"

"She don't look rich. Her horse is older than ours was."

"Are you makin' excuses?" Giddy lunged and grabbed Junior by the collar. "Pa ain't gonna like it if you back out now. You're worth. Junior. Pa's right about you."

Junior gulped. Looking in his brother's mean eyes, he saw Pa's meanness. Saw all the times Pa would grab him like this, throw him down and beat him with a switch. Giddy was no different.

Neither was Pa gonna be. Sometimes you wanted people you loved to change, even when you knew they never would.

"Sorry, Giddy." He lowered his eyes, waiting for his brother to release him. Giddy did, giving him a hard shove. Junior straightened his shirt, glancing across the fall of the land to the house where Aumaleigh McPhee sat on her sofa. Her face was in her hands.

Oh, she looked sad.

That was another lady who'd been nice to him. She'd invited him to Rose's wedding. Iris wouldn't want him to hurt her aunt—or worse, if Giddy had his way. He sat down in the grass, shaking hard. It wasn't right. He couldn't do this. He just couldn't.

And by the look in his eyes, Giddy knew that too. He drew before Junior could blink and the shot reverberated through the forest.

CHAPTER TWENTY-ONE

W ell, she had better get supper in the oven. Annie, Bea and Adam would be coming over to eat tonight. Aumaleigh tossed the last box of her parents' things out the door. It landed on the grass, to be hauled away later. She'd hired Oscar to do it.

She turned around, startling as a shadow moved alongside the house. The shadow became a man.

"Why don't you come over here nice and slow?" He thumbed back the hammer on the .45 pointed straight at her head. "Let's go in your kitchen and talk."

Panic beat through her. Her knees felt watery. She stared at the nose of the gun. It felt eerie, like one of those dreams that felt strangely real but wasn't real at all. "You're George's son."

"And you're the old lady that cheated him." Hatred twisted his mouth, stole the life from his eyes. His gaze was icy and dead.

"That was my mother." Fear made her voice thin and high, and she wondered if she could run. There had to be a way to escape. "My mother cheated your father and a lot of men."

"You ended up with it all, didn't you? All that land. All that money. You think you're better than me because of it, but you know what a dead woman is? Just a piece of dead meat." He came at her.

Run! Her brain shouted. Her body scrambled to obey. In her mind she was halfway to the barn, running for her life, but in truth her muscles had frozen. Her limbs were like water, her feet too weak to move. Fear had paralyzed her as he grabbed her by the back of the neck. His fingers dug into her hair, pain shot through her and she was airborne, slamming against the side of the house.

She managed to stay standing, but the gun was at her head before she could blink. Cold and hard against her forehead.

"I'm in charge now." His fingers gripped her shoulder, bruising, strong enough to break bone. He spun her toward the door. "We're gonna go inside and you are going to give me your money. All of it. Every penny. Or I'll gut you right in your own kitchen—"

She didn't know what made her do it. Her foot shot out, tangling with his. They both went down hard. She hit hard, knocking the breath right out of her. Time slowed down as she scrambled, pushing off the grass, free from him now. Her feet were spinning, her instincts were screaming at her to run and she could feel him rising up next to her, reaching out—

And a single gunshot echoed across the yard. Giddy Klemp stumbled as the bullet hit. Blood sprayed against the side of the house and he fell dead at her feet.

"Sorry I was late." Gabriel, astride his black gelding, held his shotgun steady as he slid to the ground. "Should have got here earlier, but we had to jump the fence."

Barney nickered, as if in agreement.

"It was perfect timing, to me." There she was, frozen in place again. This time for an entirely different reason.

Gabriel caught Giddy Klemp at the shoulder and rolled him over with his boot. The body was limp, there was no life there, but he checked anyway.

"Yep, he's dead. He's not going to be bothering you anymore." He lowered the rifle, leaning it against the house. He pulled her into the garden, away from the blood and death. "Are you okay? Aumaleigh, talk to me."

What was there to say? There was a dead man in her yard, a man who'd been ready to do who-knows-what to her. She was trembling, then quaking hard. Relief washed through her as cold as ice.

"Oh, Gabriel. You came." Her brain seemed to finally catch up to what was going on. "I've never been so glad to see anyone before."

"I'm always gonna be here for you. You don't ever have to worry about that." His hand cupped the side of her face, but it was more than a touch. It was a brush to her soul. Her spirit sighed with recognition, her one true match.

The next thing she knew she was in his arms, pressed safe against his chest. It was homecoming and joy and gratitude all at once, but that wasn't the reason she was crying. Tears blurred her vision, fell hot on her cheeks, but it was the emotion alive and growing in her heart. Love rushed in—sweet, sweet love.

The grass was greener, the flowers brighter, the sun incandescent as his strong arms held her tight. His heartbeat thudded against her ear. Every inch of her was aware of him as they pressed together. Her skin tingled. She felt breathless. As if she were on the edge of a precipice and about to fall.

"I heard a gunshot echoing through the valley and I was afraid for you. And then when I saw that gun to your head—" His voice broke, and he pressed his face into her hair. "I didn't know if I could save you in time. I don't think I could bear losing you."

"That's something you don't have to worry about." She leaned back in his arms, searching his gaze. "I've gotten used to having you for a neighbor. I'm not going anywhere."

"Good to know. Since I'm in your good graces, maybe this is a good time to ask. I'd like to amend our agreement."

"Which agreement would that be? The one where we agreed to be friends?"

"That's the one." Gabriel took a shallow breath. Boy, his heart was thundering a hundred times a second. His entire heart rode on her answer. "I'd like to come calling."

"You want to come courting?"

"If it's all right with you." He tried to keep how desperate he felt out of his voice—desperate from fearing he couldn't save her, desperate from imagining just for a second his future without her. "It might not be so bad this time. I'm not as wet behind the ears."

"What exactly does that mean?" She arched a brow, as adorable as could be.

"I've got experience behind me. I've been trained up some. I'm not as dumb as I used to be."

"Not from what I've seen." she teased dryly.

And then they were laughing together. The affection shining in her bluebonnet-blue eyes stymied him. Just made him melt. He was nothing but tenderness—so, so sweet—and much deeper the second time around.

Did she feel this way too?

He leaned in, following the whispers of his heart. Her eyes widened—maybe surprised, maybe not ready—but she didn't push him away. Their lips met lightly, softly, touching in the gentlest of first kisses.

This is the way it's going to be, he wanted to tell her, he tried to tell her with that kiss. Did she feel the reverence he had for her? The adoration? He didn't know.

And then her hands lighted on his shoulders, such a sweet touch pushing him away to end their kiss.

"Soul meets soul on lover's lips." She smiled through her tears. "Ours is a love that is more than love."

"You have no idea how good that sounds. What it means." His gray eyes darkened, showing all of his heart. His true, true heart. "You are my first love and my last. I'm going to love you every day for the rest of my life."

"That sounds perfect to me."

The world brightened, the sun blinded and all she wanted was him. Just Gabriel—her other half. She could see their future—family, grandchildren, and growing old together side by side. Laughing and loving the way they were always meant to be.

She was going to love every moment—every single one.

EPILOGUE

Morning at the Kincaid house came early, and these days she didn't do early mornings as well as she used to. Daisy sipped a steaming cup of fresh coffee, hoping it would give her the kick she needed to get everyone fed and out the door. It didn't seem to be working. Her entire body felt exhausted, dragging, tired to the bone.

But this exhaustion wouldn't last for long. She cracked eggs into the fry pan, watching them sizzling in the bacon grease and smiled to herself. After the new year, they would be welcoming another member of their family. That thought was enough to make her smile all the way down to her soul.

Life was going to get interesting. She threw away the egg shells and grabbed the spatula. While the new sun peaked between the curtains and spilled onto the kitchen table, she imagined her life to come.

Well, to put it more accurately, she imagined her plan to come. She wanted five girls, who would grow up just the way she did, playing princess tea parties and running all over the yard with their stories of adventure and fun.

Just think of the chaos when she had her own sisters over! Their kids would join hers in the backyard. The McPhee Clan would have a whole new generation, a new chapter of love and stories and happy futures to come.

Footsteps thudded across the floor, coming closer. Beckett was pulling up his suspenders as he strode into the kitchen. Freshly washed and shaven, he looked handsome and strapping. Her wonderful husband. Love, pure love, set her heart aglow. She flipped the eggs and set down the spatula before waltzing into his arms.

"Good morning." She tilted her head back, ready for his kiss. "You are right on time."

"I aim to please. I know how you get when I'm late for grub." Beckett's eyes twinkled, and his mouth hitched up into that smile she loved so much. "You abuse me. Take the switch to me."

"Yes, one day I will. So you'd better show up to meals on time."

His chuckle became a kiss that curled her toes and won her heart all over again. Who knows how long they kissed—she wasn't counting the minutes—until the distinct scent of something burning caught her attention.

"Oops. I think that's your toast." She broke away from his kiss and his arms to rescue his food.

"What's the penalty around here for burning a man's food?" His arms came around her at the stove as she grabbed his blackened toast from the oven rack.

"I owe you two kisses." She dropped the toast on a cloth napkin and scooped on the two eggs. "Guess I'll have to pay up tonight."

"I'll make sure you do." His gaze glittered, full of mischief. "You'll pay up or else. With interest."

"I look forward to that." She handed him his sandwich, poured him a cup of coffee and handed him his hat on the way out the door. He kissed her cheek and strode through the yard. Her heart tugged, missing him already.

If anyone had told her a year ago that she would be standing here today in sunny Montana Territory happily married, a stepmother and expecting a baby, she never would have believed it. Never. Those hard days in Chicago seemed like a century ago. Fading away compared to the incandescent brightness of her life.

Love had done that.

"Ma?" Hailie rubbed her eyes with her fists, adorable with her sleep tousled hair and her ruffled nightgown. "I'm real hungry."

"You are?" Daisy went over to brush a shock of hair out of the girl's face. Motherly love filled her full, brimming over. "I happen to have some extra crispy bacon. I cooked it extra crispy just for you."

"You did?" Hailie flashed her dimples.

"Yep. Come over here and I'll fix your plate." Daisy went to take a step but Hailie lunged, hugging her hard and holding on tight. The girl didn't say a word, but no words were necessary.

With some joys, they are best said with the heart.

* * *

The Rocking M was a lovely sight. Aumaleigh took a moment to drink it all in. Dams and their foals dotted the lush green hillsides, the mares grazing and the babies frolicking nearby. Farther out, cattle grazed, calves chasing each other playing their little calf games. A few men on horseback patrolled the fields, keeping an eye out for the wildlife that liked to snack on vulnerable foals and calves.

The three barns were busy. Hammering rang in the yard as someone was repairing stalls, just routine maintenance. Cal, the stable boy was pushing a wheelbarrow to empty near the manure pile. Burton and Dale were working horses in the arena. Beckett and Kellan were unloading a wagon full of grain from town.

The bright sun, the warm breeze, the color of the grass and the feel of this busy, prospering place. She'd grown up on a ranch, and she'd worked her whole life on one. But as with all things, this too had to come to an end.

Perhaps it was fitting with all that had happened with the Klemp brothers. Giddy intended to scare her into giving him money she no longer had. Junior, who'd crawled onto the road for help and was found by a couple deputies, had told all. He'd confessed to his role in it, but Milo had promised to ask for leniency from the judge. After all, Junior had saved Milo's life.

Junior seemed like a misguided but not a truly bad man. He had promise. She'd made sure Milo told Junior he had a job at the Rocking M when he got out of prison.

A horse's whinny caught her attention. Phil, one of the ranch horses, stretched his neck over the top rail of his fence and batted his eyes, knowing he was a good looking guy no woman could resist.

Because he was right, she laughed and went over to rub his nose.

"This is the last time I pet you as my horse," she told him. "Be good, Phil."

Boots thumped on the ground behind her. Beckett strolled up. "We got the feed stored. After lunch, we're heading out to ride the fence line in the summer fields. Got to make sure they're in good repair."

"Great. Would you make sure all your men come in for the meal? I have an announcement to make." She gave Phil one final pat. There was Josslyn, waving at her through the open kitchen window, signaling lunch was ready. "I'll go ring the bell."

"Sure thing." Beckett tipped his hat, looking a little curious. But if he had questions, he didn't ask them.

Wishing she could slow down time, just a little, to hold on to this place she loved a bit longer, she reached up and rang the dinner bell. The clatter carried on the wind, alerting cowboys everywhere. They dropped their work, they left their animals and they headed in.

"Are you sure you want to do this?" Josslyn asked. She'd come out onto the porch, maybe sensing how hard this was going to be—that's the kind of lifelong, good friend she was.

"I'm ready." She took her friend by the hand. "C'mon, let's go feed that horde of cowboys together one last time."

The kitchen smelled delicious, of herbed, roasted chicken, butter-fried potato coins, fresh buttermilk biscuits and molasses baked beans. Orla carried two serving bowls into the dining room. On her heels, Louisa dashed behind her. Annika, who'd answered the advertisement, hurried after with a pitcher of lemonade. Not one to stand around, Aumaleigh grabbed a platter of chicken pieces and headed through the house.

The cowboys came like a tornado. Thumping on the floor, banging against the walls, booming voices telling jokes, or discussing ranch business, or complimenting them on the delicious looking food. Chairs scraped against the wood floor as they were drawn out, cowboys settled in and the pandemonium began. Cowboys reached, they snatched, they stuffed things into their mouths, emptying platters and serving bowls at an alarming rate.

"They're like locusts," Annika commented, hurrying away to fetch a fresh pitcher. "They're eating everything in sight."

Aumaleigh laughed, walking around the tables with a basket of biscuits.

"It tastes extra good today," Kellan told her around the roll he'd stuffed in his mouth.

"You made my favorite rolls," Burton added, slathering one with butter.

"I'll take two before they're gone," Beckett said with a wink, helping himself to the basket.

When the men were served and busy scarfing down the food on their plates, she circled around to the front of the dining room. She grabbed a spoon and banged it on an empty glass.

Conversations silenced. All eyes turned to her.

She cleared her throat. "I've decided to sell the ranch."

"What?" Kellan dropped his fork.

"No!" Tiernan thumped his fist on the table. "Don't do it. I like working here."

"Where on earth will I go?" John murmured to Burton, who sat next to him.

Aumaleigh held up her hand for silence. "Do you really think I wouldn't look after you? After all these years of feeding you? I've gotten mildly attached to you cowboys."

"*Mildly* attached?" Kellan arched a brow. "Only mildly? I think you're kidding us. You love us. Admit it."

"Okay, I do." She opened the sideboard drawer and pulled out a thick stack of papers. "Which is why I've split all of last year's income from the ranch between us to give everyone a bonus. It's based on seniority and hours worked. That includes the kitchen and house staff."

Orla gasped in surprise.

Burton's jaw dropped.

John cleared his throat. "Did you say you split *all* the income from last year?"

"Yes." It was a substantial amount. She spread the paperwork across the top of the waist-high sideboard. "When you're done eating, come get the envelope with your name on it. This is a thank you from my family for all the hard work you've given to this ranch.

"Today is the last day the Rocking M will be owned by a McPhee. I've decided to sell the ranch to the people my mother promised ownership to and then cheated. Burton, John, Kellan and Beckett. I've taken one dollar out of each of your bonuses in payment, per Nathaniel's advice. This ranch is now yours."

Cheers broke out. Beckett met her gaze, giving her a sincere, heartfelt nod of thanks. Kellan stood up and whooped in delight, shouting his gratitude. Burton came over and kissed her cheek. John bowed his head, swiping a tear from his eye.

Oh, she was going to miss these men. But finally the McPhee legacy was one she could be proud of.

* * *

"Thanks, Aumaleigh." Louisa still clutched her check, holding on as if she didn't want to let go. "You don't know what this does for me."

"You earned it." She gave the girl a hug.

The clank of dishes being washed and dried followed her out the kitchen door. As she tied on her sunbonnet, she found her feet dragging. It was hard to close the door on this chapter of her life, but the one ahead of her would be good too. And it wasn't as if she were leaving behind these people she loved.

Well, her time here was officially over. She straightened her shoulders, took one long last look around and headed over to the barn.

"I've got Buttons hitched and ready for you." Cal, the stable boy held out a hand to help her up.

She accepted, settling onto the seat. "Do you have plans for your bonus?"

"I'm buying two of the mares here. I've wanted them so bad for so long. Burton gave me a fair price. It's a dream, really. I'm gonna keep 'em here and start my own herd."

"Excellent. You'll be a great success, I know it." She seized the reins. While he tipped his Stetson to her, she drove out of the barn and into the bright kiss of the warm sun.

"Aumaleigh?" The smoky baritone rolled over her, making her shiver. Anticipation trilled through her like a song as she turned, needing, wanting, craving to see him—her Gabriel.

Her heart soared when she saw him ride into sight, so perfect astride the back of his black horse. His Stetson was tipped at an angle, the brim slashing down to hide half his face. But that only emphasized his flawless smile and the dimple in his chin.

"Hey, there." He reined his horse to a stop. He was there, beside her, towering over her, all she could see. The sky, the sun, the world—it had faded away and there was just him.

There would only, always, be just him. Her soul filled with that knowledge, deep and without end.

"How did it go?" he asked.

"Wonderful and sad all at once." She shrugged. "And freeing. Like the best part of my life is ahead of me."

"That's because it is. I'll make sure of it." His fingers curled around her elbow, strength and gentleness combined. He leaned toward her. His kiss was welcome, familiar and sweet. His lips brushed, they caressed, and she wrapped her arms around his neck, holding on. She loved this man, how she loved him. Every day and every way, she loved him a little bit more.

It was her turn to ride off into the sunset, this was her happily-ever-after. She was going to live it so there were no regrets. It was never too late for dreams to come true.

Heart in heart and full of joy, they rode off together through green fields and golden sunlight.

The McPhee Clan continues in *A Place In The Heart,* Oscar's story. Coming later in 2015.

48557211R10118

Made in the USA
Middletown, DE
16 June 2019